SERVANT

The Goodpasture Chronicles
Book 2

R.J. Halbert

Eald Talu House

To Kelton and Kennedy, though life will take you away on grand adventures though dark valleys and over high mountains, may you look for the ancient paths to lead you home.

Servant
The Goodpasture Chronicles

This is a work of fiction. Unless otherwise indicated, all the names, characters, businesses, places, events and incidents in this book are either the product of the author's imagination or used in a fictitious manner. Any resemblance to actual persons, living or dead, or actual events is purely coincidental.

ISBN (Ebook): 978-1-963366-10-5
ISBN (Paperback): 978-1-963366-08-2
ISBN (Hardcover): 978-1-963366-09-9

Printed in Canada

Published by:
Eald Talu House
(A Division of Novus Press Works)
Nashville, TN 37203

To Rhonda, my co-author in fiction and in life. When we began "The Goodpasture Chronicles," we thought we knew exactly where the story would lead. But like life itself, our best-laid plans gave way to unexpected twists and turns, while the Keane family came alive to teach us in ways we never imagined. What started as a reaction to trauma became a beautiful journey of revelation and hope. Through all of life's surprises since finishing "Caretaker," the sweetest has been creating this world with the love of my life, Rhonda. Nothing brings me more joy than writing the next chapters of our lives together. What began as healing became hope, what started as a story became prophecy. As we 'listen to the whispers,' let's continue to write the ending we're dreaming of.

-Jason Halbert

Life has a funny way of imitating art, or in our case, art has a powerful way of impacting life. This unexpected shift in direction has changed me for the better. Trust and patience have carved a road of hope and healing through the hardest grief and pain. This story could not be told without my co-author, partner, husband, and best friend, Jason. We are big dreamers together, but even we did not see this big dream coming. The end is near. What is happening?!?!

P.S. Our moms would be so proud.

-Rhonda Halbert

Contents

Dedication v
From the Authors vii
Prologue xi
Chapter One 1
Chapter Two 5
Chapter Three 19
Chapter Four 27
Chapter Five 41
Chapter Six 53
Chapter Seven 67
Chapter Eight 77
Chapter Nine 89
Chapter Ten 99
Chapter Eleven 111
Chapter Twelve 123
Chapter Thirteen 137
Chapter Fourteen 145
Chapter Fifteen 159
Chapter Sixteen 171
Chapter Seventeen 187

Chapter Eighteen 199
Chapter Nineteen 211
Chapter Twenty 221
Chapter Twenty-One 231
Chapter Twenty-Two 235
Epilogue 245
Acknowledgements and Thanks 247
About the Author 250

PROLOGUE

"SIXTEEN...SEVENTEEN...EIGHTEEN?"

Zach stopped climbing the steps and closed his eyes tight.

But there are only fifteen, he thought. *Did I miscount? Now I have to start over again.* The thought unnerved him. Eyes still closed, he pictured the stairwell, the landing at the top of the stairs, the hallway that led to his room. *Eighteen steps are too many. This isn't right.*

As he turned around to climb the stairs once more, Zach opened his eyes and was even more confused. He was surrounded by fog creeping down from above. Looking down, he couldn't even see his feet.

"What is hap—" he began to say aloud, then quickly stopped. His voice sounded different. It was hollow and echoey, like the way it sounded in the stairwell of his school gym. *No, not quite like that*, he thought. More like a cave.

And why is the fog back...inside? Can fog form inside a house?

"Mom?" he said in a whisper, fearing the sound of his own voice. "Dad?" he added, even more quietly.

"Zach..." a faint whisper replied. But it wasn't Mom or Dad. It came from above, below, and inside all at the same time.

The fog continued to swirl around him; he didn't dare move. The risk of falling was too great. *But falling to where?* he wondered.

Is the house acting strange again? Acting...like a sentient being? He allowed himself a half smile at his use of the word *sentient*. He had only just looked it up yesterday to confirm its meaning after hearing a teacher at school use it when randomly theorizing about the TARDIS from *Dr. Who.* He was pretty sure he already knew the word. Dictionary.com had proved him right.

He decided to test his voice again, this time listening for clues.

"It's bigger on the inside," he said aloud. *But the inside of what?* he wondered. The words bounced off the walls and landed at his feet with a thud. "Something is definitely wrong," he added. This time, he couldn't quite muster a half smile. He had been so certain that something was still off about the house, and his family—even after Marshall had found a solution to the old wiring that had nearly killed his mom.

"Mom?" he ventured again in full voice, but with a noticeable quiver from holding back tears. This time there was no answer.

A familiar feeling started to settle in…*fear.* He lowered himself to sit down and began to cry. Immediately he noticed the stair beneath him was not wooden. There was no carpet runner to soften heavy footsteps. He brushed his tear-stained hand against the hard, smooth surface, picking up dirt on his fingers. Though the air around him tasted dry and gritty, the stair was cool to the touch. Polished and yet imperfect at the same time…like stone.

That confirmed it. He was not at his house. He was somewhere else.

He could be anywhere!

Panic began to chip away at his curiosity. Sensing the panic coming on, he pictured it as a dragon and began to fight it off with an imagined crossbow. "Khalas! Not now!" he offered as his rallying cry. The command had always worked for his mom.

But the dragon was relentless. His mind trick wasn't going to work this time. He shook off the imagined battle and focused instead on his breathing.

Deep inhale, slow exhale.

Deep inhale, slow exhale.

Deep inhale…

Dust choked his throat and he coughed.

Okay, Zach, just think. What is actually happening to me? I was just heading to bed. Now, where am I?

A faint, deep voice echoing off the walls and floor answered his thoughts. *"You're with me."*

At that thought, the fog dissipated, and his surroundings materialized. He was sitting on a step halfway up a long stone stairway. As the fog continued to clear, a dim flickering light came into view below him at what he presumed was the bottom of the stairs.

A thought came over him. But it wasn't his own. *Down*, he thought. *I need to go down. Down is the way home.*

He rose unsteadily to his feet, almost falling when he reached for a railing that wasn't there. He shuffled closer to the wall side of the staircase, then leaned against it as he descended, one step at a time, counting backward as he went.

"Seventeen, sixteen, fifteen..."

He felt the coolness of the stone under his bare feet. A stray memory distracted him from his counting. *Dad's not going to be thrilled to find my dirty socks on the living room floor.*

He had been watching TV. A History Channel show about the Bermuda Triangle—people just vanishing into thin air, never to be seen again. He choked on a laugh as he recognized the irony in that choice.

"Sixteen...no, fifteen?" Panic began to creep into his thoughts again, causing his heart to race: He'd lost count. He paused his descent.

Deep inhale. Slow exhale.

Deep inhale. Slow exhale.

I can do this. I can do this.

With great difficulty, he decided to stop counting as the realization that he was not home deepened. He slowly continued down the stairs until his feet landed on the floor. This, too, was clearly made of stone. The flickering light was coming from a torch attached to the wall along a hallway directly in front of him. The right side of the wall, he noted. He felt the need to keep track of every detail.

He turned to look back up the stairs. They seemed to go on forever.

Is up the way home? he wondered.

"Mom? Dad?" He waited for a reply but once again heard nothing. Then, "Ariel? Ariel, is this some kind of trick? Are you doing this to me?" He knew the instant he said it how insane that idea was. His sister was clever and prone to pranking him, but he couldn't imagine how she could have orchestrated his current circumstance. He must have been dreaming this whole thing.

That's it! This is just a dream! A realistic, vivid dream.

Zach was so certain he had solved the puzzle that he almost missed the figure darting across the endless hallway, a shadow just beyond the reach of the torch.

His heart pounded in his chest. His panic returned full force.

Was the shadow human? Animal?

Or monster?

This dream was about to become a nightmare.

ONE

EVERYTHING WAS DIFFERENT here. Akolo inhaled deeply, trying to find even a hint of home in the foreign tapestry of scents—sharp and bitter, nothing like the warm bread and river mud of home. Strange voices bounced off walls too high and too wide, speaking words that scratched at his ears. Even breathing felt different here, as if the air itself knew he didn't belong.

Akolo closed his eyes and recalled the events of the past few weeks. Or had it been months? He pictured the conquering army—their swords drawn, confidence painted on their faces with wide eyes and bitter sneers, almost as if they were enjoying it. He trembled when he revisited the moment they separated him from his family.

He remembered being taken to the temple building, left there alone under watchful guard. He strained even now to hear the strange sounds that came from the grounds surrounding the holy place—the one his family helped construct after the previous invaders destroyed the original temple. His father had described that temple's beauty as "beyond words." The only temple Akolo had known was still massive—a building that intimidated most who visited. He could only imagine something even more magnificent.

He shook as the memory of those sounds came into focus—the clashing of metal upon metal, yells of conquest, screams of defeat, and finally, the echoing eerie silence that seemed to last for ages.

Then he pictured the tall man who came to stand just outside the door. This was a man of great power and honor, surely. His face was stern, yet not entirely unkind. But how could anyone who leads a bloodthirsty army be kind?

The words he heard the strange man command just outside the temple room continued to haunt Akolo: "Keep the boy. We are going to need him."

What did he mean? Need me for what? And what did they do with my family?

All armies are the same, he thought. All they bring is bloodshed and heartache.

He was afraid his family was dead. If not by the swift sharp swords of the conquering army, then surely by the careless strikes of the frightened men who were losing the battle. In a flash, he was back home, listening to his parents from the comfort of his bed, old enough to hear their words, not quite old enough to understand what they meant.

"We've lost so much," his mother said. She was on the verge of tears. That much Akolo knew for certain.

"Yes, but the temple has been rebuilt," his father said. "The rituals continue. We have not abandoned our God."

"Sometimes I wonder if God has abandoned us," she said, almost in a whisper.

"No! What are you saying? Of course God is still with us."

"But he let the invaders win..."

Akolo would never forget the long silence that followed. In that moment, he feared his parents had discovered he was eavesdropping. Finally, his father spoke words he would repeat many times in the years to come.

"There are no winners in war, only losers," he said.

Akolo sobbed.

They should have killed me, too, he thought, wiping away another dusty tear. Anger and heartache battled in his soul. Most of the time he couldn't distinguish one from the other.

"Abba? Imma?" he cried aloud, his voice aching with every word. The shadow that fell across his dimly lit doorway shifted ever so slightly. Akolo was once again under guard, but this was no temple. He looked around the small windowless room but saw only the rough-hewn mat that barely passed for a bed, the empty plate that once held a small hunk of stale bread, and a pot that gave off a stench so vile it stole Akolo's breath and made him want to retch.

This, he concluded, is a prison cell.

He could make a run for it—he was fast; his mother always said so.

Said so.

His mother. His father. His entire family...gone.

Akolo released another painful sob.

He pictured the leader of the conquering army again—the tall man with the unreadable expression who saved him from certain death. The man who *didn't* save his family.

Akolo slid his hand into his pocket and found the vibrant gemstone—the one the high priestess had dropped at the altar during their frantic escape from the temple. Its dark body caught what little light filtered through the entrance, the play-of-color effect dancing across its surface like trapped fire. He was surprised, but thankful the soldiers hadn't discovered it when they captured him. He rubbed it like a talisman, then imagined pulling out his favorite sling and hurling a stone at the guard, blinding him. Or at least breaking his nose.

He gripped the stone tight.

But there was nowhere to run. Nowhere to go.

He didn't even know where he was.

TWO

"ZACH, ARIEL, BREAKFAST!" Ian called up the stairs, then returned to the kitchen table. As always, before enjoying his coffee, he scrolled through his favorite '80s playlist on the iPod Shuffle Lyana gave him on his last birthday. *Perfect!* he thought. He clicked on Heart's "These Dreams" and played it through the new speakers he had installed in the kitchen when Marshall was rewiring the house.

Spare a little candle
Save some light for me
Figures up ahead
Moving in the trees
White skin in linen
Perfume on my wrist
And the full moon that hangs over
These dreams in the mist

The song continued as Ian sipped his coffee and stretched his neck to work out the kinks from a good night's sleep. Well, his wife's good night's sleep anyway. Ian had twisted himself into a pretzel to accommodate Lyana's sprawl, rather than gently nudge her to her side of the bed like he typically did. She deserved an undisturbed night of sleep. And he didn't mind, really. Watching his wife sleep peacefully had always been something he looked forward to. But never so much as now, after what she'd endured—after what they'd all endured in the past months. So maybe he had a stiff neck—it was still a good night.

As the signature drum fill set up the chorus, a grin spread across his face. He remembered Lyana's patient voice coaching him: "Don't chase the melody, Ian. Find your own part." He'd been practicing ever since Lyana's impromptu family music lessons—Ariel rolling her eyes, Zach enthusiastically getting into it, all of them crowded around the old piano. This morning, for once, he finally nailed it—his voice finding the sweet spot below Ann Wilson's powerhouse vocals, creating the kind of harmony that sent chills down his spine.

These dreams go on when I close my eyes
Every second of the night I live another life
These dreams that sleep when it's cold outside
Every moment I'm awake the further I'm away

Ariel sauntered into the kitchen and slumped into the chair next to Ian, disturbing his imaginary concert.

"What's for breakfast?" she mumbled.

"What's for breakfast? Um…that was going to be my question," said Ian.

"Huh?"

"It's International Make Breakfast for Your Parents Day," said Ian, a small smile coming to his face.

"Sorry, no can do," said Ariel, curling her lips into a smirk. "It's a school day and I have a big test. Besides, that's not a thing."

Ian took another sip of his coffee, relieved, in a way, to see his teenage daughter back to her snarky self after such a long season of uncertainty.

"It's a thing now," said Ian. "I've just declared it. I look forward to seeing what you and Zach make for us." He looked over at the stairs, expecting to see Zach, but it was Lyana coming down to join them. He pointed to the coffeemaker on the counter. "Freshly ground and everything."

Lyana smiled and walked over to pour herself a cup.

"The kids are making breakfast for us today," Ian said to her. "I've declared it International Make Breakfast for Your Parents Day."

Ariel harrumphed and scooted her chair back. "Nope. Still not a thing, Dad," she said, then walked to the refrigerator and opened it, staring inside.

After a couple minutes, Ian turned to Ariel. "I'm fond of scrambled eggs and bacon, if you're trying to decide what to make. Or are you just trying to cool the house down?"

Even though her back was to him, Ian was sure she rolled her eyes at him. She finally reached into the fridge and pulled out a pizza box, then plopped it onto the kitchen table before sitting down.

"Eat up," she said, pointing to the box.

"Pizza? For breakfast?" said Ian.

Ariel glanced up at him and raised her eyebrows. "You're welcome," she said, then grabbed a slice of pepperoni.

Lyana walked back to the table and sat down with her steaming cup of coffee. "Sounds delicious," she said, then pulled a slice from the box.

"See?" Ariel pointed her slice of pizza at her mom. "Mom gets it."

Ian shook his head. "Guess I'm outnumbered." He grabbed a slice of pizza and took a bite. "Wow, you made this all by yourself? Kudos to the breakfast chef."

Ariel stripped a piece of pepperoni off her slice and flicked it at Ian. He caught it, then stuffed it into his mouth.

"Nice catch," said Lyana.

"Zach's missing out," said Ian. He looked over toward the stairs. "Maybe I should check on him…"

"Don't get up. I got this," said Ariel. She walked over to the base of the staircase, then, with a mouth half-full of pizza, shouted, "Hey, Zach! Pizza for breakfast!"

They all waited for a response. None came. Ariel shrugged, then returned to her seat.

"I tried," she said.

"Must be exhausted from… What exactly was he doing last night?" asked Lyana.

Ian stood and walked over to the living room. He bent down and picked up a sock. "Watching TV. And leaving his socks on the couch."

"Gross," said Ariel.

"Speaking of gross, Ariel," began Lyana, "weren't you supposed to clean your bathroom yesterday?" Lyana raised an eyebrow.

"That's not my mess. Zach…"

Ian interrupted as he returned to the table, "…is using makeup now? And moisturizers? That's new…"

"Okay, *some* of it is my mess." She offered an exaggerated sigh. "Fine. I'll do it." Ariel took a long swig of orange juice. "Later."

Ian knew exactly what "later" meant in Ariel's vocabulary: It would take at least three more reminders. A knowing look from Lyana cemented that certainty. She smiled at Ian and shook her head ever so slightly. Ariel's reluctance to do chores meant things were back to normal. At least as normal as could be expected in a house that had been trying to kill Lyana just months earlier.

Ian turned his thoughts to Zach. Maybe he wasn't feeling well. Getting up at the last minute on a school day wasn't entirely unusual for the smarter-than-his-age middle schooler, but the word *pizza* was like Pavlov's bell to Zach. Ian knew he might be worrying unnecessarily, but the season when everything fell apart was still fresh in his memory, despite how well things had been going lately. He scooted his chair back and stood. "I'll just check on Zach. Make sure he's up. Or at least make sure he's not being swarmed by bees again." The memory of that day made Ian shiver. They'd almost lost Zach.

"Tell him he has to help with the bathroom cleaning," Ariel shouted after him. "Later, I mean," she added.

Ian nodded and took the stairs one at a time, silently counting them as he went, just as Zach always did. It was Zach's way of maintaining a modicum of control. Of balance. A hazy memory from the previous night flashed in Ian's head. He was lying in bed with Lyana when he heard Zach counting aloud his steps on the way up to his room.

Fifteen... He didn't stop at fifteen. He always stops at fifteen.

Ian stepped onto the landing. The fifteenth step. A wave of nausea swept through his stomach. He shook it off. "I'm overthinking again," he said to himself. He walked up to Zach's door and knocked.

"Hey, Zach, we're all eating pizza for breakfast. And it's a school day, remember?" He waited for a response. None came. Ian grabbed the doorknob and turned it, then gently pushed the door inward. "You feeling okay, buddy...?" Ian stepped into the room and froze. Zach's bed was empty, still made up the way Zach liked to make his bed in the morning—with pillows in the middle of the bed and the comforter pulled up over them. "I just like the way it looks," he'd said, as if that explained everything. Ian walked over and gently pushed on the lump in the middle of the bed. Sure enough, it was just the pillows. He surveyed the rest of the room. The laptop on Zach's desk was resting atop a stack of books—school textbooks, it appeared—lifting it to a "standing desk" height. Ian wondered when Zach had started doing that. There were clothes on the floor next to his dresser and the closet door was half-open. A crumpled potato chip bag rested on the floor just next to the otherwise empty trash can. That seemed odd. Zach preferred order to chaos. Or at least an orderly chaos. He checked the closet, looked under the bed, then stood in the room staring at the spot in the wall where the bees had been hiding months ago. Marshall had repaired the wall so expertly it was nearly impossible to identify the exact spot. Nothing else seemed out of order.

He left the room and walked to the kids' bathroom. It was indeed a mess, but there was no evidence of Zach. Ian walked a little more briskly down the stairs to the kitchen. He tried his best to sound calm, but fear was bubbling just under the surface. "Zach's not in his room. Not in the bathroom either."

Lyana stood suddenly, her chair tumbling to the ground behind her. "Zach?" she called out. "Zach?"

Ian walked over and picked up Lyana's chair, then rested his hand on her shoulder. "I'm sure it's nothing. Maybe he decided to take a morning walk." *He could have gotten up early and headed out*, thought Ian. But that didn't seem like something Zach would do. Zach sometimes got himself in trouble—Ian recalled the time he and Ariel had sneaked into Marshall's house—but lately he'd been extra careful to let his parents know if he was going out.

"Could he have gone to a friend's house?" asked Lyana. Zach didn't really have close friends. There were a couple of kids in his class who were friendly toward him, but his brief season as a "celebrity" after recovering from the potentially fatal bee attack had begun to fade. He was just a regular kid now, a kid who usually kept to himself. At the last parent-teacher conference, Ian and Lyana learned he was closer to his teachers than his peers.

"You mean last night? No, I heard him coming up the stairs. And besides, he would have told us," said Ian.

"Maybe he forgot today was a Friday," said Lyana.

"Zach forget the date? Yeah right," said Ariel. "He's obsessive at marking the days on his calendar."

Ian nodded. "I'll check outside. Maybe you two could just sweep the house to make sure…" *To make sure what?* thought Ian. *That the house hasn't swallowed him up?* "He's probably just playing hide-and-seek and just forgot to tell us." Ian's attempt at a joke fell flat, as it should have. It was a poor attempt to lighten the quickly darkening mood.

Ian had started toward the door when Lyana called to him, "Maybe he's out visiting Marshall?"

"Good idea. I'll check," said Ian. Marshall had become more than just "the caretaker," as folks around town called him. After helping the Keanes with Zach in the hospital, through their trials with the house and the old wiring, and Lyana's strange illness, he had become a friend, but remained mysterious in his personal life. It still made no sense to Ian—this supernatural event—but he had been hopeful all that was in the past—that Marshall's brilliant idea to rewire the house had ended whatever it was that possessed Lyana. *Was that the right word? Possessed?* Ian shook the image of his catatonic wife out of his head as he walked briskly around the house. He passed the garden, then stopped to stare at their favorite bistro table and chairs, remembering the meaningful moments he and Lyana had shared there throughout the years. Somehow that little three-piece sitting area had lasted from Kentucky, to Boston, and now Littleton. Ian ran his hand along the back of one of the chairs, then snapped back into focus, continuing around the side of the house, pausing again at the chicken coop.

"Zach?" he called out, peering through the wire fencing. He shook his head. *Of course he isn't hiding in the chicken coop.* Ian continued searching the grounds, calling out Zach's name and then pausing to listen for a response. None came. After making a quick search of the grounds, Ian headed back toward Marshall's cabin, trusting his memory of the map Ariel had drawn for him. They rarely saw him outside of his modest one-room shack. It seemed like an odd living situation for a man who possessed numerous marketable skills. He was a gifted carpenter—an artist, really—and, at least for the Keanes in their time of need, a clever electrician. He occasionally performed odd jobs around town, even at Zach's school, but otherwise kept to himself doing... *What did he do with his time?* Ian wondered.

Ian crossed into the woods, then followed an almost invisible path until he reached the cabin. He hesitated before knocking on the door—noticing the symbol etched there. He was surprised he hadn't noticed it the first time he had stumbled onto the cabin with Zach. At a glance, it would have been easy to miss for an untrained eye. But he should have instantly recognized it—an ancient and primitive version of the ouroboros—the snake eating its own tail. It was similar to the carving on the bracelet Ian had brought home for Zach after lecturing at one of his seminars in the Middle East. But it was the same variation of the symbol on the cabin door that had appeared around the Tudor-style house they had called home now for just over six months. Zach drew it after seeing it on his bedroom wall, and he found it again etched on the lamppost in the front yard. How was it that he hadn't noticed that before?

When no one answered, Ian turned around to head back to the house. He took one step, then stopped. *Could Zach be hiding in the cabin?* Another shiver ran through his body. He was so over these kinds of shivers, exhausted by the inexplicable events that had defined so much of their time in their new house.

He started to turn back toward the door when he heard Marshall's voice calling from behind him.

"I'm not home," said Marshall. Ian turned around and waited for the old man to approach. Marshall carried himself with a rare kind of inner strength, and in this moment, also a rather bold outer strength: He was carrying an axe on his shoulder. Not for the first time that morning, Ian shook off an uninvited thought and focused on the issue at hand.

"Hey, you haven't seen Zach, have you?" Ian said, working hard not to stare at the axe blade.

"Has he gone missing?"

Ian was taken aback. "Um...why would you say that?" Ian couldn't read Marshall's expression.

"Well, you just asked if I'd seen him. I presume that's because you're looking for him and haven't found him yet. Therefore...missing."

"Right." He nodded absently toward the cabin. Marshall looked over Ian's shoulder, then back at Ian.

"And you think he might be in my cabin?" This time Marshall's expression was totally readable. He looked a little put out with Ian.

"No, well...I don't know. I know he likes to go exploring..."

Marshall nodded, then walked past Ian. He paused at the door and examined the trim toward the top. "I would be very surprised if he's in here," he muttered, then opened the door and gestured for Ian to enter first. "If he is, he must have sneaked in while I was out."

Ian stared at the axe that was still on Marshall's shoulder. Marshall smiled and gently set the axe down on the ground outside the front door. "Don't worry, Ian. I haven't murdered anyone..." He paused for effect, then gave Ian a look that would have scared Jack Nicholson. "Yet."

Marshall laughed and slapped Ian on the back and the two entered Marshall's home. It took a moment for Ian's eyes to adjust to the dimly lit space, but it didn't take long to determine that Zach wasn't there.

"Could be wandering along the stream," said Marshall. "He collects rocks and things, doesn't he?"

Ian nodded, picturing the growing collection of random items that filled Zach's bookshelves.

"If we split up, we can cover more ground," said Marshall. He paused in the doorway and turned around. "You coming?"

Ian took one last look around Marshall's tiny cabin and followed him outside. He would have liked to have stayed longer and ask Marshall about the dozens of books, *in dozens of languages*, that overflowed the shelves, or the many wood carvings, old electronics, and glass jars and bottles of every size that littered the small worktable.

He decided to save those questions for another time when he wasn't distracted.

The two men headed in different directions, each calling out Zach's name.

• • •

Lyana called out to Ariel, and they met in the kitchen.

"Any clues?" asked Lyana.

"None." Ariel was fidgeting with a scrunchie she'd pulled out of her hair. "You don't think…" She paused.

"Don't think what?" Lyana asked, though she knew what Ariel was about to say.

"What if…the house…is…you know, doing things again?" Ariel tugged harder at the scrunchie, twisting it this way and that.

"Don't let your thoughts go there again, Ariel. Marshall and your dad repaired all the wiring that was the source of whatever was going on. It's all in the past now."

"Is it?"

"Of course it is." Lyana pulled Ariel into a hug that she needed at least as much as Ariel. "I'm sure Zach is fine. He's probably out counting birds or rocks or something and lost track of time. He'll be back. You'll see."

Ariel pulled away from the hug. "I guess you're right. I mean, things were finally getting back to some kind of normal…"

"That's a good way to describe it," said Lyana. "'Some kind of normal.'" Ariel had been the slowest to find any peace after the crazy events of the past few months. Lyana attributed much of that to her being a typical surly teenager. But it was more than that. Despite claiming to be "all in" on their move from Boston, Ariel had never fully embraced the move. It was more like she was still trying to find the good in it. This was totally understandable, of course. Lyana herself had wondered for a moment if the move had been a terrible idea. But it was only a moment's regret. Despite all she'd been through, despite what they'd *all* been through, she was more convinced than ever that this was exactly where they needed to be. She only wished Ariel could feel that way too.

"Do you remember the kid from science class Zach was talking about at supper a few nights ago? Umm…Henry, I think it was? Zach said Henry's brother Nathan was in your class. Maybe you could call him and ask…"

"Nathan? Ew, no. I'm not calling *him*. Nathan is a narcissistic moron. Trust me, I googled it."

"Ariel, that's not a nice…"

"But it's true, Mom. He's not a good person. Maybe Henry is cool, but his brother? The opposite of cool. And besides, why would you think I had Nathan's number? I would never."

"Okay, okay. Fine. What's their last name? I'll find their number and call."

Ariel huffed. "Hampton. But he's not there, Mom. There's no way Zach is hanging out with Henry. Or anyone from school. And how would he even get there? Dad said he was here last night, so… what, did he get up early and call a friend to come get him so he could hang out before school? That doesn't make any sense at all. Besides, he doesn't have that kind of friend."

That truth landed hard on Lyana's heart. She knew this, of course, but it still hurt to realize her son struggled to make friends.

A garbled whisper caught Lyana's ear.

"What was that?" Lyana asked.

"I said he doesn't have that kind of friend," said Ariel, scrunching her face into a familiar teenage scowl.

"No, I mean after that."

"I didn't say anything after that."

But there was a voice. Wasn't there? Maybe it was just the wind. Lyana could always tell when the wind had picked up. The house made a peculiar sound on windy days and nights.

"Maybe we can look around the house again?"

Ariel sighed. "Mom, he's not here, okay?"

No, he's not, thought Lyana.

"Well, I guess we just wait for your dad, then." Lyana walked into the kitchen. "Are you hungry? Want something to eat?"

"I just ate two slices of pizza. I'm not hungry."

"Right, sorry."

Ariel just stared at Lyana, her expression a curious blend of concern and boredom.

"I'm going to my room to finish getting ready for school," Ariel said. When Lyana didn't reply, she added, "Call me when the little jerk shows up so I can yell at him."

"Ariel…" began Lyana, but she stopped herself. This was not a time for correction. "I'll come find you the minute Zach is back."

Ariel bounded over to the stairs and took them two at a time. When her bedroom door closed, it wasn't quite a slam, but almost. Lyana bit her tongue yet again.

After a few minutes of wandering back and forth from room to room, Lyana decided she had to busy herself with something or she'd go crazy—again. She walked over to the pantry to search for a cake mix. When she glanced at the old mirror that graced the back wall of the small room, she once again thought she heard a voice. But the words were indistinct.

Please, not this again, she said to herself.

•••

Marshall had walked up and down the edge of the stream for nearly an hour before meeting back up with Ian in the clearing behind the house. Neither of them had found any clues as to Zach's whereabouts. Ian then left to go back to the house and Marshall had returned to his cabin.

He walked over to the bookshelf and picked up the old bracelet with the ouroboros symbol carved into the dark stone. The leather straps that held it had been replaced more than once, but the stone barely showed signs of wear.

Marshall squeezed the stone in his hand and looked up as if staring through his ceiling into the sky.

"This is not how I thought things would go," he said aloud. "I don't know what to do."

He closed his eyes and whispered. "*Be with me.*"

THREE

"COME."

It was a single word, and a command. Akolo crawled off his sleeping mat and stood. His muscles ached and the only food he'd eaten since they had arrived after a long journey was that stale hunk of bread. He started to stretch, to work his muscles back to life, but a grunt from the guard cut his morning routine short. Was it morning? He couldn't tell in the windowless room.

Akolo followed the guard out into a hallway that stretched forever in both directions. Evenly spaced torches lit the hallways, their fiery reflections flickering onto the clean white surface. Akolo slowed his steps and reached out to touch the wall. It was nothing like the rough stone of the temple building back home. This was smooth—almost as smooth as the goblet he had once held while helping his father in the temple. His father had said the goblet was made of glass. It seemed almost like sorcery that something could be so smooth and so clear. Lost in his thoughts, Akolo stood there stroking the shimmering wall.

A tear came to his eye. How far were they now from home? How many days had they marched to get to this strange place? He was already so tired of all the tears. He wiped the tear away with the back of his hand. The guard, who had continued walking ahead of him, stopped and turned around.

"Keep up," he said.

The man spoke Akolo's language, but with an accent. He sounded like the man who had led the conquering army. The man who had said, "We are going to need him."

Akolo didn't dare ask where he was going. The guard's abrupt manner made it clear he wasn't eager for conversation. As they walked along the hall, Akolo noted all the doorways on either side of it. Some had closed wooden doors; some had no doors at all. But even more curious was just how empty the place appeared to be. All this space, all these rooms—and no people to fill them. This was the opposite of what he'd known growing up. At home, people flowed in and out of the city like the water of the Jordan River itself.

They approached a stairway and the guard paused, then pointed, directing Akolo to climb the stairs. Akolo hesitated. What was he walking into?

"Go," said the guard, nudging him forward with the hilt of his sword. It was a small sword, but decorated with colorful stones that glittered in the light of the flickering torches. Akolo slipped his hand into his pocket and wrapped his fingers around his stone again. Then he began to climb the stairs. As he ascended, the air became cooler, and a blueish light filtered down from above. At the top of the stairs, he walked through a doorway and stopped, staring in wonder at the expansive courtyard before him. It was clear from the color of the sky above that it was early morning. Akolo took in a deep breath. The air smelled of green plants and flowers, but he saw only a few trees neatly arranged around the perimeter of the courtyard.

The guard led him across the neatly manicured grounds to the biggest door he had ever seen. It was completely covered in gold with images made of colorful stones and was at least four times his height and nearly as wide as it was tall.

A soldier could ride his horse through that door and not have to duck.

They walked through the door into a grand room. Wide columns of stone were interspersed throughout the immense space. They held up a high ceiling decorated with intricate woven patterns of blue and gold. The walls were shiny white, like the walls below ground, but here, that white was interrupted in places by floor-to-ceiling panels painted with patterns to match the ceiling. To the right and left, Akolo saw openings that led to more hallways. Ahead of him was an entrance to yet another room.

The guard started walking toward the doorway at the very back of the room, then gestured for Akolo to follow. Akolo had been so mesmerized by everything around him, he almost missed the guards standing at attention on either side of that doorway. He tried to take in the entirety of the scene. *This grand hall is a gathering place. A hundred people could fit in this room. But what is this room we're heading to?*

"You have an audience with the king," said the guard. "You will bow before him."

A throne room, he thought. *This is a palace.*

They entered the throne room. The guard guided him to turn left and walk to the end of the surprisingly narrow area, but Akolo was again stopped by the magnificence before him. The scene of a great battle stretched out before him in either direction along the back of the throne room wall. The carved stone depiction was so detailed he could almost hear the sounds of the battle and smell the fires burning in the background.

Akolo glanced to his right and saw a blank wall. *What battle would this king have carved into this space?* he wondered. He swallowed hard, then turned to face the throne that sat at the far end of the room to his left.

The throne was elegant, but empty. A tall man with his back to Akolo was talking with someone just to the side of the throne. Akolo stopped a few feet from the man, as directed by his accompanying guard. The tall man turned toward Akolo. It was the man with the curious expression.

The man who had separated him from his family.

Akolo's knees were shaking. He knew he was expected to show respect to this leader—this king. But the anger inside was bubbling up faster than he could quell it.

"Where is my family?" He nearly spit the words out. The guard who had brought him to the room grabbed the hilt of his sword, but the king stopped him.

"Put your sword away," the king said, waving his hand with a simple gesture. His voice was commanding but calm.

Akolo repeated his question, but this time his voice was quivering. "Where is my family?" His head fell forward, and tears once again filled his eyes.

The king stepped toward Akolo and gently lifted his chin.

"What is your name, child?" he asked.

Akolo hated the feel of the man's fingers on his chin, but he stopped himself from shaking them off. "Akolo," he said.

"Tell me about your family," the king said.

Akolo hesitated. Did he not remember separating him from his family during the siege on Akolo's home? He didn't trust this man.

The king removed his fingers from Akolo's chin and stretched up to his full height. Akolo felt like he was standing before a giant. The king nodded.

"Your family served the high priest, did they not?" he said.

Akolo shook his head. "My mother and sisters served the high priestess," he said.

"And your father...he was an advisor to the king?"

Akolo nodded.

The king paused as if in deep thought before continuing. "In war, there are always casualties," he said. "Do you know what that word means?"

Akolo shook his head again.

"We liberated your city," said the king. "But there is a cost to liberation. Always a cost." The king folded his hands behind his back and began walking back and forth as he spoke. "Your family was part of that cost. They are gone." He stopped walking and turned back toward Akolo. "The god you serve…does this god have great power?"

Akolo didn't know what to say. He had asked his mother many times about the God they served. She had always answered, "Our God is a great God. He is good and fair. He will protect us." But Akolo was rarely satisfied by such a simple answer, so he would keep asking questions. Usually, she would simply reply, "Someday you will understand." But one time, she added, "Akolo, it is good to ask questions. But sometimes the answers are difficult. Our God is great, but he is also mysterious." Akolo could still picture the look on his mother's face. She was the kindest person he had ever known, and she always spoke the truth.

"Yes," said Akolo, finally.

"Then I would like to know this god. And you will help me."

The king gestured with a flip of his hand and the guard nudged Akolo to turn around and leave the throne room.

Akolo resisted and opened his mouth to reply, but he couldn't find the words. He didn't want to help this man. He just wanted his family back. The guard nudged him again, and Akolo shuffled forward, his head bowed. Mindlessly, he left the throne room, crossed the floor of the grand room, exited into the courtyard, descended the stairs, and walked down the hallway. The guard stopped at the room with the straw mat and nodded for Akolo to enter. He took one step, then stopped.

"What did the king mean about the cost of lib…liberation?" he asked. "What happened to my family."

"It means your family is dead," said the guard. There was no emotion in his voice. He gestured again for Akolo to enter the small room. He walked over and dropped onto the mat.

Then it is true. My family is gone.

Where was Akolo's good and fair God now?

Akolo wept.

• • •

Zach closed his eyes tight and counted to ten. Before opening them, he silently prayed that he would find himself in bed. That this had indeed all been a crazy dream.

But when he opened his eyes, he was still standing at the bottom of a long stone stairway, looking at a hallway that stretched on forever. The glow from the distant torch beckoned him. He took one step, then two, then three. He counted every step he took until he found himself standing next to the flickering light. It wasn't a simple wooden torch after all—the flame was coming from a clay bowl filled with some kind of oil.

"Oh, wow," he said quietly to himself. He had seen this sort of thing before. Zach had always been intrigued by his father's studies of ancient cultures. He loved to sit and listen to his father talk about some new discovery he'd made while researching information for a new course he would be teaching. His favorite stories were about his father's visits to archaeological digs. "It's almost exactly like Indiana Jones," his father would say. "Except fewer Nazis," he would always add, expecting (and getting) an eyeroll, and sometimes a giggle, from Zach.

"At least there are no snakes. I know how much you *love* snakes," Zach would comment back with a smirk.

Zach recognized the source of flickering light as an oil lamp. His father had brought one back from one of the digs he visited. Zach could picture it sitting on the shelf in his father's study, right next to the bright yellow clay pot Zach himself had made in elementary school.

"It looks a lot like my third grade art project," Zach had said when presented with the small clay pot.

"Ah, but it's so much more. You're holding a lamp, Zach. Someone held this very lamp twenty-five hundred years ago!"

The look in his father's eyes in that moment was one of wonder. It was a favorite of his father's looks. Zach had quickly and carefully handed the lamp back to his father, afraid that he might drop it and destroy such an ancient treasure.

"Can you imagine a time when there was no electricity? When the only light at night was provided by a lamp like this?"

No, Zach couldn't have imagined that at all. Not as he watched his father hold the simple clay object between his fingers and turned it this way and that. But now, he was staring at something so similar, it might as well have been from the same artisan.

Twenty-five hundred years.

That's a long, long time ago. Zach searched his memory banks for anything else he knew about that period in ancient history. He ran his fingers along the wall, tried to remember what he'd read in his father's books about the building materials of the time. *Could this be marble?* he wondered. The material was smooth, but not as polished as the marble he'd run his fingers across at the Boston Public Library. No, this was something else.

The sound of approaching footsteps pulled him out of his memories and back to his current, confusing reality. "What exactly is this place?" he wondered aloud. There were two darkened doorways on either side of the hallway in front of him. He made a quick decision and darted into the one on the right, then crouched in the shadows.

Zach had suspected something was still off about their house. The literal fog had lifted from their property, but he still had questions about the place they now called home. There was something off about Marshall, too. It was like Marshall knew something he wasn't telling them. Sure, he'd been the one to save his mother, to save them all, in a way. But...

Zach's racing thoughts hit a wall. The weight of his current circumstance landed on him with a thud.

What if I didn't just travel to a foreign land? he thought. *What if...* He could barely form the words, even in his mind. *What if I've traveled to a foreign time?*

Zach found the possibility equally exciting and frightening. *Is such a thing even possible?* He loved time travel stories, but this wasn't a story. This was his life! Zach realized he was absently twirling the bracelet he wore on his left hand. He looked down at it and saw the symbol that had kept appearing on their property. A snake eating its own tail. A symbol of life, death and rebirth. The Ouroboros. He had looked it up.

The footsteps drew closer. Zach held his breath.

I'm going to be late for school, he thought. *No, not late. Early. Twenty-five hundred years early.*

FOUR

IAN WALKED INTO the kitchen. Lyana was seated at the table, her hands wrapped around a cup of coffee. She seemed lost in thought. He knew the answer to his question before asking it, but he asked it anyway.

"Any luck?" he said.

Lyana shook her head. Ian sat down across from her and reached out his hands. She removed hers from the coffee cup and gently grasped his.

"Did you or Ariel think of anyone you could call?" he asked.

"No," she said. "I mentioned the boy, Henry, that Zach was talking about the other day, but...she's certain he wouldn't be hanging out with him." Lyana shook her head again. "Oh, Ian, what if he's..."

"Zach is fine," interrupted Ian. "He's eternally curious, but he's also resourceful. I'm sure he's just out adventuring somewhere."

"On a school day?" Lyana pulled her hands back and returned them to the coffee cup. "You were out in the woods. You didn't see him?"

"Well, no. But it's a big forest..." Ian stopped when he realized what he'd just said.

"What if he's…what if he's in trouble? Hurt or something? You know how he is—some things are challenging for him."

"He's only been gone a little while…"

Lyana stood suddenly, her chair scraping the floor with a piercing screech. "Ian, we don't *know* how long he's been gone." She started pacing in the kitchen. "He could have been gone for hours. We should call the police…"

"It's too soon for that," said Ian. He pointed to Lyana's coffee cup and raised an eyebrow. She nodded, so he picked it up and took a sip. It was tepid, but he didn't flinch. He needed caffeine and didn't care in that moment what form it took.

"What did Marshall say?" asked Lyana. She had stopped pacing and was staring out the kitchen window.

Ian's thoughts returned to Marshall's cabin. There was something about the small shack that troubled him. He pictured the books in Marshall's bookcase. They were old books—the kind of books you'd find in the basement of a library—or in the rare books section. What would a carpenter want with all those books? Was he a collector? He wondered once again why anyone would choose to live that way. Especially someone who had money. *He had money, right?* thought Ian.

"Ian?" Lyana's voice brought Ian back to the present. "Where did you go just now? I spoke to you, and you didn't respond. You seemed…lost."

Ian straightened his shoulders and stretched his neck left, then right. "Lost? No, just thinking, that's all." Had she really spoken to him? He hadn't heard a thing.

"So, what are we going to do now? Just wait?"

Ian pursed his lips. "Mmm…no. Not just wait." He stood. "I'm going to drive around and see if he's out on the road or something."

Lyana nodded. "Yes, that could be it. Maybe he decided to walk to school?"

"Yeah, maybe," said Ian with uncertainty in his voice. But it was a few miles to the school, and he couldn't imagine Zach choosing to walk there.

"Take Ariel with you," said Lyana.

Ian nodded. "Good idea." Ian stood and started toward the stairs, then stopped and walked over to Lyana. He pulled her into a hug. "It's going to be fine. I know it."

Lyana didn't respond, but she hugged Ian tight before pushing him away and pointing toward the stairs. "I don't want her sitting up there alone, you know? She was anxious about a big test today, but I don't think she wanted to miss school." Lyana paused.

Ian slapped his hand to the side of his head. "We forgot to take her to school," he said. He shook his head. "I can't believe we forgot that."

"It's okay. I called the school, and I already apologized to her. Honestly, I can't tell if she's upset or happy about it," said Lyana.

"I'll go get her," said Ian. "She can be my lookout."

A few moments later, Ian walked down the stairs, Ariel lagging behind. Lyana was in the pantry looking for something when they passed her on the way to the garage. They climbed into the car. As they backed out of the garage, Ian turned to look at his teenaged daughter. Her expression was unreadable, but that had been the case for a while now. She had always been a smart and thoughtful kid—a great big sister to Zach, but ever since they'd moved, her moods had become more and more unpredictable. *Par for the course,* Ian had told Lyana one evening recently when they were talking about Ariel. *She's moody, right? Isn't that how all teenage girls act?* He'd expected Lyana to agree with him. Instead, she'd just offered a closemouthed smile and patted him on the back like she was patronizing him.

"Keep your eyes peeled," he said. They began heading down the long driveway.

Ariel huffed. "What does that even mean?" she said. Ian knew she didn't really want him to answer, so he bit his lip.

As they drove into the shadow of the trees, Ariel opened her window. She turned toward it and yelled, "Zach!" She repeated his name over and over. There was almost a violence to her tone. It was sharp, decisive, and maybe even a little bitter.

When they reached the end of the driveway, she dropped back down in her seat and folded her arms in front of her.

"What if he's dead?" she said. This time her voice was the opposite of decisive.

"Why would you even say such a thing?" said Ian, aghast. He paused at the intersection, wondering if he should turn left toward town, or right, deeper into the forest. He turned left.

"We have to consider all possibilities, Dad," she said.

Ian shook his head. "No. We don't. Zach is fine. And we're going to find him." He was driving slowly, scouring the side of the road, hoping no speeding cars would pull up behind him. Ariel was still staring straight ahead. "Please, can you just look for him out your window? Two sets of eyes are better than one..."

"Fine," she said. She turned toward the window and yelled out Zach's name again.

They drove along the road for a while, then pulled over at a park on the edge of town. Some kids were playing catch with a football on the baseball field. *Probably homeschooled*, thought Ian. *Why else would they be at the park on a school day?*

Ian turned to Ariel. After calling his name a few times, she'd stopped and slunk back into her seat.

"This is pointless," she said, breaking the awkward silence.

"It's not pointless," said Ian. He reached up to brush Ariel's hair from her face. She reflexively pushed his hand away, then turned to face Ian directly.

"What if he doesn't want to be found?" she asked.

"What do you mean?"

"What if he's sick of this stupid town and ran away? Have you considered that?"

"Okay, Ariel, clue me in here. What's this really about?"

Ariel huffed again, then suddenly opened the car door and climbed out. Ian turned off the ignition and followed her. She stomped over to the aluminum bleachers behind the backstop and sat on the bottom plank, then put her face in her hands. Ian sat next to her. He considered putting his arm around her, then decided not to. He was less sure lately when it was best to offer a hug and when it was best to give her space.

"I don't like it here," she said, finally. Her voice was calm, collected. She spoke as if she'd been rehearsing her words. "Mom loves the house. I mean, it's a really cool house, don't get me wrong. But hello? It literally almost killed her! You do remember that, right? The bees swarming Zach? That wasn't normal, Dad. And what about Marshall, who just happens to know exactly how to fix everything but won't explain anything? There's something seriously wrong with that guy. I don't care how much he's helped us. I don't trust him!" She took a deep breath, sighed. "So why would Mom want to stay? Why should any of us want to stay? That's the thing I don't get, Dad. I just don't get it. Somebody please tell me why we're not already back in Boston?"

Despite her typical teenage unpredictability, Ariel had seemed to be doing fine. Her grades were good, and she'd made friends at school. Yes, the family had been through a lot in the past half year, but that was behind them now.

Wasn't it?

Ian didn't know what to say, so they sat there without talking for a while, listening to the kids shout and cheer while they tossed the football around the field. He was just about to initiate conversation when the football bounced up against the chain-link backstop in front of them with a loud clank that made them both jump. One of the kids—a preteen boy—rushed over, stared at Ariel for a second, then gathered the football and left. Ariel stood and started to head back to the car. Ian quickly followed.

"I want to go home, now," said Ariel. Ian wasn't entirely certain what she meant, but he didn't ask for clarification.

They drove in silence back to the house. Ariel was out of the car before he'd turned it off. When he walked into the kitchen after her, she was already halfway up the stairs, heading to her room.

"Lyana," called Ian. She didn't respond. He walked throughout the first floor, looking for her. His heart started to beat faster. Had she gone missing, too? He was just about to head upstairs when he looked out the window and spied her sitting outside at their bistro table that overlooked the garden. He went outside and joined her.

"You didn't find him," she said as he sat down across from her.

"No," he answered.

She took a deep breath, closed her eyes and lifted her face to the heavens.

"You know, I really love the smell of the air out here," she said. "It's..." she paused. "Life giving."

For a moment, Ian was taken back to the city—to the smell of automobile exhaust, the redolent richness of rain on dirty sidewalks, the tantalizing scents coming from the restaurants that lined the streets. Boston had a unique smell to it. Maybe all cities did. But she was right. As much as those city smells—most of them good—had made him feel at home when they lived there, the scents at their new home were almost overpowering in their comfort. The smells at their forest home weren't any less complex than those of the city, but the scents out here worked together somehow, rather than competed for attention. Especially now that it was spring. Ian took a deep inhale through his nose and caught the slightest smell of the chicken coop. *Well, most of the smells anyway*, he thought.

"Something's bothering Ariel," he said. His voice was an affront to the momentary calm they'd been enjoying.

"I know," said Lyana.

"She's having second thoughts about our move."

Lyana opened her eyes and looked into Ian's. "Not second thoughts, Ian. She doesn't want to be here at all. She's been playing the part. Trying to be okay with everything. She even said things were getting back to 'some kind of normal' earlier. But the truth is..."

"This doesn't feel like home to her," Ian finished.

"Oh, it's home," said Lyana, her voice full of conviction. "This is undeniably our home." Lyana sighed. "But yeah. It doesn't feel like home to her. I wish Ariel could see this house the way I do."

Ian knew this was where they were supposed to be. But he couldn't deny a few lingering doubts. The house was still so much of a mystery. Then again, mysteries usually compelled Ian forward—he was drawn to them, like Zach. He...

"Hang on," he said. "I think I might know where Zach went." He stood, then started toward the door. Before opening it, he turned to Lyana. "Do you think you should talk to Ariel and get to the heart of the matter?"

Lyana nodded. "Of course." She stood, walked over to him and gave him a hug. "I hope you're right about Zach."

Ian forced a smile and went back through the house. *And I hope I'm wrong*, he thought.

• • •

Walking up the stairs, Lyana could hear music coming from Ariel's room. She recognized the song as one of Ariel's favorites.

Hard to be sure
Sometimes I feel so insecure

And love's so distant and obscure
Remains the cure
All by myself
Don't wanna be
All by myself anymore

"It's not Celine's version," said Lyana.

"I found this on the internet. The original artist, I guess. Eric something."

"Carmen?"

"Yeah." Ariel was lying on her bed, her journal in front of her, next to her pillow. Lyana opened her mouth to speak, but Ariel held up her hand. "Wait. Listen to this part."

The chorus had just finished, and the piano continued to play, accompanied by a sweetly melancholic string section. Lyana had heard this version of the song before but didn't recall such a long instrumental interlude.

Finally, the vocals returned, gently at first, then passionately following a drum fill almost as iconic as the one in Phil Collins's "In the Air Tonight." A moment later, the song faded to silence.

Ariel rolled over and looked up at the ceiling. "It's the same song, but…also it's not."

"What do you mean?" asked Lyana.

"Celine's version is like an anthem. I mean, it's a big song because she has a big voice, and I know it's sad, but…"

Lyana waited.

"But this version?" Ariel paused, seemingly at a loss for words. She took a deep breath. "This is so much sadder," she finally choked out.

Lyana pulled the chair from the desk and sat on it, facing the bed. She reached over to rest her hand on Ariel's. Ariel allowed the touch for a moment, then lifted her hand to wipe away a tear.

"That instrumental section is familiar," said Lyana. "I think it's based on something by Rachmaninoff..."

Ariel abruptly slapped her journal closed and scooted away into a seated position, her back against the headboard.

"I don't trust him," she said, her voice resolute.

"Who, Rachmaninoff?" Lyana said, unable to hide a small smile.

"No, not him," Ariel said with an intolerable inflection.

"Do you mean...Dad?" offered Lyana.

"Not Dad." She huffed. It was her go-to sound of late. "Marshall."

"Why do you say that?"

Ariel stared off into the distance, unwilling to meet Lyana's gaze. "And I don't like how you two have been buddy-buddy lately," she added.

Lyana was taken aback. Had she and Marshall been "buddy-buddy" lately? Sure, they'd been talking more—and she'd been enjoying his company and his wise words, but Ariel was overstating things. This wasn't an entirely new behavior for her. She had always been good at creating drama out of nothing. She wasn't quite a drama queen, but she was definitely drama queen adjacent.

"Why don't you trust him?"

Ariel sighed. "I don't think he's entirely truthful," she said. "He lives in a tiny cabin in the forest like some kind of crazed hermit. And what does he actually do during the day? What's his job?"

"He does odd jobs around town, but I think he's mostly retired..."

"Do you hear yourself, Mom? 'He does odd jobs around town.' That's like the perfect cover for a creeping tom...or a serial killer."

Lyana's eyes went wide. Then she tried, unsuccessfully, to stifle a laugh. "Creeping tom?"

Ariel huffed again.

"Did you mean peeping tom?" asked Lyana.

Ariel shook her head, then rolled her eyes. "Peeping tom, creeping tom. What's the difference? They're both..."

"Toms?" said Lyana.

This brought a half smile to Ariel's lips. "Yeah. They're both Toms." She looked at Lyana and her half smile faded. "I...I don't like it here, Mom."

"Oh, honey, I know it's been a rough few months, but..."

"You love it here, don't you." Ariel's words were more accusation than question.

"And you will grow to love it too," began Lyana.

"Why?" asked Ariel.

"Why will you love it too?"

Another exasperated sigh slipped from Ariel's lips. "No, Mom. Why do *you* love it? This house almost killed you."

Lyana sat back in the wooden chair, noticing the way it wobbled ever so slightly. "I love the way the house looks, the way it's laid out. The wood beams, the stonework. If only the walls could talk. I mean, it's just a great house. We have all this land around us, and you know how much I love the garden and the chickens and the creek and our community... It's, it's everything I've ever dreamed of. And there's something else." Lyana wasn't quite sure how to express the "something else."

"What?" asked Ariel.

"I'm not sure how to explain it, but I just know this house was meant for us."

Ariel seemed to consider Lyana's words, but then shook her head. "No, I don't know." She rolled over on her stomach and reached for her journal. "I think I'm done talking for now," she said. "Besides, apparently I'm 'sick' today, so I should probably get some rest."

"Ariel, I told you we were sorry we forgot..." began Lyana.

"Forget it. I'll just have to make up the test next week."

Lyana stood and scooted the chair back under the desk. "I noticed the chair is a little uneven. I can have Dad fix that if you want."

"Why not ask your buddy Marshall to do it?" said Ariel. Lyana opened her mouth to respond, but Ariel cut her off. "Kidding, Mom. But I don't want it to be fixed. I like that it wobbles."

Lyana nodded. "Okay." She walked out of Ariel's room and headed back downstairs to wait for Ian's return.

Please be okay Zach, she whispered as she walked through the house.

The house whispered back, *He will be okay*, and a chill ran down Lyana's spine.

• • •

Ariel turned on her music and flipped to the place she'd left off in the journal and began writing.

> *March 26, 2010*
>
> *Dear Diary, I'm going to stop starting each entry with "dear diary" because that's starting to feel juvenile. So anyway, here's the thing: The house I live in is trying to kill my family. It feels like that, anyway. I know I wrote about this before, but now that my brother is missing, I need to write about it again. Oh, and my brother is missing. I should have led with that.*
>
> *Zach* probably *is fine. I mean, it's disgusting how resourceful he can be sometimes. He's probably building a fort out of rocks and sticks somewhere. But because of the insane house stuff we went through (see other entries on this—I don't need to repeat myself here), I'm not totally confident about that. What if the house is doing crazy stuff again? What if it swallowed Zach up?*

Ariel paused and looked suspiciously over at the old intercom box on the wall by the door. She pressed pause on her music and listened intently. Was there crackling coming across the intercom? Wait…it sounded like faint music with foreign lyrics. She squinted, as if that might help her hear better. The music quickly faded away. A moment later she shook her head. No, that's just the sound of creaks and aches of an old house. *That's all it is.*

She returned to writing in her journal.

> *Also? I'm missing a math test today. I'm not sick. Mom and Dad just forgot to take me to school. Because of the Zach thing. To be honest, I'm not exactly torn up about that. Maybe a few more days of studying will make me less stressed about it.*
>
> *I'm trying to figure out what's going on with my mom. She should be more upset about Zach being missing. Dad's doing his best to keep cool, but I know he's having a hard time. I could tell by the way he didn't know what to say when we were parked at the baseball field earlier.*
>
> *I just don't get why Mom is so in love with this place. Yeah, it's a cool house. But…I'm looking at the intercom on the wall right now, and as cool as that was the first day we moved in, now it's creeping me out.*
>
> *That reminds me: I made a faux pas today (I think that's how you spell it). I called Marshall a "creeping tom" instead of "peeping tom." He comes across as a kind, quiet man, but something is off about him. I'm not afraid of him or anything. I don't really think he's a peeping tom. But… yeah. I don't know how to describe it.*
>
> *Creeping tom, I guess.*
>
> *Meanwhile, Garrett spoke to me yesterday in third period. I mean, it was just one word, but that counts, right? He saw me doodling in my notebook—I was drawing a*

zombified giraffe because I'd already finished my worksheet—and that's when he said, "Nice." Garrett is a strange guy. Dresses like he's half preppy, half goth, and when he talks—which isn't often—he sounds British, except he's not. He's from NYC, or at least that's what I heard him say once. Maybe he's just a good liar. Anyway, you gotta see him to understand what I mean. Oh, and for the record, it's not like I like-like him or anything. He's just...interesting.

FIVE

AKOLO WALKED UP the stairs and into the courtyard. Instead of heading toward the grand auditorium and the throne room beyond, his guard directed him to a doorway directly across from the stairs. As Akolo stepped through the door, he found himself in a small garden. The rich scent of flowering plants made him pause. He took in the smell with a long inhale through his nose before the guard gently prompted him forward. They walked through the garden and came upon a single-story building that stood alone on the palace grounds. This building wasn't as elaborately decorated as the palace itself—it almost looked half-finished. A large tent stood at one end of the building, its opening billowing in a gentle breeze. Four guards in full uniform stood outside the tent opening. A growing crowd was kept at a distance by another flank of soldiers.

Akolo's guard stopped him just before reaching the tent. Moments later, three bearded men walked into the scene and stood by the tent flap. The long blue robes they wore were decorated with gemstones and patterns woven from golden threads. The tallest of the men looked directly at Akolo. His gaze was so intense that Akolo had to turn away. Akolo knew instinctively these men were the religious leaders of this place, of this people. They carried themselves with the same kind of seriousness that he had witnessed from the high priestess back home. The one with the most elaborate hat wore a black patch over one eye. *Surely, he is the high priest*, thought Akolo.

But what is beyond that tent? he wondered.

The high priest and his two associates stood just outside the tent, facing the crowd. The high priest nodded at a guard near the tent and that guard produced a rope he'd been holding. Then the high priest nodded to one of his associates. The man walked up to one of the guards keeping the crowd in line and said something to him that Akolo couldn't quite hear. The man seemed agitated by whatever was said, but set down his spear and walked up to the tent opening. There, the other guards tied the rope to one of his feet, then stepped back, waiting.

The high priest then began to speak.

"You are performing an important duty today," he began, addressing the man who stood by the tent with a rope tied around his ankle. "Beyond this entrance lies a great and ancient mystery, and you have been chosen to help solve it." He turned to the murmuring crowd. "When we liberated the people of the Jordan valley from their barbaric overlords, our great leader rightfully took ownership of their religious artifacts. We have placed them just beyond this tent in a temple so that we might learn more about the god of these people. Our great leader and king is a wise man, and eager to learn about *all* the gods."

He turned again to the soldier who had been chosen. "Are you a good and godly man?" he asked.

The soldier paused before nodding resolutely.

"Then perhaps this god will speak to you."

The high priest gestured toward the tent. The soldier got down on his hands and knees as instructed, then began to crawl through the opening. Two guards held on to the other end of the rope, letting it slide through their hands as the man moved forward. By this time the crowd had filled in around Akolo and he could hear their whispers.

"I heard a dozen soldiers were killed while bringing the artifacts to our city," said one.

"I heard it was two dozen," said a second man.

"We already have enough gods," said another.

Akolo's guard turned toward the whisperers and offered a stern growl. All three swallowed hard and backed up a step.

Moments later, a terrifying sound came from beyond the tent. The sound was a muffled scream, as if the man was being strangled. Quickly, the two guards outside the tent pulled at the rope. The man who was on the end of it bounced across the ground like a rag doll. Akolo leaned forward to get a better look, then wished he hadn't when he saw the man's face—it was white as a tunic and frozen in fear. This man was dead.

The high priest didn't seem at all fazed by this. He simply nodded at the guards, and they picked up the body and dragged the man away. Then he turned to another guard who stood by the crowd. The man shook his head, then dropped his sword and tried to escape through the crowd. He was quickly captured by the other guards and brought back to stand before the high priest.

"Why are you so afraid?" asked the high priest. The man mumbled a response and the high priest asked, "Are you a good and godly man?"

The reluctant soldier shook his head. "I stole a coin from a shopkeeper when I was a child," he said. "I am not worthy…"

The high priest held up his hand to stop him from speaking. "You have admitted your sin. Perhaps this is a god that values honesty." Again, he directed the guards to tie the rope to the man's ankle. The soldier was trembling when he got down on his knees and began to crawl under the tent flaps. This time, the rope moved more slowly through the guards' hands. The crowd's persistent murmuring gave way to expectant silence.

Even though Akolo knew what to expect, he was still shocked by the scream that soon followed. The soldier was dragged out from the tent, but Akolo didn't watch. He turned his head and tried to erase the image of the first man's face. Still, he couldn't ignore the sound of the guards gathering up the soldier and carrying him away.

Akolo ventured to speak to his guard. "Why did you bring me here?" he asked.

The man simply said, "Just watch. And wait."

His words caused Akolo's stomach to drop like a stone.

• • •

Zach woke up in darkness and, for a moment, was certain he'd sit up and find himself in his room. But the hard stone floor told him otherwise. He was still in this ancient place. He stood stiffly, trying to work out the kinks in his muscles, then looked out into the hallway. There was no sign of anyone there, so he gingerly stepped out and walked back to the stairs he'd descended hours earlier. There, he paused. Something drew him in the other direction—down the long hallway that was only sparsely lit by oil lamps. Standing at the bottom step, he turned and began walking down the hallway, counting each step. He also counted the doorways, beginning with the one on his right where he'd hidden from whoever was in the hall the night before. The farther he went, the more he felt an almost imperceptible pull in that direction. At the ninety-ninth step, he immediately stopped. He heard a voice whisper, "*Please be okay, Zach,*" and it sounded as if it came from somewhere close by. There was a closed door on his right. In the dim light he thought he could make out a symbol carved into the door. It looked like a rough-hewn version of the ouroboros. But when he reached his hand to touch the carved outline, it vanished.

"Well… that was weird," he mused to himself. He continued his journey down the long hallway, and in a matter of minutes finally reached the end. There was no door there, just a solid wall. He turned back around and walked toward the stairs, pausing to glance at the ninety-ninth step door to look for the ouroboros again. It was not there.

When he got to the bottom of the stairway, he looked up and saw what seemed to be daylight streaming in. He looked down at his clothes and realized he would look entirely out of place if this was indeed some ancient time period. At least he wasn't wearing his sneakers. That would've been an instant giveaway that he wasn't from around here. But his T-shirt and jeans wouldn't fit in either. He returned to the room where he'd fallen asleep and looked around. It was empty except for a couple of crates that he soon determined were also empty. Zach heard his name whispered again. He followed the voice across the hall to a room with an open doorway. He explored the room and found a pile of ragged, dirty cloaks and tunics.

"Checkpoint!" he said to himself with a faint smile. Something about all of this felt unreal, as if he was in his favorite video game, *World of Warcraft*. Could he be trapped in some kind of game? *In real life, things don't appear just when you need them*, he thought. Battling the shadows, he shuffled through the pile and found a tunic and robe that looked to be his size. He changed into them, guessing at how they fastened. He felt strangely naked, even though he had kept his T-shirt and underwear on. He buried his jeans neatly under the pile of clothes.

He stepped out into the brighter light of the hallway and gasped when he looked down at his robe.

"That's not dirt," he said. "It's blood!" He returned to the room and shuffled through the clothes, looking for something else to wear. He tried hard not to think about what happened to the people who had worn these clothes as he searched through the pile for something that wasn't bloodstained. Finally, he found something relatively stain-free and put it on. He walked back into the light and looked down, afraid of what he might see. But this tunic was merely dirty. No blood stains on this one. He breathed a sigh of relief and thought, *I just leveled up!*

"Up," he repeated aloud. "What if up is the way home?" he wondered. He laughed to himself. "I'll never hear the end of it if I walk into my home wearing...this," he said. He shrugged and started up the stairs, hoping he would have a chance to be so embarrassed.

At the top of the stairs, he found himself facing a big courtyard. He glanced around and, seeing nobody, walked into the open space. Across the way, he saw an open doorway that led to a small garden. He ran across the courtyard, battling nerves and trying to keep his curiosity in check, and stepped into the garden. Beyond the garden, another open courtyard beckoned. A small crowd had amassed there, but Zach couldn't see what they were looking at.

His stomach twisted into a knot. This scene looked familiar. Zach exited the garden and slipped in among the crowd, hoping no one would notice how out of place he looked with his much whiter skin. His ears perked up when he heard people in the crowd talking in low voices, but they were speaking a language he didn't recognize. Zach knew before he could see it what the people were looking at.

There, in front of him, was a large blocky building fronted by a tent.

Zach swallowed hard. This was exactly the scene he had witnessed in a dream months earlier. A dream that, quite unbelievably, his sister had experienced as well. *Would it all play out the same way?* he wondered.

Zach weaved in between onlookers and found an opening where he could get a better view of what was going on. Sure enough, the bearded men from the dream were there. But where was the young boy? Zach took a deep breath and wondered again if he was merely dreaming. But no, he couldn't shake the smell of sweat and dust. This was all too real.

And that's when he saw the boy—the one from his dream. A guard was urging him forward. The leader of the bearded men—a man with an ornate hat and a menacing patch over one eye—bent down to speak to the boy. The crowd noise increased. People seemed surprised by this action. Ariel had said something about soldiers going into the tent and being pulled out, dead. Zach was relieved he'd missed that part of the dream.

But just as in the dream, when the boy's ankle had been tied to the rope, he looked over and caught Zach's gaze. It wasn't a look of recognition, but one of curiosity. Maybe because Zach looked out of place. He knew he should slink away, find someplace to hide until he understood more about what was happening to him, but the memory of that dream kept him frozen in place, staring ahead as the young boy got down on his knees and started to crawl into the tent. The dream had ended before either Ariel or Zach learned what happened to the boy.

Zach's heart raced.

What if he doesn't make it?

• • •

The only instruction Akolo had been given was, "Go into the temple. Ask what sacrifices this god demands. Bring the answer back to me." The high priest had then smiled at him as if this was nothing. As if Akolo hadn't just witnessed six soldiers crawl into that tent, then be pulled out moments later, stone dead.

"What if I don't hear an answer?"

The high priest's expression didn't change. He nodded at a nearby guard, who began to tie the rope to Akolo's ankle. Akolo looked nervously around at the amassed crowd, searching for anyone who might speak up for him—for anyone who might step in and save the day. A boy about his age, maybe a little older, caught his eye. The boy was fair-skinned, and he wore ill-fitting clothing that resembled what Akolo's people wore, rather than what the people of this foreign city were wearing. He looked just as frightened as Akolo felt.

The guard pushed Akolo to his knees, then pointed at the entrance. Akolo glanced back at the high priest, who seemed to scowl at the guard's abruptness, then began crawling under the tent flap, feeling every pebble under his knees as he went. The flap closed behind him. He paused to let his eyes adjust to the darkness, then inched forward until he was at the entrance to the temple building. Unlike the temple building back home, there were no steps to climb, so he continued into the room on his knees. Once inside, he stood. The air inside the temple was wet and tasted odd—like the way the air tastes in a thunderstorm just before a lightning strike. The rope remained slack. He was safely inside.

Instinctively, he reached into his pocket to touch his stone, to feel the coolness of it and calm his growing anxiety. But the stone was warm, almost hot. He pulled it out of his pocket and held it in his hand. Slowly, like the coming of dawn, the stone began to glow. It wasn't a bright light, but it was enough to reveal what stood before him. The temple room was vast, much bigger than it had appeared from the outside, with a high ceiling. But except for a large box in the very middle of the room, it was empty. Where were these "artifacts" that the high priest had talked about. Maybe inside the box?

He stepped closer to the box and his stone glowed brighter.

Akolo studied the box. It was as long as he was tall, half as wide as it was long, and came up to his chest. Two long poles stretched across the long sides of the box and extended beyond it. *For carrying it*, thought Akolo. He recalled the overheard comment about soldiers dying while bringing this box to the palace and shivered. Akolo had been near the temple artifacts when he helped his mother and sisters prepare offerings but had never been this close. He wasn't afraid then; his mother was always nearby. And though he expected to be afraid now, he felt a strange sense of calm.

A soft sound emanated from the box. Not quite a hum, but something sweeter. Like a song. Akolo took another step toward the box and reached out his hand, stopping short of touching it. As he examined it more closely, his nerves began to settle. The box was elegant but simply decorated, with swirls carved neatly into the sides and top. There were a few places along the sides that looked like they once held gemstones, but now they were empty holes. The box's lid looked heavy, like it might take two men—or more—to lift it. The longer he stood in its presence, the more at peace he felt.

A wave of comfort that felt like a gentle hug washed over Akolo. It was so familiar. It nearly brought a tear to his eye.

"Imma?" he whispered.

A voice answered him, not with spoken words but somehow inside Akolo's head.

Welcome, servant, the voice said.

Akolo looked at his stone. The colors inside the stone swirled like it was alive. He carefully set the stone on top of the box and knelt next to it, thinking this is what his mother or father would have done.

"What...what sacrifices do you demand?" he asked. But there was no response. A moment later, he felt a gentle tug on his ankle. He grabbed the rope and tugged back to let them know he wasn't dead. Then he collected his stone, stood, and backed away from the box before getting to his knees and crawling out into the tent and then through the tent flap into the bright sunlight.

The high priest was looking down at him with an expression Akolo could not quite read.

"You stayed a long time," he said, a severe look on his face. "Did you hear anything? What sacrifices does this god demand?"

Akolo's throat was dry. He cleared it, then spoke, carefully choosing his words for fear the wrong ones would doom him. "I did not get an answer." The high priest's left eyebrow went up, almost comically high. Akolo fought away the smile that threatened to appear on his lips, then added, "But I did hear a voice!"

"And what did this voice say?" asked the high priest.

"It said..." Akolo hesitated. *What if it's not what the high priest wants to hear?* he thought.

"Speak up, boy."

"It said, 'Welcome, servant.'"

Akolo thought he was going to be punished, but then the high priest smiled. "The king will be pleased," he added. He placed his hand on Akolo's head and suddenly pulled it away as if it burned. Then he laughed. It was the kind of laugh that sometimes scared Akolo—not one of joy but one of surprise. The high priest turned to Akolo's guard, who was staring wide-eyed at Akolo. "Take him back to his room. And feed him well."

His guard led Akolo through the crowd of open-mouthed onlookers. Gasps and muffled conversation followed him as he made his way back to the small garden, then back into the palace courtyard. He had tried to find that boy again in the crowd, but he was nowhere to be seen.

Not long after he had been returned to his room downstairs, his guard brought him a plate of fresh fruit and bread and a goblet of cool water. The guard stared at him for a moment after delivering the feast, then returned to his post outside the door.

Akolo ate the food slowly, savoring every bite. It was the best meal he'd had in weeks.

But what had just happened? he wondered.

Akolo's stomach was full of food, but his head was full of questions.

What was in that box? Why did his stone glow? And why did he feel so safe in that place, when so many others before him had not even lasted a minute?

He reached into his pocket and pulled out his stone. The glow had faded, but for a moment, he was sure he saw the swirling colors.

He had felt his mother's presence in the temple. Or maybe he just really missed her. Oh, how he wished he could talk to her now, ask all his questions.

"Welcome, servant," the voice had said.

What does that mean?

• • •

Before he could escape, a soldier grabbed Zach's arm. Zach didn't understand what the man was saying, but the tone of his voice didn't sound particularly pleasant. Zach stretched his neck to see if he could find the young boy, but he'd already been led away from the temple. He needed to talk to that boy. He needed to know what was happening.

But instead, he was being dragged along to who knows where, by a soldier in a strange land. Zach's insides felt like they were all out of order, like he was about to implode. Nothing about this scenario made sense. As he was pulled along, he closed his eyes, willing himself to wake up.

But when he opened his eyes, the waking nightmare remained. He was standing before the man he had concluded was indeed the high priest. The man gestured for the soldier to let go of Zach. Zach had to find something to latch onto, something to give him even a small measure of control, so he started counting the gemstones on the priest's robe. Anything to avoid looking at the man's singular dark eye.

"One, two, three..." he counted aloud.

The man tilted his head, watching Zach, then laughed. Zach couldn't think of anything funny about the situation. He continued his count, "...eighteen, nineteen, twenty..."

A few minutes later, a different soldier led him away from the tent. The crowd had already dispersed, so the two of them walked alone back through the small garden, into the vast courtyard, and then down the stairs where this whole crazy adventure had begun.

Zach was ushered into a small room. There, sitting on a straw mat, plucking the seeds from an unusual-looking fruit and tossing them in his mouth, was the boy from the tent.

The boy from his dream.

The boy stared at Zach for a moment, curiosity filling his eyes, then reached out to offer Zach a handful of seeds.

Zach took the proffered mystery seeds and popped a few into his mouth.

As he bit down, the little juice capsules popped and exploded, spilling red down his chin and onto his tunic. When he looked down, he noted just how much the stain looked like blood. But the random thought was short-lived—he was too entranced by the flavor of the fruit.

It was the best thing he had ever tasted.

SIX

IAN PRIDED HIMSELF on his ability to navigate new territory. Twenty years of archaeological work had honed his sense of direction to near perfection, but his own property's woods seemed determined to confuse him. Every path looked different each time he walked it, as if the forest was deliberately rearranging itself. When they'd first moved to Littleton, the property had been shrouded by a persistent fog that seemed to only appear as they reached the gate at the end of the long driveway. At first, Zach had a different theory every time they returned home as to what could be causing it, much to Ariel's annoyance—everything from moisture content in the soil due to previous cattle on the land to high pressure buildup from the surrounding hills. Eventually, the regularly appearing fog became so routine they barely noticed it.

After Lyana was miraculously healed of what doctors thought was Lewy body dementia, both the metaphorical and the literal fog had lifted around the Keane household. But there remained a sense of mystery to the property—not only with the house itself but the grounds surrounding it. Ian couldn't quite put words to the mystery, but it lingered, often intruding upon his thoughts while trying to write another chapter in his latest book. He would be typing away, following the outline he'd scratched out on a yellow legal pad, when his fingers would stop—sometimes mid-sentence—and he would be compelled back to that moment months ago when he relived a tragic moment from his childhood. Time had transformed his memory of that event from something he was certain really happened into something that must have been a trick of the mind. A hallucination brought on by the leaking chemicals from the ancient house wiring, he surmised. Or maybe just one sip too many…

When he snapped out of those reveries, he'd be staring at the computer, wondering if minutes or hours had passed. So far, it had always been just minutes, though this realization brought him only so much relief.

The door in the dirt must be somewhere around here, he thought as he searched the grounds. *Why is this so hard to find?*

"Ian."

The sound of Marshall's voice caught Ian off guard. He turned suddenly, nearly losing his footing on the damp ground.

"Marshall," he finally said when he'd caught his breath. "That door… What was it, a bomb shelter? A storm shelter?"

Marshall walked toward him in his deliberate way. He was never in a hurry to get anywhere or to answer a question.

"It was…" Marshall paused.

It wasn't a difficult question. This had been Marshall's property, after all—land his uncle had built on decades earlier. Surely, he should know everything about it.

"It was a long time ago," he finally answered.

Ian lifted his hands in frustration. Zach was missing and time was their enemy. He needed answers, and right now. "How is it possible you don't know this? It's on your property!" He shook his head and sighed. "Sorry, I'm just a little stressed about Zach." He looked this way and that. "And where is it? I was sure it was right here." He pointed to the ground in front of him.

Marshall's eyes went wide.

"You think Zach may have gone to the door," he said.

Ian nodded, afraid to put words to his growing fear—that Zach had somehow opened the door and gone into the shelter, or whatever it was, only for the door to close behind him, locking him inside.

This time, Marshall moved quickly, walking past Ian and further into the woods. He made a sudden right turn, then stopped. Ian followed and looked down to see the door in the dirt, partially covered by rotting leaves from the previous autumn. It didn't look as if it had been disturbed, but Ian's heart raced, nonetheless.

He walked directly to the rusty handle and reached down to grab it. Marshall remained at the base of the door, hands folded together as if in deep thought. Ian tugged. The door didn't budge.

"Help me out here, Marshall," he urged. Marshall hesitated a second longer, then nodded and stepped up next to Ian. Together they tugged at the handle, but the door didn't open. After a few failed attempts, Marshall reached over and put his hand on Ian's shoulder.

"Rusted shut," he said. Then he added, "If we can't open it, then surely Zach didn't either."

This made logical sense to Ian, but he had to try one more time. He pictured Zach trapped inside, scared and alone, and pulled again, using all the strength he could muster, but unsurprisingly the door refused to budge. Ian dropped down on the ground next to the door and put his face in his hands.

"I don't know if this is good news or bad," he said. He looked up at Marshall. "Where could he possibly be, Marshall?"

Once again, Marshall looked deep in thought. Ian climbed back to his feet, brushed the dirt and leaves from his backside, and turned toward the caretaker.

"We need to organize a search party," said Ian. He was resolute. He would call the police and hope for help there, too, but didn't want to count on it. After all, Zach had only been gone for a few hours.

"Lloyd can help with that," said Marshall.

"Yes!" Ian slapped Marshall on the back. "That's a brilliant idea. Lloyd knows everyone in town." Ian started walking away, then paused. He turned back to Marshall.

"That way," Marshall said, pointing in the opposite direction Ian was heading.

"Right," said Ian. He took off in the direction Marshall indicated, moving as swiftly as his body could take him. When he stepped into the clearing and saw his house in the distance, he paused to look behind him, but Marshall hadn't followed. Ian checked his watch: 3:15. They would have to move quickly.

He pulled out his cell phone, made sure he had a signal (it wasn't a certainty in the woods), then punched the call button for Lloyd's diner. A woman's voice greeted him after the second ring.

"This is Ian, Ian Keane," he said before she even finished her greeting. "I need to talk to Lloyd. Is he there?"

"Hello, Ian," said the woman. "He's with a customer, but he shouldn't be long. How are you..."

"I'm sorry, Amanda, is it? It's about Zach," said Ian. "He's missing. We have to arrange a search party. I mean, I need Lloyd to help set up a search party..." Ian spoke rapidly, driven by the adrenaline of an urgent idea.

"Oh, wow. And yeah, this is Amanda. I'll go interrupt him." Ian heard the phone hit the counter, then waited for Lloyd's voice.

"Ian," Lloyd said. "What's all this about?"

Ian explained the situation, and Lloyd, being Lloyd, quickly took charge of things. He told Ian to just wait at the house. He'd gather as many people as he could, and they'd meet him there as soon as possible.

Ian hung up as he finally reached the back door of the house. He leaned against the siding and tried to slow his rapid breathing. Lloyd was going to help. Ian had help now.

We'll find Zach. Of course we will.

But what exactly would they find?

Ian shook the poison thoughts from his head.

"He's fine," he said aloud. "Zach is just fine."

• • •

"We're heading out now," called Lyana. When Ariel didn't reply, she walked to the bottom of the stairs and called up to her. "Did you hear? We're heading out."

A moment later, Ariel appeared in her doorway. "I heard you, Mom," she said. She didn't say it with a snarky attitude, though. This seemed like a small victory.

"I don't know how long we'll be, but it really would be good if you were to hang out downstairs..."

"I know, I know...in case Zach returns while everyone is out looking for him."

It was a short-lived victory. The attitude was back. But it was probably well earned. After all, Lyana had already gone over their plans earlier, before Lloyd and a dozen other people had arrived.

"We'll find him," said Lyana, looking up at her teenage daughter from the bottom of the stairs. "I know we'll find him."

The words were intended to ease Ariel's anxiety, but Lyana was really just trying to convince herself everything was going to be okay.

For a second, Ariel looked as though she might cry, but then she took a deep breath to compose herself and replied, "Please do." She put on a brave smile, then turned and went back into her room.

Lyana was about to remind Ariel yet again not to stay in her room, but before she opened her mouth wide enough to fit her foot, Ariel called back, "I'm just getting my headphones, Mom. I'll be down in a sec."

Lyana waited for Ariel at the bottom of the stairs. As Ariel descended, Lyana saw her lips move; it looked as though she was silently counting each step. This brought a lump to Lyana's throat.

"I'll just hang out in the living room," said Ariel, after giving her mom a quick hug. When she plopped onto the couch, she turned back to Lyana and added, "You know you can call me when you do find him, right?"

Lyana nodded. "Of course. The very second we do, you'll know."

"K. Good." Ariel stared down at her phone. The living room seemed eerily quiet for a Friday afternoon. Usually, Zach would be playing a video game, or Ariel would be watching a show. Or the two of them would be arguing about who had the rights to the TV.

Lyana stared at her daughter's head for a moment, wondering what must be going through her mind.

"I'm so sorry about the school thing," she began.

Ariel huffed. "Mom, go find Zach, okay? You've already apologized a hundred times. I'll make up the test next week. Just go!"

Lyana nodded and turned to go. As she reached the front door, she heard a voice whisper, *It's not what you think.* Lyana turned to look at Ariel, but she had already disappeared under her headphones and was bopping in time to a song Lyana probably had never heard of.

It's not what you think, the voice whispered again.

A voice had indeed returned. A chill ran through Lyana's veins, but she didn't have time to process what that meant.

She had to find her son.

• • •

Ian stood there on the lawn, stammering his instructions to the group. *This is so unlike Ian*, thought Lyana. He was always so organized, so in control. But he was rattled. They all were, of course, but this was way out of character for Ian.

"I'm sorry," Ian said to the small crowd. "I guess I'm not exactly sure of the best approach..." His hands were shaking.

Lloyd stepped up and put his hand on Ian's shoulder. "If I may," he said to Ian. Ian nodded and Lloyd took over. He made sure everyone had flashlights and a compass and bear spray and paired people up so they'd each have a searching buddy, then gave explicit instructions on how to search, what to look for, and how to report back if they found any clues about Zach's whereabouts.

Lyana had been paired up with Lloyd, and once they were a few yards into the woods, she dared ask the question that was foremost in her mind.

"Is the bear spray really necessary?" she asked, hoping for an answer that didn't escalate her fear level.

"Probably not," he replied. "Haven't heard reports of bears in these parts for a while. As long as people don't leave out their pic-a-nic baskets, the bears are perfectly content to stay away."

Lloyd turned to Lyana and raised an eyebrow.

"Pic-a-nic baskets," she repeated. Lyana allowed a small smile to grace her face. "That's a very old reference."

"Wasn't sure you'd get it," said Lloyd. "I have a soft spot for the old cartoons."

Lyana marveled at Lloyd's demeanor. From anyone else, such a lighthearted comment could have come across as inappropriate, considering the stakes. But coming from Lloyd, the gentle humor felt like a kindness. Perhaps something he'd needed himself years ago after the loss of his wife and daughter to a tragic car accident.

"Lloyd," she said. Her voice broke, so she repeated his name. "Lloyd, can I ask a rather personal question?"

Lloyd didn't hesitate. "Of course."

"How did you..." She paused. "How..." She struggled to find the words.

Lloyd read her mind. "When I got the news about the accident, I didn't want to believe it. No one wants to believe someone they love could be gone so quickly, so...unexpectedly." He stopped walking and turned to Lyana. "Grief is a funny thing. It doesn't go away, not really. It just...changes shape. I still miss them. All the time." He placed his hand gently on Lyana's shoulder. "But this isn't the time to grieve Zach. He's not gone. He's only missing." He turned from Lyana, perhaps to hide a tear, then began walking again, resolute.

Lyana brushed away her own tears, then jogged to catch up.

They continued on in silence. The light passing through the trees was like liquid gold. Lyana marveled at the spread of trees before her—it was a dense forest. Maple trees mostly. And birch—both black and yellow varieties, if her memory served.

She paused, called out Zach's name, then listened for a reply. None came. Lloyd had stopped when he heard her call, then waited for her to catch up to him again.

He pointed to a towering tree on their left. "Do you know trees?" he asked.

"That's an oak, right?"

"Red oak," he said. "Beautiful, strong giants. You can count on trees like this one. They're steady. Reliable." He turned to look directly at Lyana. "We're going to find him, Lyana."

She nodded, unable to form words.

Lloyd checked his compass, then started walking again. Lyana fell in behind him.

It wouldn't be long now before they would need their flashlights.

• • •

Ariel had pulled off her headphones soon after everyone left. As much as she wanted to disappear, it didn't feel right to hide in her music. Not with Zach still missing. And besides, maybe Zach would show up after all.

She wandered into the kitchen to look for something to eat. She hadn't eaten much all day. She picked up a box of donuts and looked inside. There were two left.

No, that's not it.

She went to the refrigerator and stared inside, hoping something would call out to her. But nothing did. Not the container of leftover lasagna. Not the carton of strawberries. Not even the chocolate cake. She opened the fruit drawer and pulled out an apple, lifted it to inspect it, then returned it to the drawer. She closed the refrigerator door and walked over to the pantry, nearly scaring herself to death when her image appeared in the mirror that sat at the back of that small room.

"Why is that even here?" she said aloud. She stepped into the pantry, moving cautiously as if something might be lurking there. The wiring that had nearly killed her mother was situated behind the pantry wall. Marshall had fixed that, of course. But he couldn't erase Ariel's memory of her mother's blank face. Of the panic she felt while her mother screamed in agony from...whatever it was that had taken hold of her.

Ariel shivered and exited the pantry. She didn't know if she'd ever be able to erase those images.

Marshall.

What was it with him, anyway? thought Ariel. "He should have known about the wiring." She spoke aloud just to break the eerie silence.

Unable to find a snack that could satisfy her hunger, Ariel wandered back to the couch and dropped down into it again. She picked up her phone and her headphones and considered listening to music, then stopped herself.

"This house is too quiet without you, Zach," she said, aloud again. She wondered what Zach would do if the tables were turned—if she were the one who'd gone missing. For just a moment she considered heading upstairs to try the intercom. Zach probably would have done that, but it made zero sense. She sighed. Would they even look for her if she went missing? Ariel shook her head at such an inane question.

"Of course they would," she said. "Why would I even think that?"

When no one answered her rhetorical question, she decided to turn on the TV. When it came on, it was on the History Channel. Ariel was about to change channels when she had an idea. A Zach-like idea.

What were you watching last night, Z?

She picked up her phone and started searching the internet for a listing of the shows that were on the History Channel on Thursday night.

"I was studying while you were still downstairs. I must have fallen asleep before you came up. What time did I fall asleep?"

She scrolled through the listing she'd found and laughed out loud at what she discovered.

History's Greatest Mysteries: Expedition Bermuda Triangle. Of course it had to be something like that. But what does that mean?

She sighed and clicked off the TV.

"Nothing. It means nothing." She slid down off the couch onto the floor in front of it and folded her arms around her knees. "Where are you, Zach? Where did you go?"

A loud sound startled Ariel. Her heart started racing.

"Mom? Is that you?"

There was no response. The wind whipped up, gently rattling the living room window. "Ugh. I hate this place," she snarked aloud as she stood back up and tried to calm down.

But she wasn't calm. She was restless. Ariel headed down the hallway toward her father's study. "Anyone in there?" She peeked around the half-open doorway. Everything looked as it always did—the shelves were filled with heavy old books, ancient artifacts, and family mementos, a sharp contrast to the sleek computer monitor that dominated the desk space. She knew he was writing again, but he didn't talk about it much.

She stepped into the room and sat in his office chair. The computer keyboard beckoned. She tapped the spacebar, and the monitor came to life. He hadn't password-protected his user account—the monitor revealed a Word document. She almost turned away, but the formatting on the page grabbed her attention. This didn't look like one of her dad's other books—the ones on ancient civilizations and cultures.

No, this was…different. She read the first paragraph, then the dialogue that followed.

This was a novel! Her father was writing a novel.

She read the rest of the page that was visible on the screen, stopping cold when she saw the word *attic.*

Was he writing a novel based on the unbelievable events of the past few months? *Why would he do that? He gets to tell the world, and I've had to keep it all inside!*

"Wait," she said aloud. "The attic!"

Driven by adrenaline and a rapidly growing panic, Ariel scooted away from the desk and raced out the door and up the stairs. When she got to the middle of the overlook, she paused and stared up at the pull-chain for the attic ladder.

"Please don't be up here, please don't be up here…" she repeated to herself as she pulled on the chain. The ladder made an ungodly squeal as it unfolded in front of her. She placed a foot on the bottom rung and stepped onto the ladder, pressing it firmly against the floor. Step by step she climbed, listening after each rung for sound from above, afraid of what she might hear. Halfway into the dark space, she reached up to grab the string for the attic light. She closed her eyes and pulled, listening to the subtle "pop" of the bulb coming on.

"Please don't be up here, please don't...." She opened her eyes and scanned the storage space. There was no sign of Zach. Apart from the boxes they'd stored up there when they first moved in, the attic was empty. She climbed the rest of the way up and walked gingerly across the plywood floor to examine the boxes more closely. She recognized the Christmas tree box and the boxes of Christmas decorations right away. Ariel involuntarily shuddered as she recalled their most recent Christmas—the strangest Christmas she'd ever experienced. There were two boxes marked "old clothes" and another marked "junk I can't throw away" in her father's handwriting. That made her smile.

She turned in a circle, looking around the open space. The angled roof made it difficult to stand except in the middle of the room, but she began to wonder what it would be like to turn this into her own private hideaway. A place to escape. As quickly as she'd gotten the idea, she shook it off. Too claustrophobic, she decided.

She was about to return to the ladder when she saw a couple of boxes off to the side. They looked dilapidated, like they'd been there a long time. She walked up to the first box and opened it. Inside was a strange device. She lifted it out and held it up to the light. One end of the device featured what looked like goggles. They were attached to a wobbly handle below and a length of metal half a foot long that ran from the nose to a simple metal frame that lined up with the eye holes.

"I know what this is," she said aloud, her voice sounding strange in the unfinished space. She dug further into the box and pulled out something that resembled a heavy-duty shoebox. She slowly lifted the lid.

"Yes!" she said. She gathered the device under one arm and the box under the other and carefully made her way back down the ladder. After returning the ladder to its hiding place in the ceiling, she carried the items downstairs. She sat on the floor in front of the couch and studied the device. She could just make out the words printed on the underside of the frame: "The London Stereoscopic Company." She turned her attention to the box. At one time it must have been a fancy box, but now it was scratched and chipped and smelled of mold. She opened it and saw a different name printed on the inside: The Kilburn Company. The box was filled with stereoscopic slides.

The original virtual reality device, thought Ariel.

She chose a slide at random and read the words printed along its bottom edge: "3113. View in Mr. Hunnewell's Grounds, Wellesley, Mass." She slid it into the stereoscope's frame, then lifted the viewing goggles to her eyes. It took a moment, and some nudging of the frame backward and forward along the metal rack, before she could focus.

"Wow," she said. It was an image of neatly trimmed shrubs lined up on multiple terraces like a fancy garden display. A 3-D image. She tried to recall the name of the toy her dad had told her about once—View-something. This was just like that, but really old.

She started going through the slides one by one, marveling at the simple magic such an ancient device could provide. Some of the slides had dates printed on them. It was clear they were all from around the late 1800s. She came across one that didn't have any printing on it. It was a picture of a house under construction. Something about the image looked familiar. She slid it into the frame and held the device up to her eyes.

She froze.

It was their house! She studied the picture a little longer. There was a man standing next to the house, looking at whoever was taking the picture. Ariel squinted.

No. It can't be.

The man in the picture looked just like Marshall. Not a younger version of Marshall. It looked exactly like him.

She shook her head. *That's silly. It can't be him.*

"It must be a relative," she said.

"Who must be a relative?" The sound of her mother's voice coming from the kitchen startled Ariel. She hadn't heard them return.

"Sorry, it's nothing," she said. She pulled the slide from the device and, without thinking, surreptitiously slipped it under the couch. She would come back for it later. Ariel looked out the living room window and saw that night had fallen. *How long have I been looking at these?* she wondered.

Lyana came over and sat down on the couch behind Ariel, who was still sitting on the floor. Ariel leaned back and her mother placed her hands on Ariel's shoulders.

"You didn't find him," Ariel said, not daring to look at her mother's face.

"We had to call off the search. It isn't worth someone else getting lost."

Ariel suspected her mother was merely parroting what someone else said—there was little conviction behind her words.

The front door opened. Ian was standing there, talking with someone just outside of view. He thanked the person—*probably Lloyd*, thought Ariel—then he closed the door. He stood there facing the door for a moment, then turned and walked resolutely down the hall. Ariel heard his office door close. And then she heard another sound.

Her mother was crying.

SEVEN

AKOLO WAS HAPPY to welcome this new boy into his room and equally happy to share the generous supply of food he'd been given. The boy didn't say much, and Akolo couldn't understand his words even when he did speak, but there was something comforting about sharing the simple, small space with another person around his own age. Or maybe older, probably, but not by much. After enjoying some pomegranate seeds, the boy had pointed to himself and said, "Zach." Akolo had repeated the gesture, offering his own name in return. So, they knew that much about each other, anyway.

Zach was an unusual name, something he'd never heard before, but that fit the boy's odd appearance. While the clothing was familiar—not unlike what Akolo himself wore, Zach wasn't wearing it quite right. His skin was much lighter than Akolo's, but the hair was curly like his own. The more Akolo studied his new roommate, the more he realized, though they had similarities, they were different in so many ways. But in one way they were very much the same: They were clearly far from home.

Akolo watched with interest as Zach surveyed the room, then sat on the second mat that the guard had brought. Zach's fingers were always in motion, his eyes darting around the mostly empty room like they were searching for something. Zach lined up the uneaten seeds from the pomegranate and began organizing them on the floor in front of him into rows. Zach pointed to the first row, then held up one finger and said, "One." He then pointed to the next row, held up two fingers and said, "Two." Then he pointed to the last row and held up three fingers and said, "Three." Akolo giggled thinking about how his mother would count on her fingers to get Akolo's attention when they had to be silent in the temple. When he didn't obey, he would get an earful from her all the way home.

Akolo swallowed hard. *Home*. That word was supposed to feel warm and hopeful, but instead, thinking about home felt like chewing on rocks. It hurt his teeth just to imagine the word. Anger began to bubble up in Akolo's heart again. How could anyone be so cruel as to take away his home? His family.

Akolo made a fist and slammed it down onto the hard ground. This startled Zach. It startled Akolo, too. He had so rarely expressed this much emotion. Up until now, he hadn't had reason to be so angry.

Zach quickly returned to his organizing of the seeds. This time they were taking the shape of a circle, or a ring. Zach said something and pointed to the seed drawing. Akolo didn't understand his words, but it sounded like a question.

What are you asking?

Before Akolo could think of a way to respond, the guard stepped into the room and extinguished the small lamp that sat on a shelf near the door. The room grew dark as midnight, then, as his eyes adjusted to the darkness, Akolo made out shadows in the hallway. He closed his eyes and listened as the guard's footsteps shuffled back and forth just outside the doorway. He lay down on his mat and heard Zach do the same. It was perfectly silent for a moment, and then Akolo heard

Zach's voice. He was saying words, slowly, rhythmically. It reminded Akolo of the way his mother would soothe him to sleep.

She would keep her voice low, so as not to wake anyone else in the small house they called home, and recite poems she'd memorized from her own childhood. There were poems about flowers and birds and other animals, but Akolo's favorites were the poems about the wind and the water. The one about the Jordan River was his favorite. When he was too young to understand the meaning of the words, he fell in love with the rhythm of them. Their cadence was like a lullaby.

Akolo realized he'd been crying and gently wiped the tears from his eyes, thankful Zach couldn't see him weeping. *When can I go home?* he wondered.

• • •

Zach had been revisiting his exploration of the long hallway, counting the steps in his head until he reached the door at the ninety-ninth step. He was trying to see the fleeting image on that door and hear the whispered words again, but both were just out of reach. Had he imagined it? He gave up and listened to the quiet of the room. The other boy, Akolo, if he had heard the name correctly, was surely sleeping now—his soft whimpering had faded away, replaced by the gentle wheeze of someone deep in dreams. He reached his hand over and touched the seeds he had tried to organize into the ouroboros. It looked nothing like the symbol. And anyway, there was no reason the boy would have recognized it.

He swiped at the seeds, stirring them into chaos. It was a fitting metaphor for how he was feeling. Nothing made any sense. *What day is it? Saturday?* He should have been out exploring the woods or following the stream and looking for interesting rocks. Instead, he was locked up in this ancient room with a stranger, wondering what would come next. *Well, not technically locked up*, he mused—the door was open. But it was also guarded. *Did this guard ever sleep?*

He wished he was in his bed, his warm, comfortable bed. He'd even take being teased by Ariel over...whatever this was.

Zach had watched enough science fiction to know something about time travel. Or at least something about how fiction writers thought of time travel. If he was indeed back in ancient times, could his actions now affect something in the future? Some of the stories said so. What was the term? He searched through his brain, recalling then rejecting terms until he found the one he was looking for: the butterfly effect.

Great, he thought. *Now I'll be overthinking everything I say and do.*

He fell asleep while considering the myriad ways he could cause the end of the world.

• • •

When Zach awoke, Akolo was already sitting up on his mat, staring at him.

"Akolo," said Zach, forcing a tired morning smile.

"Zach," said Akolo. His smile seemed sincere.

Their guard walked in, and Akolo quickly stood. The guard shook his head and pointed to Zach instead, then issued a one-word command.

That must mean "follow me," he guessed. Zach stood and nodded, then wasn't quite sure how to indicate that he had to go to the bathroom. *What were bathrooms like in ancient days?* he wondered. He glanced around the room. That was when he noticed the pot in the corner.

"You gotta be kidding me," he said aloud. The guard repeated his command. Zach pointed to the pot. The guard just stood there, waiting, but offered a small nod.

Zach, feeling entirely embarrassed after he finished relieving himself in a robe in front of a guard, was reminded of the time his mom thought it would be a great idea to dress him up as a mummy for Halloween by wrapping him up in bandages. A few hours later, when he needed to go to the bathroom, he had to ask his teacher to cut a hole in his costume to resolve the issue. It was a memory Zach would never forget. At least Akolo had the sense to look away while he was peeing.

As he followed the guard into the hallway, he heard Akolo say something. Of course he didn't know what the words meant, but the tone suggested he was offering Zach encouragement. But encouragement for what?

He found out moments later when he was delivered to the front of the tent, where the high priest stood with his assistants. Zach gulped. Guards there were holding a rope.

"I don't know what you want me to do," said Zach. His insides were twisting, his head spinning. Ariel told him that in her dream soldiers were pulled out of that tent dead. Presumably, that had happened for real, too, before Akolo had gone in yesterday. Akolo had survived, but Zach knew nothing about what he was about to encounter. He thought back to what Ariel had said she'd found inside in her version of the dream.

"I knew I was in the presence of a great god," she'd said. Or something like that. She had felt safe. *But in the dream, wasn't she playing the part of Akolo?* thought Zach. *I'm not Akolo.*

The high priest was talking now, addressing Zach. Zach threw his hands up and shrugged, hoping the gesture was universal enough to make the man understand: He didn't know what he was supposed to do. The high priest then flicked his hand toward the guard holding the rope. The guard walked up to Zach and tied the rope to his right ankle. Zach winced when the man pulled tight on the rope, securing it. Then the guard walked away.

Zach was shaking now. He felt like he might throw up. *What if there really is a god in there? What if I say or do the wrong thing?*

The high priest spoke to Zach again, then pointed to the tent flap.

Zach didn't move.

The high priest walked up to Zach and bent down to him, offered some words that sounded like a mix of encouragement and demand. Zach couldn't stop staring at the man's eye patch. *Just what did it hide?* The high priest pointed again to the tent. To the temple beyond.

Zach's throat felt dry. He got down on his hands and knees, then began to crawl. Just inside the tent, he paused. The flap closed behind him and it took a moment for Zach's eyes to adjust. Maybe he could just crawl up to the temple door and stop there. He didn't have to go in, did he?

Zach crawled forward and paused at the entrance to the temple building. Because that's what it was, right? A temple? He was trying to piece together his memories of the dream and Ariel's description of her role in it. A voice came from just outside the tent. A word of command, certainly. No, he couldn't fool this high priest. He would have to go into the temple.

But how do you approach a god?

Zach remained on his knees, feeling every pebble on the ground and then every small ridge on the stone floor as he entered the temple proper. The darkness in that room was like none he had ever known. Darker even than the night he and his dad had experienced while camping at that wilderness campground. What was it called? Sutton something? Zach hadn't hated the experience, but after the trauma of realizing they'd pitched their tent on an anthill, they weren't keen on camping again anytime soon. Zach loved the outdoors—it was the perfect place to live out imagined adventures. But he could do without swarming ants…or bees…or swarming anything, for that matter.

The thought made him feel itchy all over.

As he rested there on the ground in the doorway to the temple, the pitch-black room began to glow. Slowly, the room grew brighter, kind of like the way the lights in the gym at his old school would come on. At that thought, he decided he would have rather been there than here, and he had zero love for PE class. The light seemed to be coming from the big box in the middle of the otherwise empty room. *Not a box*, thought Zach. *A chest.*

A treasure chest? he wondered. It was about five feet long, three feet wide, and three feet tall and sat on a stone slab that reminded Zach of an altar he had seen pictured in one of his father's ancient history books.

Zach realized he'd been holding his breath and let out a sigh. He slowly stood, then walked toward the chest. The closer he got, the brighter the room became, until it was so bright, he had to shield his eyes. Just then a rush of wind came through carrying a whisper.

"Zach...be with me."

Was that in my head or was that in the room? Zach wondered. He felt drawn to the glowing object and reached his hand out, stopping just short of touching it. That was when he noticed the stone on his bracelet. It was glowing, too. That made no sense. It was a simple black stone with a symbol carved into it. *How could a stone be glowing?* Zach was so entranced by this, he nearly fell when he felt a tug on the rope. He carefully slipped the bracelet off his wrist and slid it into what passed for a pocket on the robe he was wearing, hoping the cloth would hide the glow. He wasn't sure why, but he didn't want the high priest to see the glowing stone. Zach turned and walked back toward the temple doorway. As he did, the room's glow faded until it was pitch black once again. He got down on his hands and knees and continued through the tent and out into the morning light. The priest was standing there, staring at Zach with a look of surprise. Then that look turned into a broad smile, followed by a guttural laugh.

"*This* is certainly a surprise," the priest said.

Whoa! Zach shook his head in confusion and shock. Had he heard that right? He understood the high priest!

"What is a surprise?" asked Zach. The words came out sounding like English to him, but the high priest, with another incredulous look, laughed once again.

"You speak our language," he said.

Zach was about to correct him, but then he thought, *Maybe I am speaking his language*.

"You are alive," the priest said. "This god smiles upon you."

Zach looked himself up and down and nodded. "I'm alive." He hadn't realized until that moment how thankful he was that this was true. "I'm alive!"

The high priest was lost in thought for a moment. Then he said, "This is a powerful god." He nodded to himself, then pointed at Zach. "You will be useful," he added. "But that is enough for today. You look...weary."

Zach did feel unusually tired. He looked up at the sky. The sun was higher than he'd expected.

"How long was I in there?" he asked, mostly of himself. But the high priest offered an answer.

"All morning," he said. "The guards tried to pull you out soon after you went in, but they could not. Even six men couldn't budge the rope."

Zach was totally confused now. He hadn't felt them tugging except that once, right before he came out.

"You must rest," said the high priest. He turned to the guard Zach recognized—the one who stood outside the room where he stayed... where he and Akolo stayed. A wave of hope washed over Zach—would he be able to understand Akolo now? Perhaps they could talk. Maybe Zach could finally learn what was going on.

He offered an awkward bow to the high priest, unsure if that was appropriate, then followed his guard back to the room. Akolo was sitting on his mat there, enjoying a bowl of fresh fruit and a goblet filled with something that didn't quite look like water.

"I'm alive!" said Zach as he walked into the room.

Akolo's eyes went wide. "I can understand you!" he said. "How did you learn my language so fast?"

"How did you learn mine?" asked Zach. He sat down next to Akolo and reached for a piece of fruit, pausing only long enough to get a nod from Akolo. He bit into the fruit and immediately spit the bite back out. The bitterness had caught him by surprise. He looked at the fruit and realized it was a lot like a lemon. To the great amusement of Akolo, and with some effort, he pulled at the outer rind until he found the pulpy middle. He pulled at it and popped the pulp into his mouth. It was just a little sweet. And it tasted delicious.

"What is this?" he asked, holding up the mangled piece of fruit.

Akolo tilted his head, reminding Zach of a curious dog. "A citron," he said.

"And what about this one?" Zach was referring to the fruit they had shared the night before.

"That's a pomegranate. I like the way they pop in my mouth." Akolo took some seeds, threw them into his mouth, then smiled with red seeds covering some of his teeth. They both laughed.

Zach was pretty sure he'd heard of pomegranates, but he'd never actually seen one, let alone tasted one. He would have to research this unusual fruit when he got back home.

When he got back home.

His stomach dropped, and so did his face, apparently, because Akolo reached out and touched Zach's arm. "Are you okay?"

He wasn't. Not really. And, like the priest had said, he was well and truly exhausted.

"Just tired, I think." He had so many questions for his roommate. But they would have to wait. "I think I'm going to sleep for a bit."

He crawled over to his mat and lay down. He barely had time to wonder what his dreams might look like before he fell into them.

• • •

Akolo stared with wonder at the boy named Zach. How was it that they could now understand each other? He had so many questions.

Akolo finished the pear he was eating, and drank from the goblet, then lay down on his mat, staring across at Zach. As Zach rolled over, something slipped out of his tunic. Akolo waited to be sure Zach was asleep, then crawled over to investigate. It was some kind of jewelry. A bracelet or something worn on the wrist, perhaps. He nudged it, flipping it over. The familiar stone that decorated the bracelet was carved with a symbol. A snake eating its own tail. He'd seen this symbol before somewhere. He swallowed hard when he remembered where—the high priest had a similar image painted on his arm.

Did this mean Zach was one of them?

Akolo reached into his pocket and felt the coolness of his own stone.

He didn't have the words to explain it, but he knew this meant something.

He could only pray it wasn't a "bad" something.

EIGHT

IAN AGGRESSIVELY DROPPED down into his office chair and snapped at Lyana, "I need this." He had meant he needed time to himself in his office, but Lyana might have thought he was referring to the bottle on the nearby shelf. He had promised he would not drink again after he botched trying to call 911 when Zach was attacked by the bees a few months ago. Lyana opened her mouth to respond, then clearly decided against it. He was about to explain himself, but she turned and walked away without a word. He almost wished she had taken the bottle with her. He didn't know if he had the willpower to resist under these circumstances.

Zach was missing. This was a fact. He couldn't deny this, no matter how many times friends and strangers had patted him on the shoulder and offered encouraging, hopeful words. They had found no clues in their search of the woods. Not a single one.

But Ian had a clue. Or at least the hint of one. It sat in the periphery of his thoughts, just out of view. His hands trembled slightly as he stared at the amber liquid across the room. For years, alcohol had been his thinking companion, the lubricant that loosened the tight connections in his brain and let ideas flow freely. Some of his best academic insights had come with a glass in his hand, the whiskey warming his thoughts until patterns emerged from chaos. Perhaps if he blurred his thoughts even more with a drink, it would somehow come into better focus. That idea made zero logical sense, but then again, logic wasn't the ruling factor for this season of life. Zach and the bees. Lyana's dementia diagnosis. His own hallucinatory trip back in time. None of these things followed logic.

Just one, he rationalized, already rising from his chair. *Just enough to think clearly. For Zach.* The familiar weight of justification settled over him like an old coat. This wasn't about weakness or addiction—this was about using every tool at his disposal to find his son. Ian caved and poured a shot of whiskey down his throat, the familiar burn awakening his senses. *Maybe this will help focus the swirling thoughts*, he mused. He had been staring at the computer now for more than an hour. What was he waiting for, the ghosts of the internet to speak to him? He leaned forward, resting his head on the stack of books he'd been studying as research for the novel he was writing.

Trying to write.

Non-fiction was so much easier, he thought. You just lined up all the details and pretended you were lecturing to a hall full of eager students. But fiction? That was a different beast altogether.

The flashing cursor on the empty page was like a metronome, keeping time for a song he couldn't quite hear.

"Zach, where are you?" he whispered. He checked his phone for the hundredth time and saw a dozen or so messages, but none offered any clues about his whereabouts. His call to the police had led to the filling out of a report and assurances that the police would be searching for Zach as soon as they could send officers out. This surprised Ian, as he'd expected they'd have to wait twenty-four hours before they could declare a missing person case. Once again, movies and TV turned out to be unreliable sources of information. This whole situation was more like a horror movie than a police procedural. Maybe he was thinking about it all wrong.

He leaned back in his office chair and closed his eyes.

There must be an answer to this mystery, he thought.

The scent of smoke jarred him from his reverie, and he bolted from the chair and ran into the hallway.

"Lyana! Ariel!" he called out. There was no response. The smell of smoke drew him down the hall, right to the spot where he'd previously found a secret door—the door that led him to a childhood memory that had played out in front of him like a note-for-note reenactment. Ian placed his hands on the wall and began sliding them across the surface, feeling for anything that might be out of place. There was no door, but perhaps there was a seam, or some other evidence that he didn't merely imagine the events all those months ago.

He found nothing. On a whim, he backed up and gathered up all his alcohol-fueled Harry Potter courage and ran toward the wall. It did not let him through. Instead, he found a stud with his shoulder and the impact reverberated throughout his whole body. He swore under his breath—something he never did—and bent over, hands on his knees until his body felt more or less normal.

He sniffed the air and smelled smoke again. He called out to Ariel and Lyana, but they didn't respond. He walked to the front door and opened it. A gentle breeze blew into the house, and the smell dissipated as quickly as it had appeared. Ian investigated the kitchen and saw the fading smoke trail from a candle that had been set on the counter. He didn't remember a candle being there before.

Lyana must have lit it, he concluded.

He returned to the office and fell into his chair, pressed down by the growing weight of defeat.

When he looked up at his computer, the flashing cursor was no longer alone on the screen. Two letters had been typed there: BC.

I must have bumped the keyboard when I got up, he thought, rubbing his throbbing shoulder. But then something clicked in his brain.

"BC...Before Christ," he said aloud. *What if...*

Ian immediately shook the idea from his head. It was a ludicrous theory, completely illogical. Still, he filed the thought away before clicking Delete twice on the keyboard. Once again, he was staring at a perfectly empty page. He glanced at the whiskey bottle. It, too, was empty.

He was starting to feel the same way. But also like he was juggling too much information. There were too many unanswered questions, too many uncertainties, too many frightening possibilities about what happened to Zach. Ian was both empty and overwhelmed and the juxtaposition of those two truths made him feel dizzy.

Or maybe that was just the whiskey.

Where are you, Zach?

• • •

Ian awoke with a start, nearly falling out of his office chair. He stretched his neck this way and that to get the stiffness out, then looked at the computer monitor. It had gone dark after being idle. With slight trepidation, Ian clicked the spacebar to wake it up. It illuminated to the blank page where he'd left it. He didn't know what he'd expected to see—some clue about Zach, perhaps?

He glanced at the clock.

"How is it already midnight?" he wondered aloud. His voice sounded hollow, like he was in a cave. But no, that was how it always sounded in his office. The stone walls accounted for that. He stood up and nearly tripped. The stack of books that had been on his desk were scattered across the floor. He bent down to pick them up and place them on the desk. One of the books had fallen open to a spread of images depicting an ancient fortress situated on a high, rocky plateau. "Masada," he said aloud. *Established around 30 BC*, he thought. He was a professor of ancient history. He could recite dates and times in ancient history like a music fan could quote liner notes. Of course, he could do that too.

BC.

He let the letters tumble around in his head, hoping they'd jar loose the clue that was just out of reach.

"Ian."

The sound of Lyana's voice startled Ian. He turned toward the open doorway. Lyana was standing there with sleep-deprived eyes. She was wearing her white bathrobe—the one he'd "borrowed" from that fancy hotel in DC years ago when he was presenting a lecture on Bedouin traditions. He could still picture the detailed map on the screen behind him illustrating the history and spread of this ancient people. He had been especially proud of that lecture. More than half of the attendees had given him a standing ovation. And while adulation wasn't the reason he taught, he rode that unexpected confirmation of his competence all the way back to his hotel room, where he didn't hesitate to claim the elegant bathrobe as a prize for his wife. He knew he'd end up paying for it when the hotel bill was reviewed by the accounting department back at the university, but he didn't much care in that moment. He cared later, though. About $150 worth.

"You should come to bed," said Lyana. She looked over at the desk. The empty whiskey bottle was resting on its side next to the empty glass.

"I'll be up soon," he said. Lyana paused, glanced at the desk again, then turned and left. He listened to her footsteps as she climbed the stairs, quietly counting them under his breath until she reached the landing.

Fifteen.

He let out a sigh, then scooted his chair back. When he collected the whiskey bottle and the glass from the desk, he glanced at the shelves above and saw the bright yellow clay pot Zach had made back in the third grade next to an antique oil lamp Ian had collected from a dig.

As Ian picked up the oil lamp to look it over once more, the memory of smoke from earlier found its way to his nostrils. He recognized it now. What he had smelled wasn't a candle. It was a different kind of smoke—the kind from an oil lamp. He'd know that smell anywhere—he had taught an entire section on the key role oil played in the lives of ancient peoples. A smile came to his lips as he pictured students trying to light their homemade lamps during a hands-on class session. They had initially scoffed at the idea of making clay lamps—claiming he was treating them like children. But when they'd seen the results of their efforts—with a little help from Ian—their eyes had been opened to something they had previously only read about. Life in ancient times was fraught with difficulty but littered with invention.

"Hmmm…. Never noticed *this* before," Ian said. Examining the bottom of the lamp, he spotted markings that looked like thin hash marks. *No, wait. It looks more like a faded* Z, he thought.

How did he miss this? And more importantly, why had he smelled an oil lamp?

Ian added these questions to the bulging folder of questions he had filed in the back of his head, turned out the office light, and headed upstairs.

Lyana was already asleep when he got there, or feigning sleep. How could anyone sleep at this time? Their son was missing, and they had no clue where he could be.

Not one clue.

He brushed his teeth, put on his pajamas, then climbed into bed and leaned over to kiss his wife on her forehead. She rolled away before he reached her, so instead he settled into his sleeping position facing the other way and glanced at the digital clock that sat on the dresser across the room.

1:27.

It can't be, he thought. *It was just midnight a few minutes ago.*

Time, like everything else on this day, made no sense.

The last number he saw before fading into fitful sleep was 1:42.

• • •

Ariel woke to find herself still wearing her clothes from the day before. The dim blue light coming from her window suggested it was still early. She glanced over at her clock.

6:18.

Her journal was resting on the bedside table, closed, but with her pen sticking out of it like a bookmark. She didn't remember setting the journal there. She must have fallen asleep while writing.

She gathered the journal and opened to the saved page. There wasn't quite enough light coming in from the window to see the words, so she reached up and clicked on the reading light attached to her headboard. The sudden blast of light washed out the lines in her journal for a moment before her eyes were able to focus on the words. She began reading.

> *Still March 26, 2010*
>
> *Okay, this is not normal. I'm writing for the second time today. But a day like today deserves multiple journal entries. I don't know what to do. Zach is still missing. I was sure he'd show up by sunset, but no. Dad arranged a search party. Well, not Dad so much as Lloyd. They were gone for hours. I stayed here in case Zach showed up. He obviously didn't. I also did a little exploring. Found this cool old stereo viewer thing. Like really old. And a bunch of old slides that worked with it. Most were of buildings and trees and gardens and things like that. But one was a picture of this house while it was being built. I know it's this house because the lamppost is out front. Which makes zero sense by the way. The house wasn't even completed in the picture. But here's the strangest thing—there's a man in the picture who looks like Marshall. I mean, it can't be him, but the resemblance is scary. It's a grainy picture, so*

maybe I'm wrong about that. But I hid the slide under the couch when Mom showed up because...

This was where the entry ended. Ariel picked up the pen and scratched out the unfinished sentence until it was unreadable. She climbed out of bed, set the journal on her desk, and slipped into her purple bathrobe. She didn't love the color purple anymore, but the bathrobe was warm and cozy, so she could forgive its out-of-fashion look. She turned the wobbly chair to face her window and sat on it, pulling her legs up and wrapping her arms around them. She stared out the window into the backyard, watching the long morning shadows cast by the sun rising in the east.

Zach, where are you?

Movement among the shadows set her heart racing, but what emerged from the trees in the distance wasn't human. It was an animal. It paused in the morning light, then took off back into the woods, little more than a black blur.

A deer maybe?

Ariel just wanted to climb back into bed and sleep until everything was back to normal. But what was normal these days anyway? She missed her friends in Boston. And her Boston home. She even missed the sounds and the smells of the big city.

But also, she didn't miss any of that.

Ariel felt a chill and shuddered, then pulled her bathrobe tighter around her. She didn't feel at home in this house. And she didn't want to go back to before, either. Nothing felt like home.

• • •

Ariel sat at the breakfast table, staring at the scrambled eggs her mother had made. She felt like she was starving, but she couldn't eat. *Why is everything so complicated?* she wondered. Her father looked just as lost as she felt. He sat across from her, staring at his untouched breakfast. Lyana poured herself a cup of orange juice and sat with them. The silence at the table was deafening. Something was going on between her mom and dad. She didn't need to be a psychologist to notice that.

Ariel carefully selected the largest blueberry from the bowl of fruit in the middle of the table and inspected it, then popped it into her mouth. She let it roll around there for a moment before committing to biting down on it. The juice squirted out and dribbled down her lip. Most mornings, this would have resulted in a snarky comment from her brother, followed by everyone falling into uncontrollable laughter. But no one said anything.

"Mom," she said. "Did you turn off my light last night?"

Lyana nodded. "You had fallen asleep while writing in your journal, I think."

"You didn't read any of it, did you?" Ariel picked another blueberry from the bowl while watching her mother's eyes for evidence of a lie.

"No. Just set it on the bedside table and covered you up."

"You promise you didn't read anything? That's personal, you know."

Lyana shook her head. "I promise I didn't read anything." She took another sip of orange juice. "I had a journal once, too."

Ariel didn't know that. Now all she wanted was to read her mother's journals. The thought was so ironic it almost brought a laugh. Almost, but not quite.

Ian stood abruptly and took his still-full plate over to the kitchen sink and set it there, then walked away down the hall to his study like he was on a mission.

Ariel watched him leave, then turned back to look at her mother.

"Is he okay?" she asked.

Lyana took a deep breath. "Your dad is having a hard time with..."

Ariel spoke when her mother didn't finish the sentence. "And you're not?"

Lyana furrowed her brow. "Of course I am. Why would you even say that?"

Ariel shrugged.

"We're all scared and worried, Ariel," Lyana said. "But we need to stay hopeful, too, right? We need to believe Zach is going to show up soon. And that he'll be fine, and that…"

Her mother stopped mid-sentence again.

Ariel nodded. "I get it." She set her fork and knife onto her plate and stood. "Guess I'm not very hungry today." She took the plate to the sink, started to set it on top of her father's abandoned plate, then decided instead to rinse both and place the plates and silverware in the dishwasher. It was a small thing, but maybe the small things mattered. When she was done, she went to collect her mother's plate, but Lyana shook her head.

"Still working on it," she said. "I'll clean up the rest when I'm done." She set her fork down and reached over to Ariel, placing her hand on Ariel's arm. "Thank you," she said.

Ariel shrugged again. It was probably the wrong response, but all she could offer. She looked down the hall toward her dad's office and saw that the door was closed. He never closed his door unless he was on a conference call or teaching remotely. There were no classes on Saturdays, and who would schedule a conference call for before seven-thirty on a weekend?

"Hey, Mom?" she said. "Do deer live around here?"

"I think so. Why, did you see one?"

"Maybe. Out back by the edge of the woods. But it was pretty far away, so maybe it was just shadows. Or something else."

Something else.

What could that "something else" be? Ariel shook away the still-forming thought.

"We're continuing the search today," said Lyana. "People could be showing up soon. If you want to come…"

"No," said Ariel. "I'll stay here."

She didn't want to search for Zach. She didn't want to be the one who found him. Because what if he was...

Ariel couldn't even form the word in her head.

• • •

Lyana listened to her daughter's retreating footsteps as she lifted her already-empty orange juice glass to her lips. She set the glass down on the table a bit too hard, startling herself with the snap of glass on wood. She studied the glass to make sure she hadn't cracked it, then, satisfied, got up and took it over to the sink to rinse it before placing it in the dishwasher.

A flash from the kitchen window caught her eye and she blinked. A moment later, it happened again. But it was just the sun reflecting off the windchimes she had hung outside a few days earlier. She watched them gently swirling in the morning breeze, mesmerized.

Another flash and she was transported back in time to their Boston home. The front door had just slammed closed, and Ian stood before her, his tan blazer soaking wet, rain dripping from his hair. Lightning flashed, painting the room with sharp-edged shadows, lighting Ian's face in the dark room. He looked lost, unsure what to do with his hands after hastily dropping his briefcase onto the hardwood floor. He took a single step toward her.

Lyana curled up tighter in the fetal position on their couch. She wanted to scream. She wanted to cry. She was angry and sad all at the same time. She wanted Ian to hold her, and she wanted him to stay far, far away.

She had just lost the baby, and he wasn't there for her. Once again, he was off on another one of his expedition trips exploring ancient history.

He. Wasn't. There.

Be with me.

Another flash and Lyana found herself standing in her kitchen, staring out the window. They already had a name for their second child. Avril. The pain of Avril's loss was devastating and lingering, but it hit Lyana and Ian in different ways. Lyana distracted herself by focusing even more of her attention and time on Ariel, surely spoiling her. Ian disappeared into his work and began to drink more heavily.

But then Zach arrived. Their rainbow baby. Her doctor called him a miracle. There was a mixed blessing in that—the doctor also gently offered that this one was likely their last—that Lyana would not be able to have another baby. Complications during pregnancy and delivery caused irreparable scarring in Lyana's body. At the time, that was the farthest concern from Lyana's mind. She and Ian were happily lost in the wonder of this miracle, of their baby boy, Zach.

Be with me. It was the voice again.

Unexpectedly, a blanket of calm wrapped around Lyana as she remembered an old Persian proverb her grandmother taught her—*damet garm*—may your breath be warm, signaling an expression of grace and gratitude for their miracle baby.

NINE

"HOW CAN WE understand each other now?" Akolo was sitting on his floor mat, looking over at Zach. Food had just arrived, so Akolo assumed it must be morning. He wished they were in a room upstairs—one with windows—so he could tell the time of day without having to guess.

"I think it has something to do with the...what do we call it? The temple box. Is there a name for it?" asked Zach.

Akolo shrugged. "The high priest says it's a place where our...the God of my people lives." He tilted his head and stared silently at Zach.

"What? A god that lives in a box?" asked Zach.

"Who are your people?" Akolo thought back on all the foreigners who would travel to his home city on the banks of the Jordan. None of them looked like Zach. "And where did you come from?"

"I'm from..." Zach paused. "I guess I'm from really far away."

"You don't know?"

"It's hard to explain."

Akolo nodded. He understood that kind of thinking. His own circumstance was hard to explain. One minute he was at home, laughing with his siblings or helping his mother serve the high priestess; the next he was here, wherever "here" was, and his family was gone. Dead. Akolo's jaw tightened. He felt a fresh wave of tears threatening to spill out.

"Hey, are you okay?" asked Zach.

Akolo shook his head. "I miss my family."

"Me too," said Zach. His voice sounded a bit wobbly.

"You knew my family?" asked Akolo, incredulous.

"No, no, I mean…" Akolo watched as Zach swallowed, then took a deep breath. He knew what that meant. This wasn't easy for Zach to talk about. "I miss *my* family. I'm far from home, too."

Akolo choked back the tears and sat up straighter. "We're both lost boys, then," he said.

Zach picked up a pear and bit into it. "Looks like it," he said with a mouthful of fruit.

Their regular guard had been away overnight, replaced by someone new. But as they sat there eating their breakfast, their regular guard appeared at the door.

Zach looked up at the guard. "Why are we being kept here?" he asked.

The guard grunted, then cleared his throat before speaking. "You are here to serve the king."

"But what does that mean?" pressed Zach.

"It means you do whatever the high priest asks of you."

Akolo braved his own question. "Is there a room with a window? Can we be moved to a room with a window? It's so dark and scary in here."

The guard didn't hesitate. "This is where you stay."

"A window really would be nice," said Zach. This made Akolo smile.

"This is where you stay," the guard repeated. "But if you serve the king well, you *may* be rewarded for your service."

"Just what are we supposed to be doing?" asked Zach. "And where is this king, anyway?"

"That's enough questions," said the guard. He started to exit the room.

"Can you at least tell us your name so we don't have to say 'hey you' when we need something?" asked Zach.

Akolo marveled at Zach's boldness. He was really beginning to like this other lost boy.

"My name is Bijan," the guard said.

"Mine is Zach," said Zach.

"And I am Akolo," said Akolo.

Bijan grunted his acknowledgment and left the room.

After they'd finished their breakfast, Akolo and Zach were led out of their room, up the stairs, and into the grand courtyard. They sat on a stone bench and waited, while Bijan went to talk to the soldiers standing guard outside the door that led to the king's throne room.

"I saw your bracelet," said Akolo. "Last night, while you were sleeping."

Zach's expression changed slightly, showing concern. Akolo worried that he might have upset his new friend. He glanced over at the soldiers to make sure no one was looking.

"I have something, too," added Akolo. He carefully pulled his own stone from his pocket and showed it to Zach.

Zach's eyes went wide. "That's really cool! Did your father give that to you? My dad gave me my bracelet. He travels a lot and brings me special gifts from the places he's been."

"This was a stone my father once had, but he didn't exactly give it to me." Akolo paused, remembering the attack on his family in the previous temple where he grabbed it before running for safety. "It is very precious and sacred to my people," Akolo continued.

"It looks similar to the stone in my bracelet," admired Zach. "I wonder if..."

Zach stopped and pointed toward Bijan, who was heading back their way. Akolo quickly slipped the stone back into his pocket.

"The king will see you now," said Bijan. He waited while the two boys stood, then guided them into the grand hall, then further still, into the throne room. The king was standing along the back wall, running his fingers across the relief there that depicted a battle.

"Whoa," said Zach. Akolo looked over at him and saw wonder in his eyes.

The king turned to the boys and smiled. The smile made Akolo's insides twist.

"The high priest tells me you two boys are special," he began. He turned back toward the scene carved in stone. "Do you see this? One of my greatest victories." He gestured toward the scene that was as wide as two camels and just as tall. "My army is the greatest of all armies. Do you know why?" he asked.

Akolo shook his head, too afraid—or perhaps angry—to speak.

"Because we honor the gods of those we defeat. And with each victory, with all the gods behind us, we grow stronger."

Akolo glanced at Zach. He was clearly mesmerized by the scene in front of them.

"But *your* god," continued the king, "is a mystery. And that..." The king pointed his finger first at Akolo and then at Zach. His fingers were all decorated with gold and silver rings. Some also featured gemstones, including one the very same color as his stone. "...is why you are still alive."

The words hit Akolo like a blast of cold air.

"I do not yet know why, but you two boys seem to be favored by your god. And because of that, you will help me unravel this mystery. And if your god is as powerful as I believe, then my army will never be defeated. We will conquer the world!"

The look in the king's eyes was like fire. Akolo backed away but bumped into a soldier that he hadn't noticed was standing directly behind him. Not Bijan, though. This soldier was wearing full armor and holding a spear at his side.

"The high priest does nothing without my approval. You are to do whatever he says." The king then waved the back of his hand toward them. "Take them away."

Akolo and Zach were led by the armored soldier back to the courtyard, where Bijan took over and began directing them back to their room.

"Can't we stay outside for a while?" Zach's request surprised Akolo, who was still reeling from the king's words.

Bijan kept walking.

"Please," said Zach. "The god we serve"—he gestured to Akolo—"would want us to breathe fresh air once in a while."

Bijan stopped. He turned toward the boys.

"The king wants us to solve a mystery," continued Zach. "Well, we can't do that very well if we're locked up in a room, can we?"

Bijan seemed to ponder this for a moment.

"Fresh air helps me think better, too," added Akolo. Bijan scowled and Akolo second-guessed his boldness.

"Fine. You can stay here for a while," said Bijan. "But I will be watching. You may not leave this area."

"Thank you, Bijan," said Zach. He nodded toward Akolo and the two of them walked toward a circle of small trees that surrounded a fountain on the other side of the courtyard.

• • •

Zach sat on a bench, facing the fountain. It was a circular structure at least ten feet in diameter, with a tall obelisk in the middle that reminded Zach of a chess piece—a bishop. A small pool of murky water in the fountain's bowl rippled slightly in the afternoon breeze. Zach marveled at the detailed geometric patterns carved into the ring that surrounded the fountain. *Someone spent a lot of time making this,* he thought.

Akolo sat down next to Zach and sighed.

"Thank you," Akolo said.

Zach shrugged. "I want a room with windows, too."

The courtyard was vast, but he still felt closed in by the surrounding walls. He lifted his face to the sky and closed his eyes. He desperately wanted to leave this place, but where would he go? The closed door near his ninety-ninth step in the hallway called to him. Or maybe he was just hoping it was calling to him. His thoughts drifted back to the house in Littleton. To his bedroom, which had once been the source of great pain but had since become a refuge and one of his favorite places to daydream. He pictured his bookshelves, lined with collectibles and trinkets. Each item meant something to him, even if it looked like junk to someone else.

"If my God is so powerful, why didn't he save my family?"

Akolo's words startled Zach. The shift from happy, drifting thoughts to the harsh reality of his current dilemma hit him like a face slap. He was reminded of the last time he'd played dodgeball, back when they still lived in Boston. Somehow, he had survived the early onslaught of red rubber balls until he was the only person left on his team. Aaron Sanderson eliminated him with a direct shot to the face that had knocked him down and sent him, bloody nose and all, to the nurse's office. The pain had been worth it, though, because he got to sit out during gym for the rest of the semester.

"Tell me the story," said Zach, forcing himself to focus on the moment at hand.

Akolo spoke slowly, with lots of pauses. During those pauses, Zach began to count the diamond shapes carved into the ring surrounding the fountain. The counting went on in the back of his head while he listened to Akolo. *Multitasking*, he thought.

Akolo told Zach about his daily routine. About his father and siblings and the way he would help his mother with the high priestess. He became especially animated when he talked about the soldiers and about how the king himself had separated Akolo from his family.

"The king told me they're dead," said Akolo, his voice cracking.

Zach knew Akolo needed a hug or something. But he wasn't comfortable offering hugs. Especially not to strangers. Instead, he tried words.

"Maybe," he began, "maybe your parents sacrificed themselves to save you." He didn't know if that was true, but it sounded like a good thing to say.

"But I didn't want them to do that! Our God should have saved them!"

Zach had attended church with his family many times but was easily distracted during services and bored by Sunday school. He knew more about the Greek and Roman gods than the one they talked about in Sunday school. He wasn't sure if that was a plus or a minus in the current conversation, but he did recall something a pastor once said. Something that lined up nicely with what the king had just told them. "God is unknowable," the pastor had said. That had caught Zach's attention because he loved mysteries.

Except maybe the one he was currently starring in.

"The king said your god is mysterious," began Zach. "A mysterious god might do things...differently, right?"

"Isn't he your God too?" asked Akolo through tears.

What could Zach say? "No. I mean, I don't know."

"But you survived in the temple..."

Yes, he had. And this was precisely what troubled Zach the most. Why did he survive? What made him so special?

He practically laughed when he thought of that word. *Special.* The king had used it to describe them. Back home, adults sometimes used the word when talking about him. It wasn't meant to be a dig at his unique personality, but sometimes it felt that way. He was aware he had some habits that weren't "normal." But he didn't care. *Mostly.*

Zach went back to counting, this time aloud.

"What are you counting?" asked Akolo.

He pointed to the fountain. "The diamond shapes in that design."

Akolo tilted his head, reminding Zach of a curious dog. "Why?"

"It helps me," said Zach.

Akolo continued to stare at Zach, then turned toward the fountain again.

"I'll count the squares."

The two sat together for a long time. Zach smiled when Akolo got up to walk around the fountain, ticking off the number of squares as he went.

A while later—Zach wasn't sure how much time had passed—Bijan appeared and led them back to their room. Food arrived soon after. As they ate in relative silence, Zach once again tried to recall the details of Ariel's dream. She said she had a stone that glowed…

"Akolo," Zach began. "Show me your stone again."

Akolo hesitated, then retrieved the stone from his pocket. He held it out for Zach to see.

"It's a fire opal," said Zach.

"How do you know?"

"I know a lot about stones," he said. "I've done lots of research on the inter…" He stopped. "I'm pretty sure it's a fire opal. They're kinda rare, I think. Where did you say it came from?"

Akolo didn't answer immediately. When he finally did, he looked sheepish.

"I took it," he said. "I was helping my mom with the high priestess, you know, like I was telling you about, and she dropped it when we had to run. I didn't want the bad people to find it, so I grabbed it."

Zach reached into his pocket and pulled out his bracelet. He held it up for Akolo to see.

"This started glowing in the temple room," he said. "That doesn't make sense to me. I mean, look at it—it's just a black stone, obsidian, I think. Why would it glow? And how?"

Akolo started talking a mile a minute. "That's what happened with my stone too! When I went into the room, it started glowing and it felt warm and then I felt really safe, and it was all strange and cool…" He folded his fingers around the stone. "And then I came out and the stone was back to normal."

"It's that chest," said Zach. "I definitely felt something in that room, too. A kind of power. Like electricity…" He paused. "Like lightning, I mean. Maybe the king and the high priest are right. Maybe this god is a powerful god and…"

"…and he lives in that chest!" finished Akolo.

Zach smiled. "Well, maybe not exactly. Maybe the chest is where he keeps stuff." He pictured the scratched-up old wooden jewelry box Ariel had abandoned when she got a brand-new, fancier one. His most precious stones resided there now, sitting on the shelf next to his beloved (though empty) TARDIS bank.

"'Where he keeps his stuff,'" repeated Akolo. "We should look in it."

Zach shook his head. "I don't think so. I mean, I don't like people looking through my stuff at home, so I'm sure he wouldn't want us messing with his stuff. Besides, that lid must weigh a ton."

"What's a ton?"

"It's…it means a lot."

Akolo nodded. After a few moments of silence, he spoke again. "If God's stuff is in that chest, maybe he's in the room too. Maybe we can talk to him?"

Zach felt the briefest glimmer of hope. "Maybe we can." He almost said something about the voice he'd heard in the temple but chose instead to keep that to himself. He still wasn't convinced the voice hadn't just been his mind playing tricks on him. This whole situation felt like mind tricks.

There was another long pause. Then Akolo added, "I'm going to ask him about my family."

Yeah, thought Zach. *Me too.*

TEN

ARIEL LOOKED UP at the clock at the front of the classroom and willed the second hand to speed up. She had always liked school, but this was the hardest season of her academic life.

Zach had now been missing for two weeks.

She glanced over at Garrett Bondurant, not for the first time this period, the last of the day. He was focused, head down, writing something in a notebook. He turned his head to catch Ariel watching him and smiled, never even lifting his pen. Just as quickly, he returned his attention to the journal in front of him.

Ariel hadn't even flinched when he caught her gaze. On any other day, she might have been embarrassed. Or maybe even quietly thrilled. But none of her emotions were working right. Everything had gone out of sync when Zach disappeared, and the unwanted attention she'd been receiving just further muddied her emotional and mental health.

"Hey, Ariel." The voice was that of Brooke Chamberlin, a classmate who had lived up to her pretentious name with the smarmy kind of entitlement that only came from someone whose family bathed in money and was ever eager to remind people of that. Ariel had avoided her since the first day of school. She was really trying to be a better person this year and befriend people who weren't so quick to pick on those with a lesser social status.

People like Zach.

Ariel pretended not to hear Brooke.

"Ariel," Brooke pressed. "I just wanted to say sorry about your brother." The loud sigh that followed was right on brand. Brooke was the victim here because Ariel wouldn't acknowledge her heartfelt sentiment.

Brooke was just the latest in a long line of people to hurl sympathy at Ariel. The first wave of sympathy had felt sincere, because that had come from Ariel's friends, the people she chose to spend time with. Each successive sympathy wave had felt less and less sincere, eventually devolving into little more than noise. Ariel was tired of it. She didn't want to be reminded every single day that her brother was missing.

Presumed dead.

That's what the Wednesday edition of the local paper had pronounced before providing a weakly worded retraction in Thursday's paper. She wouldn't have even known about the articles were it not for her father's insane addiction to anything relating to Zach's disappearance. She understood his focus, of course. He wasn't about to stop looking for Zach simply because two weeks had passed. And he shouldn't. None of them should stop looking.

"My dog was almost kidnapped once," said Brooke, clearly unable to deal with Ariel's silence.

Ariel had had enough. She turned to face Brooke directly. "Are you comparing my brother to your dog? Are you insane?" The second line was nearly shouted. The whole class was watching, listening now. Before her teacher could intervene, the bell rang. Ariel grabbed her books and scrambled out of the classroom before anyone could call her out, or perhaps congratulate her for putting Brooke in her place. She heard lots of mumbling behind her as she left, including a neutered reprimand from her teacher, but just kept on walking. She didn't stop to catch her breath until after she'd exited the building and was standing on the sidewalk beside the parking lot where the buses had already started to congregate.

Ariel didn't want to ride the bus. She didn't want to be anywhere near her classmates in that moment.

So, she did something she'd never done before. She started walking home.

It was a five-mile walk.

• • •

"Have you heard from Ariel?" Lyana's voice caught Ian off guard. He'd been staring at the computer monitor in front of him for what was either seconds or hours. He wasn't quite sure which. Lyana appeared at the door to his study and repeated the question. This time with more emphasis. "Have you heard from Ariel? I'm worried. She isn't back from school yet. I texted, but she hasn't responded."

Ian looked up at his wife. She looked concerned. It wasn't unusual for Ariel to take her time texting her parents back, but it wasn't like her to drag it out too long. "Maybe the buses are running late?"

"An hour late?"

Ian checked the time on his computer. *How can that be? What in the world is happening to time?* He scooted his chair back and stood abruptly, then started toward the door, pausing, with obvious frustration when Lyana didn't move out of the way quickly enough.

"I'm going looking for her," he said. He grabbed his keys from the hook by the garage door and went into the garage, pulling the door behind him a bit too firmly. He stood there for a moment, gathered himself, then turned around to go back into the kitchen. Lyana was waiting there. At least she wasn't crossing her arms and tapping her foot. Not that she was the kind of person to do that.

"Sorry," he said. "I didn't mean to be so abrupt." He walked over to his wife and gave her a hug, kissing her on the top of her head. "Maybe she's at a friend's house. Have you tried calling…"

"I'll call around," she said, then she gently pushed him away. "Have you been drinking again?"

"What? No." Ian shook his head, but as he did, it seemed like his head was moving in slow motion. "Maybe a little," he added.

Lyana held out her hand.

"What?" Ian asked.

"Give me the keys," she said. She opened and closed her fingers.

"I'm fine, Lyana," he said. But was he? He'd just lost hours staring at his computer. Maybe he wasn't as fine as he thought. He dropped the keys in Lyana's hand. "Maybe she stayed after school to work on a project or something."

"On a Friday? Not likely."

"Do you think she decided to walk home? She should have called us."

"I don't know what she's capable of," said Lyana. "She's impossible to read these days."

"Call me as soon as you find her," said Ian. He watched his wife go into the garage, start the car, and back out slowly, then closed the door and returned to his study. The tumbler on his desk was empty, save for a small ring of whiskey at the bottom. He lifted the glass and swirled the liquid, watching it catch the light from his desk lamp. He took one last sip, set the glass on his desk and leaned back in his chair, nearly tipping it over. With his heart racing from the near fall, Ian gripped the desk with both hands and took a moment to compose himself.

"What am I missing?" he said aloud. "Where are you, Zach?"

He felt the weight of exhaustion pulling at him, drawing his eyes closed.

In his half-awake state, he allowed his thoughts to wander. He began sorting through all the possible scenarios that could explain Zach's disappearance, pausing only briefly on the ones that included the words *kidnapped* or *killed*. He couldn't abide those possibilities. The chief detective of the Littleton Police Department had told him that while they would continue to search for Zach, he needed to prepare for all possibilities. "Fewer than fifty percent of the people who are still missing after four days are found," he'd said.

Zach had been missing for fourteen days. Ian didn't want to know what percentage of missing persons were found alive after two weeks. He knew that number would be way too low.

Zach isn't dead. He can't be.

• • •

Ian heard a sound like hissing and opened his eyes to find himself in a small dark room illuminated only by a single torch attached to a wall across from him. The yellow-orange flame was alive with motion, swirling like a tornado. The random snap of shooting sparks made him blink erratically. He took in his surroundings. He was seated on a chair. Not his office chair, but a simple armless wooden chair. His hands gripped the seat of the chair, felt the rough-hewn wood, the threat of splinters. His feet felt cold. He looked down to see the floor was made of stone. He was barefoot. Where had his shoes gone? The frenzied flame suddenly turned blue. Gray shadows began to swirl across the floor.

The hissing sound multiplied and grew louder.

Snakes?

Ian pulled his feet up off the floor and onto the chair, wrapping his arms around them. He felt like a child trapped in a nightmare.

The shadows darkened, then slithered and swirled until they covered the entire floor as far as Ian could see.

And then, with an audible whoosh, the blue torch went out and he couldn't see anything. A bitterly cold breeze ruffled his hair and sent shivers up his spine.

"This isn't real," he said. His voice sounded wrong. Like it was coming from far away. He repeated his claim, his hope. This time the words returned to him in someone else's voice, echoing off the four walls.

Are the walls closing in?

The hissing grew louder. It sounded like it was inches from his ear. Ian dared not move.

Something cold and scaly brushed against the back of his neck.

"Ian."

How did it know his name?

"Ian, wake up!"

The room disappeared; the hissing abruptly stopped. Ian opened his eyes to see he was still in his study hugging his legs to his palpitating chest and trying to catch his breath. Lyana was standing beside him, her hand on his shoulder.

"You okay there?"

"I was just…" he began with his eyes darting around the room, but he didn't know what he was going to say.

"I came to tell you that Ariel is fine," said Lyana.

Ariel. What was wrong with Ariel?

"She's fine?" The reality of the moment began to come into focus.

"She was walking home," said Lyana. "I found her a mile down the main road."

Right, hadn't come home from school yet. "Why didn't she text us?"

"Phone was dead," said Lyana. She stepped back and looked at him with a curious expression. "Are you sure you're okay?"

Ian took a deep breath, allowed himself a moment to finish returning to the present. "I'm fine," he said. "Just nodded off for a bit. What time is it?"

"About twenty minutes since I left to find Ariel," said Lyana. She gave him her furrowed-brow look. He knew what was coming before she said a word. "You don't look well," she said. "You haven't been sleeping and you're drinking again, and you're not going to figure out what happened to Zach if you're running on fumes." She pointed to the door. "Go. Get some sleep."

"But it's not even supper time," he began. *Is it?*

"Ian, you're a wreck. And I need you not to be a wreck, okay? I need you to be clear-headed. We both do." She gestured toward the door. Ariel was standing there, looking scared.

Ian scooted his chair closer to the desk and clicked on the computer mouse. "I can't stop now, Lyana. The longer we wait..."

"Please, Ian. Just get some sleep. We'll talk tomorrow morning and make a new plan."

She started to help Ian to stand, but he brushed her off, a little too aggressively, he realized immediately. "Sorry. I'm just on edge," he said.

"Welcome to the club," said Ariel. She huffed, then disappeared around the corner.

Maybe Lyana was right. Maybe he just needed a little more rest so he could piece together the clues that were slithering around in his head, just out of sight. Like the snakes in his dream.

Had it been a dream? It all seemed so real.

Ian followed his wife out of the study and up the stairs. This time he didn't count the stairs, and that small decision weighed hard on his heart. He had been counting them every time he went up or down as a way to honor Zach in his absence. Or maybe he was hoping the ritual might somehow bring him back.

Lyana led Ian past Zach's empty room and Ariel's closed door, to their bedroom. She helped him onto the bed and pulled a blanket up over him. He looked up at her and saw the tiredness in her own eyes and suddenly felt the weight of all she was carrying. He was so thankful for the miracle that had saved her from intense suffering and death. He would never have survived even this long after Zach's disappearance without her by his side. "I love you, Ly," he said. Were his words slurred a little? Maybe. Must be the exhaustion.

Lyana offered a tired smile.

"Get some sleep," she said.

He closed his eyes, then abruptly opened them again. "Ariel! Is she okay?"

"Ian, I already told you I found her. She's fine. She just wanted to walk home, for some reason."

"Oh, right. Sorry. You did say that."

Lyana bent forward and brushed her hand gently across his stubbled cheek. "I love you, Ian." Then she left the room, turning the light off behind her.

• • •

Lyana stopped by Ariel's room to ask what she wanted for supper, but Ariel told her not to go to any trouble. "I'll just eat leftovers," she said. Then she added, "I'm worried about Dad."

Lyana thought for a second, then sighed. "So am I, honey, but he is trying. Everything he's doing is about trying to find Zach. This just isn't the sort of mystery you can solve with reason. I think that's what's frustrating him most."

Ariel nodded. "Yeah, I guess so."

"We're still not okay, you know? We have no reason to be 'okay' right now. But we need to be 'not okay' together. We need to be there for each other while we..."

"While we what, Mom?" Ariel looked truly scared in that moment with her eyes welling up with tears. Lyana walked over and sat down. After brushing Ariel's hair off her face and wiping away her tears, she cupped her daughter's chin and lifted her face to see those beautiful gray eyes.

"We're going to find Zach," said Lyana. "I don't know how or when, but we're going to find him, and he's going to be just fine."

"I hope so," said Ariel with a deep sigh. Ariel turned away and Lyana pulled her hand back, feeling the disconnect in her gut as a loss. "I'm going to read for a bit. I'll eat later," she added.

"Okay." Lyana wanted to say more, but instead just quietly left the room, pausing to close the door so Ariel could return to her isolation.

She walked down the stairs and into the kitchen, then stood in front of the pantry. Her eyes blurred into the middle distance, not focusing on anything.

She is hurting.

"What?" said Lyana. She was certain she'd heard an audible voice. But maybe it had just been her own thoughts. They were certainly plenty loud these days. And yes, Ariel was indeed hurting—she was missing her brother and going through all the usual teenage angst and still trying to excel as a high school student. They'd all decided together that she would be better off trying to maintain some kind of "normal," but now Lyana was second-guessing that decision, wondering if the emotional and mental toll was too great.

Lyana walked into the pantry, carefully avoiding looking in the mirror—mostly because she didn't want to see the bags under her eyes, but also because it still freaked her out a bit—and chose a box of Triscuit crackers. She didn't really love the salty crackers, but they reminded her of her sister, Eliza. When they were kids, they would dress up the crackers with cheese and meats and whatever else they could find in the refrigerator, then imagine they were in a five-star restaurant enjoying a four-course meal. It was a little thing the two sisters would enjoy together, even though their mother showed little interest in playing along. It was never about the Triscuits—it was all about the two girls spending time together, finding pockets of joy in a house that reeked of despair.

Lyana poured a glass of the boxed wine, grabbed her favorite cheese, and took them along with the crackers to the living room.

She sat on the couch and sipped the wine, then chomped away on a cracker with cheese. The taste made her childhood memories all the more vivid. She pulled out her phone and held it in her hand. This was going to be a difficult phone call. She should have done this so much sooner.

After a deep breath, she dialed her sister.

"Hey, Ly." Eliza was always so cheerful. *And it was a sincere cheerfulness, too,* thought Lyana.

"Hey, E," said Lyana.

"Everything okay there?"

Lyana swallowed hard, forced a smile she knew Eliza couldn't see. "Hey, I don't just call when things are falling apart, do I?"

"No, of course not. I'm just...well, I guess I'm still trying to sort through all that stuff from last year."

"I know, I know. I'm sorry...again...that I didn't share more back when things were happening. And I know I've already said this, but we really were rather consumed by everything going on, like with Zach and the bees." Lyana hadn't shared every detail of what had happened before because, despite their closeness, she didn't think Eliza would have believed it all. She was a great sister, and they talked about most things openly and without fear of judgment, but...the supernatural stuff was too much. Even Lyana herself doubted the specifics of what had occurred. She had told Eliza about her misdiagnosis of dementia, and the miraculous recovery, but she'd been intentionally vague about all the stuff with the house.

"What is it, Ly. What are you not telling me?"

This was it. The reckoning. "Zach is missing," said Lyana.

"What?"

Lyana told her sister everything she knew about Zach's disappearance and their ongoing attempts to find him.

Eliza was silent for a moment once Lyana had finished.

"Two weeks?" she finally said.

Lyana nodded, then added a mumbled verbal assent.

"Oh, Ly, I don't know what to say. That's the most awful news." There was another pause while Eliza spoke to her husband. "Sis, I can be on a plane tomorrow. There's no way I'm staying here while you're dealing with such an awful situation."

"Eliza, wait. You don't need to come. We have lots of people here helping. And we're going to find him, I'm sure of it."

There was a long pause.

"Lyana, it's been two weeks."

"I know."

"That's…a long time."

Lyana's words caught in her throat. "I know."

"How's Ariel dealing with things?"

"She's…she's hurting. Of course, we all are. But it hits her a different way, you know? She would tease Zach a lot…"

"Oh, I know how that is. It's just her way of showing love."

"She's trying her best to hang in there, but…I don't know, E. I'm having a hard time communicating with her."

Lyana pictured Eliza nodding along, perhaps sipping her tea while Lyana talked. Eliza loved tea. Lyana almost said something about how their caretaker had introduced her to a new kind of tea but stopped herself. This wasn't the time for small talk. But oh, how she wished it was.

"And Ian?" There was always a little edge in Eliza's voice when she talked about Ian. Eliza had been the one to hold Lyana together when, years ago, Ian went off the deep end, when he was consumed by work and alcohol during a time when Lyana needed him the most. Lyana often thought back to the time she and the kids had stayed with Eliza. It had ended up being a time of great healing, not only for Lyana, but, ultimately, for Ian, too. Still, Eliza was a highly protective sister, so her antennae were quick to go up if Lyana even hinted that things weren't going great.

"He's doing everything he can to solve this mystery," said Lyana. She immediately regretted the words. "Mystery" made it all sound too trite. Like something from a cheap novel.

"He's a smart man," said Eliza. "And…"

"And what?"

"And I'm sure that together you'll figure out a way to get Zach back. I don't even want to venture a guess about where he might be. But…"

Eliza stopped talking.

"But what?" asked Lyana.

"You waited two weeks to tell me." Eliza's tone was more sad than accusatory.

"I'm sorry…I just…" And what really was Lyana's excuse? Did she even have one?

"It's okay," Eliza said. Her voice sounded shaky. "I mean, it's not okay—but I get it. Sort of." She paused again. "What am I even saying? Of course I don't get it. I can't even imagine what this is like for you…" Eliza's words morphed into muffled sniffling.

"Eliza," said Lyana. "Please don't cry. It's going to be okay. I don't know how I know that, but I do."

Eliza sniffled again. This time it wasn't muffled. "And here I am supposed to be comforting you."

"Just keep us all in your thoughts and prayers, okay? I'll update the minute I learn anything new."

"Promise?"

"The very minute."

"And promise you'll let me know if you want me to be there, too, okay?"

"I will. Love you, E."

Lyana waited for Eliza's tear-muffled reply, then pressed End Call.

She took another bite of a cheese-topped cracker.

It was flavorless.

ELEVEN

ZACH SCRATCHED A mark onto the base of the wall in the back of the room. It was the twenty-first such mark he'd made.

Three weeks.

It had been a few days since he and Akolo had been summoned to the temple. Each time previously, they'd been given something to take into the temple area, to set on the chest there. First it was a goblet made of glass. Akolo seemed entranced by it. Had he never seen glass like that before? Zach decided not to ask. He had been careful not to share anything about his time travel story and didn't want to offer up any clues that might confuse or trouble his new friend. Then they'd carried a stone tablet with strange writing into the room. Zach didn't recognize the symbols, but they reminded him of the hieroglyphics he'd learned about in school and seen in one of his father's books.

His new friend.

Zach almost couldn't comprehend it. Akolo was his friend. A good friend. He hadn't had a friend like this in...well, he couldn't recall a time when he'd befriended someone who didn't look cross-eyed at him for his quirks and unique personality. Akolo actually seemed to be taken by Zach. Like a big brother.

He immediately thought of Ariel and a knot troubled his stomach. The knots had decreased in the past few days, but not because he felt any less anxiety about his impossible circumstance. He was just getting better at hiding them away in his brain somewhere so he didn't need to stare at them all the time. He knew that at some point he'd have to reckon with all the accumulating loss, sadness, and heartache. But for now, he was finding a way to survive.

The days had been long and boring, with little for Zach or Akolo to do but walk around the courtyard or pay their dues by visiting the temple. Akolo had tried speaking to the presence they felt in the temple room, but thus far they hadn't heard any kind of response. However, the power Zach experienced the first time seemed to be growing. The last time they were in the temple, Zach's pendant and Akolo's stone had glowed brighter than ever. Still, each time they'd exited the temple to return the item they'd brought in, the high priest would shake his head, disappointed. Once, the king himself was waiting for them outside the tent. The look on his face after the high priest handed him the crown Zach and Akolo had taken into the temple was something Zach hoped never to see again. It was a mix of barely contained anger and intense frustration. Zach half wondered if the king would take out his sword and kill the high priest right then and there. Instead, he'd pressed his finger into the high priest's chest and said, "You have one more week. Figure this out."

That was five days ago. Time was running out for Zach and Akolo, too.

"What do you think all of this means?" asked Zach, hoping that his young friend had better context to understand what was going on with the temple.

Akolo's expression while he was considering his reply made Zach smile. Ariel had once pointed out his similar look of a deeply furrowed brow and pinched lips while he was thinking hard about something.

"I don't know," Akolo offered after almost a minute of pondering.

"You said your sisters helped your mother serve the high priestess. Did they ever say anything about the temple? About what they did there?"

Akolo shook his head. "They never talked about it. I don't think they were supposed to. I mean, I helped them prepare offerings, but… that's all I really knew anything about."

Zach was frustrated. Though he hadn't given up the hope of finding a way back home, he'd pressed pause on that idea, choosing instead to focus on figuring out his role in this time and place. It obviously had something to do with the chest in the temple. And maybe something to do with Akolo himself. But the mystery was complicated, and even with his mind working overtime trying to solve it, he kept coming up empty.

"There *was* something," began Akolo. "Something one of my sisters said when they and my mom were heading out to the temple after sunset."

Zach raised an eyebrow, hoping the action would prompt Akolo to finish his thought. When he didn't, Zach asked, "What did she say?"

Akolo shifted his posture, as if answering the question made him uncomfortable.

"I overheard them when I was outside. It wasn't normal for them to leave at night. But that's not why I was outside," he said. "I had gone outside to see the moon. I had to see it; I really did." His voice was almost pleading. "That's when I overheard her."

"What did she say?"

"She was talking fast, like she was excited about something."

Akolo paused his story again. Zach rolled his eyes. "And?"

"She said, 'Will I notice anything different?' or something like that."

Zach sighed. "That's it? That's all she said?"

"That's all I remember. But I'm pretty sure she was talking about the temple."

Zach's hope deflated. He had no idea what that could possibly mean.

"You're upset at me," said Akolo.

Zach shook his head. "What? No. I'm not, I promise. It's just that I don't know how..." Zach paused. An idea began to form in his head. "Why did you have to see the moon?"

"Huh?"

"You said you had to see the moon. Why?"

Akolo shrugged, as if it was obvious, despite having given Zach zero context. "Because it was supposed to be red, like blood. I'd overheard my mother say something about it earlier..." Akolo paused again. "I wasn't supposed to hear that either," he admitted, looking especially sheepish.

"And was it?" asked Zach. Excitement was bubbling under the surface. He was onto something important.

Akolo's eyes went wide. "Yes! Well, maybe not quite red, more pink, I guess. But it was bright! I only saw it for a moment, though. I must have gasped when I saw it, because my sisters stopped talking. I was sure they were going to find me, so I sneaked back through the window and went to bed. I can be really quiet when I need to."

Zach nearly laughed at that. Akolo had been anything but quiet these past weeks. He was always asking questions, but since Zach couldn't answer many without revealing something about where, or when, he was from, Akolo filled their conversations instead with stories about his village, his friends, and especially about the river that ran behind the house where he lived. Zach had liked hearing those stories the best. As he listened, he pictured the stream that flowed behind his house in Littleton and all the adventures he'd already enjoyed while walking along its banks. Akolo would have made a great adventuring companion back home.

"I really don't think they knew I was outside," said Akolo, talking mostly to himself.

"You're sure the moon was red? Or pink?" said Zach, fighting the growing homesickness that threatened to take hold.

"Yes! You should have seen it."

Zach smiled to himself. He *had* seen it. Or something like it anyway. A blood moon. He was almost certain that was what Akolo had witnessed. The offhanded comment from Akolo's sister was starting to make sense. Maybe the "something different" was related to the lunar event. Could that be it?

Zach searched his memory for what he knew about blood moons. They didn't happen often, he knew that, and it had something to do with a lunar eclipse.

What if…?

"When did you see the red moon?" asked Zach. "How long ago was that?"

Akolo put on his contemplating face again. "It was at the beginning of the harvest season."

"When was that?" asked Zach.

Akolo scrunched his eyebrows tight. "Don't you know?" he asked, incredulous. "Don't they have harvest season where you're from?"

Zach pictured the last autumn he'd experienced and shuddered. Zach's family had moved to Littleton in the summer in time to get settled in before school started in the fall. It was soon after that everything started to unravel. "Um, sure, we have harvest season," he said, fumbling for a believable lie. "It's just, I think it's different than here."

He'd already told Akolo he was from "very far away," so he hoped that would be enough to excuse his lack of knowledge about the local calendar.

"Maybe two hundred days ago?" Akolo offered. He didn't sound too sure.

"It's called a blood moon," said Zach, pleased with himself for solving at least one part of the mystery. "And I think… I mean, I don't know, but I think a blood moon has something to do with the temple."

"Really? What?"

This is where Zach's guess fell a bit short. What could it mean?

"We need to talk to the high priest." Zach surprised himself with this statement. He was more than a little scared by the man and his minions.

"Why?"

"I think I know what he wants us to do, but I need to be sure."

He didn't really know much at all. But sometimes a hunch was all you needed to head in the right direction. Zach hoped this was the right direction.

He swallowed hard. He also hoped he was wrong.

• • •

Akolo stood just behind Zach, praying the high priest wouldn't stare at him with his singular dark eye. It seemed almost black at times, though Akolo knew this must just be a trick of the light.

As Zach spoke with the high priest, Akolo glanced at the surrounding area. The temple building was in the middle of a square. Smaller buildings surrounded the temple and the tent that remained in place in front of the temple doorway. The crowd had thinned considerably over the past weeks. What had initially seemed like some kind of big event had shrunk into something that interested fewer and fewer people. Only the high priest and his companions and the soldiers regularly showed up. Today there were only a few curious onlookers in attendance, most of them hanging back, looking bored. The king had visited just once. The crowd had been much more attentive then. Akolo could still hear the audible gasp from the crowd when the king confronted the high priest. That had sent shivers down Akolo's spine.

Zach finished talking to the high priest and turned back to Akolo. He guided him by his arm away from the high priest's long shadow and began to speak.

"He knows about blood moons," said Zach. "The thing is, they're kind of impossible to predict. From what I know, and what the high priest told me, they might get one or two a year."

"I don't know what that means," said Akolo. He loved talking with his new best friend, but often found himself at a loss for understanding his meaning. Akolo attributed it the fact that they were from different countries, with different traditions, even though they both spoke the same language.

"The king wants our god's power, right?" said Zach. Every time Zach spoke of the god as his God, it sounded off to Akolo. Like he didn't really mean it. Then again, Akolo didn't quite get it either. All he had to go by was the way his mother and father had talked about their God. Most of their conversations had to do with crops and harvests. And protecting his people.

Akolo scowled. *A lot of good that did my family*, he thought.

Zach continued. "The high priest shared something with me that was really interesting. He said that when they'd conquered another nation, they'd done something similar with that nation's artifacts… I mean, like the chest. The holy stuff."

Akolo nodded, though he still wasn't quite following.

"When they brought something into the place where they were keeping the holy things, that thing became more… Well, it was hard to really understand his meaning, but I guess more powerful? Like stronger or better."

"I still don't understand."

"Like, a sword for example. If they brought a sword into the holy place, or whatever they called it, that sword would be, I don't know, 'imbued'? I think that's the word."

"What does that mean?" asked Akolo.

"It means it could kill more people."

Akolo was both intrigued and frightened by the idea.

"So, he thinks…our God can do the same?"

Zach nodded. "Yes. But here's the thing…"

Akolo looked around as if Zach was about to point to something. When he continued talking, Akolo shrugged it off as yet another example of Zach's strange way of speaking.

"I think he's right. I think our god's power can imbue things. But…"

Zach paused, and a wide smile came to his face. It seemed an odd expression to have when talking about weapons and killing.

"I think it only works on certain days. I mean, I could be way wrong about all this, but it all fits. I'm pretty good at solving puzzles, you know? My sister always hated that…"

Zach's smile fell. But just as quickly, it returned.

"It's the blood moon!" said Zach. "That's when things can be imbued!"

Akolo's head was spinning. Did this mean the high priest wouldn't need them anymore? No, that didn't make sense. No one else could enter the temple. So of course they'd still need them.

Or at least one of them.

"And that's not all," said Zach. Bijan came over and began ushering them back toward the courtyard, and, ultimately, their room in the lower level. "The high priest said he would ask the king if we can have a room with a window! Because then we can watch for the blood moon!"

Bijan, who was obviously listening in, snorted. Like he didn't believe that would happen.

Akolo ignored the guard. *A room with a window.*

"That's great news," said Akolo. And it was, but his insides were swirling with uncertainty. On one hand, it was a relief to know what his purpose might be in this strange land. But on the other, he didn't like that purpose one bit.

They finished their return trip to their room in silence. But once Bijan had stepped outside, Zach gestured Akolo over and whispered one final revelation.

"You know how we haven't gotten any answers from the god in the temple?" he asked.

Akolo knew that all too well. At first, he'd been hopeful, but when no answers came, he'd begun to lose hope. Yes, there was something unusual about the temple—he felt the presence of a great power every time he went in. But no matter how he worded his questions—in a whisper, in a thought, in a quiet hope—he heard only silence in return. He was beginning to doubt his first visit, when he was certain he'd heard God's voice speak to him. "Welcome, servant," the voice had said.

Maybe he'd just imagined it.

Zach continued, "Well, a blood moon would be the perfect time for a god to speak, don't you think? Maybe we can finally get some answers."

"When is the next one?"

"Soon, I think."

Soon, thought Akolo. *Maybe I will finally have an answer to my biggest question: Why didn't you protect my family?*

• • •

Zach waited until Akolo was snoring before he crawled over to the corner of the room where he'd been marking the days. He recounted the marks, then subtracted them from the number the high priest had given him. Akolo's guess of two hundred days had been a little off. The last blood moon happened two hundred and twelve days before he'd arrived here. The next one was long overdue. At least that's what he'd concluded after his conversation with the high priest. Zach's instincts had been spot-on. The high priest knew a lot about the phases of the moon. He used different words to describe them, but Zach was good at context clues, and it didn't take long for him to decipher that the next full moon was just three days away, give or take a day. If this one was accompanied by a lunar eclipse, they'd have their blood moon.

He had his question ready for the god of Akolo's people. He'd already asked it a half dozen times before, but silently. This time he would voice it aloud.

Worried that he might only get one question, he had initially considered, "Will I ever get home?" But he couldn't bear the thought of hearing "no," so he'd quickly eliminated that question from consideration. If he'd learned one thing from Marshall since they'd moved into the house his uncle built, it was the value of asking open-ended questions.

"Open-ended questions always give you more information," Marshall had said when they were out on one of their adventure walks around the property. "And they can also lead to meaningful dialogue," he'd added. "Even new friendships."

Zach had tried this out once on the school playground, when he'd wanted to join in on a game of kickball. His interest in playing was itself a rare thing, and he second-guessed himself at least half a dozen times before gathering the confidence to walk over to the kids assembling on the baseball field.

"What do I need to do to join the game?" he'd asked, feeling more than a little foolish for his awkward wording.

"You don't have to do anything. You can be on my team," one of his classmates had said.

It might not have been the smoothest conversation he'd ever had, but at least he didn't have to endure a soul-defeating "no."

It was open-ended questions that had provided him with all the information he needed to figure out the blood moon thing, too. The high priest was surprised by all of Zach's questions but answered each one thoughtfully. He even complimented Zach on his cleverness. Zach was convinced this is why he agreed to talk to the king about moving them to a room with a window.

Marshall was right.

Zach missed him almost as much as he missed his family. Marshall had, in a way, *become* family.

Zach silently rehearsed his question once again.

How do I get home?

TWELVE

"DAD, ARE YOU coming to breakfast or not?"

Ariel's voice sounded far away, like his own voice in the dream from yesterday. It was yesterday, wasn't it?

Ian checked the day on his computer screen. Saturday. Two weeks and one day since Zach disappeared and he still felt like he was miles away from solving this puzzle.

"Where are you, Zach?" he said with anguish in his voice, for the hundredth time at least.

Movement by the doorway caught his attention. He looked over to see Ariel standing there, her arms folded across her chest like a cliché. "This is like the fourth time I've called you for breakfast. Do I have to be the adult now?" Her tone only had the slightest hint of playfulness in it. Mostly, it was a tone of exasperation.

"Sorry, sorry," he said, scooting his chair back. "I'm just a little…"

"Preoccupied," said Ariel.

She wasn't wrong.

Ian started walking toward the door but saw something flash in his peripheral vision. He felt his heart rate rise as he looked over at his computer. But it was just an advertisement flashing on the screen where he'd paused his internet search.

"Your precious computer isn't going anywhere, Dad. C'mon. You definitely need to eat something."

Ian nodded and followed his daughter down the hallway to the kitchen. Lyana was standing by the stove, wearing an apron, spatula in hand. A stack of too-dark pancakes sat on a plate next to the sink. When Ian sat down, Lyana casually lifted the plate and dumped those overcooked pancakes into the sink. Then she turned back to the griddle and flipped a half dozen fresh pancakes and neatly arranged those onto the now-empty plate. She brought the plate to the table and set it down next to a paper-towel-lined plate that looked like it once held more than a few pieces of bacon. Only two remained.

"Sorry," he said. He was going to say more, but there was nothing more to say. The words lodged in his throat like they always did when it mattered most—when Lyana needed him to be present, to be the husband who knew how to comfort instead of analyze, to feel instead of think his way through a crisis.

He'd already apologized plenty in the past few days, sometimes for things he knew he'd done, but just as often for things he didn't recall doing or saying. The apologies had become as empty as they'd been all those years ago when he'd returned from that expedition in Egypt to find Lyana hollow-eyed and grieving alone. *I'm sorry I wasn't here,* he'd said then, the words falling flat against the magnitude of losing Avril. *I'm sorry I didn't know.* As if not knowing somehow absolved him of the fundamental failure—that when his wife needed him most, he'd been halfway around the world, drunk on the thrill of some ancient pottery shards while she bled away their daughter's future.

The pattern was sickeningly familiar: Crisis hits, Ian retreats into his head, into research, into a bottle, anywhere but into the messy, terrifying work of being emotionally present. He could lecture for hours about ancient civilizations, their rituals of grief and loss, but ask him to sit with his own wife's pain—his own pain—and he became as useful as those broken pottery fragments he'd been so obsessed with studying.

What if I say the wrong thing again? The fear paralyzed him now just as it had then. Better to apologize for surface infractions than risk opening the deeper wounds, the ones that never quite healed because they'd never been properly tended. Better to search obsessively for Zach in databases and forums than confront the possibility that he might lose another child—this time to his own inadequacy as a protector.

He tried to convince himself Zach was safe and sound somewhere. He just had to be. Ian couldn't think about any other option. Despite this, he was becoming more and more frustrated with Lyana. She continued to be way too at peace with the awful reality they were living in.

"I'm going into town after breakfast," said Lyana.

Ian poured too much syrup on his pancakes, then began to scrape some off with his fork before digging in and taking a bite. With his mouth sufficiently full, he simply nodded.

"Take me with you," said Ariel. She didn't have to say the rest of what she was thinking. Ian could see it in her eyes. *I need to get away from this place.*

On one level, Ian understood this feeling. The house, the property, everything about the physicality of this place screamed Zach's absence. Zach took up a lot of space, made his presence known in dozens of ways. He was complicated, sometimes preferring to keep to himself, but also full of wonder and constantly spouting theories or riffing on the latest thing he'd discovered online or while out adventuring in the woods. Every day Zach remained missing, the house felt less and less like a home and more like the parking lot of an abandoned theme park. But Ian couldn't leave. What if Zach suddenly reappeared and no one was home? Besides, this house had something to do with his disappearance. Ian was becoming more convinced of that with every passing moment.

"Okay," Ian said, finally responding to Lyana and Ariel.

"You can clean up after breakfast," said Lyana. "And I don't just mean the dishes, Ian."

Ian furrowed his brow. "What do you mean?"

"She means you need to take a shower. With lots of soap," said Ariel. She pinched her nose to emphasize the point.

Ian couldn't remember the last time he took a shower. Perhaps she was right.

"The beard has potential, though," said Lyana, a small smile coming to her face. "Maybe you should keep growing that until it turns into something."

Ian pinched at his chin, feeling the stubble there.

"You think so?" he said.

Lyana tilted her head and shrugged.

After the girls left, Ian began cleaning up from breakfast. He rinsed the dishes, then flipped the switch for the garbage disposal. The whole house seemed to vibrate. He flicked the switch off, then on. Again, the house vibrated.

This isn't right, he thought.

He flipped the switch on and off a few more times, and each time he felt more than just the sink vibrating from the running disposal. Ian thought back to the events that led to an entire rewiring of the house months ago and wondered if maybe they'd missed these wires.

But no, he'd used the disposal plenty of times since then.

Ian flipped the disposal on one more time and it hummed like normal, now quite empty. The house didn't shake at all this time.

"I'm not getting enough sleep," he said. It was as true a statement as any. Most nights since Zach's disappearance, he was rooted to his chair in the study late into the night, scouring the internet for anything that might offer a clue about his son's disappearance. He even tried to access the dark web, though he quickly abandoned that idea when he realized he had no idea what he was doing. Whenever he finally went up to his bed, he'd lie awake next to his wife, sometimes for hours, running every possible scenario he could think of through his head, fighting off any that ended with Zach's death.

He can't be dead. That's not how this story plays out.

Ian left the stack of partially rinsed dishes on the counter, then headed upstairs to take a shower. Halfway through the shower, he remembered that he hadn't put the dishes into the dishwasher. He scolded himself for his distractedness and made a mental note to finish cleaning up the kitchen after his shower was done.

After he was out of the shower and dressed, he went right back to his study and plopped down on the chair. He let his eyes wander around the room for a moment and they landed on one of the books in his shelf. It was a book he knew well—he'd been a consultant for the project and received his first publishing credit on the acknowledgments page. His contributions to *The Rise and Fall of Ancient Empires* included detailed analysis and reasoned conjecture about the nature of family units and community culture. Early in his teaching career, he was touted as a "rising star" in academic circles. The recognition only fed his desire to become something even more—to become the top expert in his field. And he nearly reached that pinnacle, but the cost was too great. He almost lost his family.

Ian reached for the bottle of whiskey that sat on the shelf in front of him. The last bottle. He briefly considered dumping it down the kitchen sink, then shook off the thought as "overreaction." Besides, it wasn't cheap whiskey. Instead, he poured a glass and took a long sip, savoring the complexity of the flavor, imagining the story that led to its bottling. *Everything is born of stories,* he thought. He took another swig, then methodically closed every tab on his computer screen until only one remained. His novel. The last time he'd written a word in his novel was the day before Zach disappeared.

The cursor blinked at the end of a half-finished sentence:

She stared at the blank wall…

What does she see? he wondered. *Where was I even going with this?*

Ian lifted the glass to his lips to take another sip, but it was empty. His eyelids felt heavy. Sleep called to him. He could almost hear its voice…

• • •

Ariel made a beeline to the booth in the far corner of the diner and sat down. Her mother had said she'd be back to pick her up in an hour. Ariel didn't even ask what her mother was doing. She didn't much care anyway. It was hard to care about anything these days.

She pulled out her phone and started mindlessly scrolling through stupid videos, anything to fill the silence. The diner felt eerily quiet without the usual lunch crowd chatter—just her and the ancient jukebox in the corner that Lloyd kept feeding quarters. Back in Boston, she'd never even seen a real jukebox outside of movies. The whole concept seemed ridiculous: paying money every time you wanted to hear a song when you could just download whatever you wanted for free.

Lloyd's taste leaned toward classic rock that was even older than the supposedly "vintage" stuff her parents inflicted on her during family car trips. She could tolerate most of the '80s songs—some were actually pretty good, though she'd never admit that to anyone—but anything from the '70s or earlier usually sent her reaching for her headphones.

But the opening strings drifting from the speakers now made her pause mid-scroll. That sweeping orchestral intro tugged at some buried memory—maybe from one of those family music nights when Mom would insist on "expanding their musical horizons" while Dad made popcorn. The melody was hypnotic, building and swelling like it was trying to carry her somewhere else entirely. But the weight of the lyrics from The Verve's "Bitter Sweet Symphony" hit her harder than they should have.

Well, that was depressing, she thought. But something about it felt brutally honest. She was trapped in this weird small town, in this impossible situation where her brother had just vanished, where nothing made sense anymore and she couldn't do anything to fix it.

That feeling about being a million different people made her chest tight. She *was* different people now—the Boston girl who had friends and knew how everything worked, the Littleton girl trying to fit in, the sister who was supposed to protect Zach but failed, the daughter watching her parents fall apart. Which one was really her?

The song kept building, those strings pulling at something deep in her chest, and she realized she was crying. Because the song was right—sometimes you really couldn't change, couldn't fix anything, could only stand there and watch everything spiral while some beautiful, heartbreaking song played in the background.

It was at least ten minutes, which equated to about three songs, before Lloyd came out from the kitchen and saw her sitting there.

"I'm so sorry," he said. He was brushing flour-dusted hands against his apron. "I didn't notice you come in. The bell..." He pointed to the front door. "It stopped working yesterday. And I already sent Amanda home for the day."

The song had pulled her so deep into thoughts of Zach that Lloyd's sudden appearance made her jump. Her phone slipped from her hands, clattering onto the table. Heat flushed her cheeks as she quickly snatched it back up, hoping she looked more casual than she felt.

"It's fine," she said with a practiced shrug, the same one she used when teachers caught her daydreaming in class. "I'm just killing time until Mom's done with whatever it is she's doing."

Lloyd walked up to the booth and stood there. The smell of vanilla found her nose. She loved the smell of vanilla.

"Can I get you anything?"

"My brother, maybe?" she said. She felt a knot in her stomach the moment she spoke the words, but she couldn't take them back.

"Oh, Ariel, I wish I could do that for you. Your family means so much to me, to all of us here in the diner." He spread his arms to indicate a crowd of employees behind him, but the diner was empty except for Lloyd and her.

Heartache flooded her throat. She didn't dare speak or she'd become a blubbering mess.

Lloyd didn't press the issue. He just nodded. "I'll get you some sparkling water. That's what you usually get, right?"

She nodded, then shook her head. "Yes, but no. I'll take a Dr. Pepper. Lots of ice."

"You got it," he said, then was off to the kitchen.

Ariel looked down at her phone. The battery was at 9 percent. She shut down the browser and set the phone screen down on the table, silently criticizing herself for forgetting to charge it. Lloyd returned a moment later carrying a to-go cup and set it on the table in front of her.

"May I join you?" he asked, pointing to the bench across from her. Before she could reply, he continued, "We don't need to talk about anything if you don't want to. But I'd like to sit with you if you don't mind. Maybe I can soak up some of that heartache by proximity."

Ariel nodded and Lloyd slid into the booth seat across from her. Ariel liked Lloyd. He was like a cross between a wise older friend and a grandfather figure. He had been generous to the family, and kind, too. It was he who had arranged to have people line the streets and cheer for Zach after he'd been released from the hospital following his near-death experience.

Seeing that moment in her memory released the tears she'd been holding in. She buried her face in her hands and sobbed.

Lloyd said nothing. He just sat with her.

Minutes passed. When the tears subsided, Ariel looked up to see Lloyd with his hands folded, his eyes closed. Was he praying? He opened his eyes, then reached across the table to slide the Dr. Pepper toward her.

"Might need to refill those tear ducts," he said, a small smile appearing on his face.

She pulled the cup closer and sipped. It tasted like heaven. She hadn't had soda for months, the lingering result of choosing to fit in with a group of girls at her old school in Boston who had declared soda a "peasant's drink." Everyone who wasn't in that circle was considered a peasant. She'd gone along with it mostly because it was a healthy choice but also to maintain her credibility within the group. Looking back on it, she realized she was just chasing status.

"What do you think happened to him?" she said, staring intently at the cup in her hands, unwilling, or unable, to look into Lloyd's kind eyes.

"My answer is probably the same as yours," he said. "I don't know."

Ariel nodded and took another long sip of Dr. Pepper, but she drank it too fast, and a burp escaped her lips.

Lloyd smiled. "Very nice," he said. "We'll have to hold a burping contest sometime. But not today. We'll wait until…"

He paused, but Ariel finished the sentence for him. "…until Zach can join us."

"Yes. We'll wait until then."

Ariel managed a small smile. "He'll leave us in the dust," she said with a giggle.

"I don't doubt it," offered Lloyd. He reached his hand out and Ariel took it. He squeezed her hand gently, then excused himself. "There are muffins to be made," he said. "Stay as long as you need to. Call out if you want anything."

Lloyd disappeared behind the counter and into the kitchen.

Ariel sipped her Dr. Pepper.

Come home, Zach. Please come home.

• • •

Lyana noticed that Ariel seemed slightly less angsty when she collected her from the diner. She didn't dare bring it up, though, lest she burst that bubble of relative peace. Instead, she simply enjoyed the uncluttered silence while they drove home.

Lyana's brief season of calm was cut short by the unwelcome discovery that Ian had only half cleaned up from breakfast. She finished the job, not caring how much noise she made as she dropped the plates into the dishwasher, rinsed out the sink, wiped the breakfast table clean, then returned the syrup bottle to the refrigerator. It was a stupid little thing to be upset about. There were so many bigger things worthy of frustration or anger. But in that moment, it felt good to be angry over a stupid little thing.

"Ian," she called out. She walked to his study. The door was open. He was slumped down over the desk. Her heart skipped a beat, but then she saw his chest rising and falling. He was asleep. She considered waking him and guiding him upstairs to their bedroom, then decided against it. A stiff neck seemed like fair payment for not cleaning up breakfast. She chided herself for that thought. It wasn't like her to be so petty or vengeful. Still, she decided to leave him alone.

She returned to the kitchen and stepped into the pantry to look for dinner inspiration.

Trust.

There it was again. The voice.

Lyana grabbed a nearby shelf to steady herself. The voice was coming from inside her, but also outside of her. It resonated in her head and through the walls at the same time. It was all around her, consuming her.

Could it be…the house?

The pantry mirror had been a trigger for the strange encounters she had a few months ago. She hesitated, then turned her head to look at her reflection. As she fearfully waited for something to happen, she recalled the image she had seen in the mirror shortly after moving into the house: a girl holding a stuffed lamb. She and Ian had bought a stuffed lamb for their unborn daughter. She could still feel the joy that bubbled up when Ian pulled the stuffed animal from the shelf and held it up to her, tilting its little lamb head while squeaking out in a sweet voice, "Can I be your daughter's best friend?"

Lyana couldn't resist. The lamb came home with them.

Their daughter didn't.

Lyana was almost four months pregnant when she lost the baby. Lyana took in a deep breath, steadying herself, recalling again the feeling of loss like a gut punch. Her disappointment in Ian started to bubble up yet again. She shook the thought from her head. No, there was no way he could have known this would happen. He was just away on another expedition, doing his job. He would have been there for her if he had known.

Ariel was a little over a year old at the time. Ian and Lyana had waited to tell her about the new baby, and then it was too late.

Trust. There it was again.

Had she ever really considered how horrible Ian must have felt to be so far away when they lost the baby? He had been their rock, their protector.

Something shimmered in the mirror.

"Is that you, Avril?" she hesitantly asked aloud. She strained to see a glimpse of the girl again, but nothing appeared.

She reluctantly turned away from the mirror and left the pantry.

Lyana collected the food scraps from the container in the refrigerator, then went out to the garage to add them to a bucket of chicken feed. As she walked the fifty feet from the house to the chicken coop, something felt off. It was too quiet. Usually, the chickens made all kinds of racket when they heard her coming. She stopped just outside the fenced-in pen. The smell was all wrong, too. The chicken coop had a distinct smell. This was different. Fear bubbled up into her throat. She knew that smell. That was the smell of blood.

Lyana opened the gate, then walked up to the coop. She peeked inside but saw no chickens. Fear growing inside her, she walked slowly around to the back side of the coop that faced the forest. She was frozen in her tracks by what she saw.

Blood. Feathers. And not a single living soul.

"Ian!" she shouted. She retreated, nearly tripping over something. She looked down to see the decapitated head of a chicken looking straight up at her. She screamed, then ran back to the house, yelling again, "Ian!"

• • •

Ian sat at the kitchen table, his head in his hands. He looked defeated. Ariel had run up to her room soon after Sheriff Blackstone had arrived. Lyana let her go, but knew she'd have to go talk to her soon.

Sheriff Blackstone stood and placed his hand on Ian's shoulder.

"I'm sorry," he said. "I know this makes things…more dire."

Ian just kept shaking his head.

"But you don't really know what did this," said Lyana, more hopeful than certain.

"Mrs. Keane," said the sheriff, "you're absolutely right about that. We don't know. But it's pretty clear that whatever did that to your chickens was… How can I put this? A wild animal. A dangerous wild animal."

"That doesn't mean Zach…" She couldn't finish the sentence.

"No, of course not," said Sheriff Blackstone. "I just need you to be realistic about the possibility that…"

Ian shot up from his chair and shouted. "That what? That my son was killed by a bear? Or a wolf? Just what are you saying?"

"Ian, calm…" began Lyana.

"Don't you dare tell me to calm down," shouted Ian. Lyana had never seen him this upset. It frightened her. Ian turned to the sheriff, who had his hands out in front of him, encouraging Ian to take it down a notch. "You don't know what did that." Ian pointed a finger toward the garage door, then pointed it directly at the sheriff. "*You* need to do more! You need to multiply your efforts to find my son! You need to…" Ian's anger quickly turned into fear and desperation.

He leaned forward against the kitchen table, hung his head, and let the tears come flooding out. "I'm sorry," he said. "But there has to be something else you can do." His sadness had fully morphed into pleading.

Lyana looked from Ian to the sheriff and offered her own pleading look.

"Ian," he said. He turned to Lyana. "Mrs.…Lyana. We're doing all we can. I know it doesn't seem like much, but…" Sheriff Blackstone barely choked out the next words. "We'll keep looking."

"Thank you, Sheriff Blackstone," said Lyana. She led him to the front door.

"Ben. Please call me Ben," he said.

Lyana nodded. "Ben. Thank you for coming out so quickly. And thank you for continuing to look for Zach."

"Of course." He turned to leave, then stopped, turned back to Lyana. "I know it goes without saying, but I'm going to say it anyway—please don't venture out into the forest without proper…protection."

She nodded again. "We'll be careful."

"And you might want to check on that daughter of yours." He nodded toward the stairwell. "I have a daughter about her age. When they get real quiet, that's often when they need us most, you know?"

"I do," said Lyana.

They said their goodbyes and Lyana closed the door behind him. She pulled a chair around the table to sit next to Ian and wrapped her arm around him. She felt every shudder as he sobbed, but her own tears failed to fall.

Trust, said the voice in her head.

But trust what?

THIRTEEN

"IF THIS DOESN'T work, we're toast," said Zach.

Akolo scrunched his face into a question. "What does that mean? What is…toast?"

Zach laughed. The sound bounced around the temple walls like a racquetball. He'd only played the game once, but once was more than enough. The black eye he sported for two weeks afterward had been a painful reminder that he wasn't cut out for racquetball. Or most sports, really, though he hadn't hated the track and field unit in gym class.

"It means we're in big trouble if I'm wrong about the blood moon," said Zach. When Akolo's puzzled look didn't subside, he added, "And toast is just a different way to eat bread."

"I-still don't get it."

"Don't worry about it."

"But you just said we might be in big trouble. That sounds like something to worry about."

Zach dropped his smile and looked directly at Akolo, trying his best to appear both confident and calm, though he felt neither. "Let's not worry about it, okay?"

Akolo nodded.

Zach gently placed the water-filled goblet on the chest and then stepped back. Then he pulled his bracelet from his pocket and held it out in his hand, gesturing for Akolo to do the same with his stone. This was a ritual for them now—a way to gauge the power that ebbed and flowed from the chest, from the god who inhabited this space. If their stones glowed bright, that meant the god was near. If they barely glowed at all, well, they didn't quite know what to think of that.

When their stones began to brighten, Akolo unexpectedly took Zach's empty hand in his. Zach initially recoiled at his touch but recovered quickly enough to not slap the hand away. He squeezed it once, then dropped Akolo's hand and stood there next to his friend in silence, watching, waiting.

But for what? Would anything look different on this, the night of a blood moon?

Their stones continued to glow, but nothing was happening to the goblet. Zach's hope began to deflate. Then, slowly, the water in the cup began to brighten. Light flowed upward from the goblet, spreading out into the air above, like a flashlight's beam revealing dust motes. In a matter of minutes—or was it hours; time passed differently in the temple—the light was so bright Zach had to turn away.

Then, without warning, the light emanating from the cup went out. It took a moment for Zach's eyes to adjust, but when they finally did, he saw that only his and Akolo's stones continued to glow.

The temperature in the room dropped suddenly and Zach shivered.

"Why is it so cold?" asked Akolo. But by the time he'd finished speaking, the stifling heat in the room had returned.

Zach took a deep breath, trying to gauge a familiar taste in the air. He tasted this once before, back when Marshall started rewiring the house. Thankfully, it wasn't nearly as bad as the awful smell of the old wires *before* he'd replaced them. A vivid memory of his mother's screams began to bubble to the surface as he recalled the stench of melting plastic and urine. He struggled to close the door to that memory.

"Zach, look!"

Zach didn't realize he'd closed his eyes. He opened them to see the goblet glowing, just like their stones.

"Did it work?" Akolo asked.

Zach let out a huge sigh. "I think so. I think we're golden."

"Like the goblet?" said Akolo.

"Yes, like the goblet."

They stood there in silence for a moment. *No, not quite silence,* thought Zach. He could hear Akolo's rasping breath, and his own, of course. But there was another sound. One he'd heard once before in this room: a gentle hum.

God is singing.

"Did you ask your question?" Zach asked.

"I almost forgot," said Akolo.

Akolo's lips began to move, then stopped.

"Don't you want to know?" asked Zach.

Akolo shook his head. "What if I don't like the answer?"

Zach knew this feeling all too well. He hadn't dared ask *his* question for the very same reason. What if there was no way home?

• • •

Akolo's heart raced. He wanted to reach out and grab Zach's hand again but decided instead to slip his hand into his pocket to touch his gemstone.

The king had returned from another conquest (so they were told) and was standing behind a long, narrow table, soldiers on either side of him. The high priest and his companions were directly across from the king. The goblet had been placed between them on the table. It was still glowing, though more faintly than before.

Akolo wished he could just disappear into the wall behind him where he and Zach stood, watching.

"What does this mean?" asked the king.

The high priest cleared his throat loudly before answering, "I can't be sure..."

"You can't be sure?" The king's voice was calm, but to Akolo it sounded a lot like a shout.

"We think the goblet has been imbued," the high priest continued.

"And the water?"

"And the water, too," he added.

"Then drink," commanded the king.

The high priest hesitated. He turned to face the boys. "First, we must be certain it's safe," he said. He pointed to Akolo. Zach grasped Akolo's tunic, holding him back.

"I don't know if you should..." Zach whispered.

"I'm not afraid," Akolo whispered back. He was, though. He was terrified that something awful was about to happen. But what choice did he have? The king's men were standing at the ready, their hands on the hilts of their swords. Defying the high priest would be the same as defying the king.

Akolo walked forward. The high priest and his companions stepped aside, creating space for Akolo to step up to the table.

"One small sip," said the high priest.

Akolo reached for the goblet and took it in both hands. He lifted it to his lips and sipped. The water was sweet and fragrant, like honey. One sip and he wanted more, but he gently placed the cup back onto the table, then backed away. All eyes were on him. He looked over at Zach and offered a shrug. Zach's expression was unreadable.

"How do you feel?" asked the king.

Akolo wasn't quite sure what words to use. The feeling was something he'd never experienced before. He felt... "Strong," he said. "I feel strong." And it was true, he'd always thought of himself as small and weak. But in this moment, he felt powerful. He didn't want the feeling to subside.

"Watch him for an hour, then report back," said the king. He waved his powerful hand and the high priest and his companions turned toward Zach and Akolo, ushering them out of the throne room. Bijan met them at the doorway.

"Watch them," the high priest commanded. Bijan nodded. "And report back to me in an hour. Tell me everything you observe."

"Of course, your holiness," said Bijan.

Bijan guided the two boys through the grand room and into the courtyard. He sat them down at the fountain and then stood at attention nearby. Akolo didn't like the way he was staring at him.

"Well, what is it like?" asked Zach.

Akolo studied the fountain, and instantly he knew exactly how many diamond shapes there were. How many squares. If he squinted just so, he could almost see the water flowing from the fountain, even though it hadn't once worked since he'd started visiting the courtyard.

"I see things. And I *know* things," he said. That was the best way he could describe it. Because that was exactly what he felt. He saw things better, understood things better. It was like the water had given him not only a feeling of strength but a sharper mind as well. And a strange feeling of peace—something he hadn't felt for months.

"Did it really work?"

Akolo smiled. "Yes! We will not be toast!"

Zach nodded. The look on his face was not one of joy, however. He looked serious, solemn.

"This is good news, isn't it?" asked Akolo.

Zach took a deep breath before responding. "I hope so."

Hope.

Now there was a word Akolo could get used to.

• • •

Zach and Akolo stood before the king. This time, the high priest and his companions stood behind the boys. Zach felt more vulnerable than usual. The king hadn't chosen him to sample the water. Was he no longer needed? The thought hit his stomach like one pancake too many. He'd known *that* feeling far too many times before.

After the high priest shared the news that Akolo was just fine, in fact, that he felt smarter, stronger and wiser after drinking just one sip of the water, the king lifted his hand, signaling the end of the high priest's speech.

"I knew we saved you for a reason," said the king, looking directly at Akolo.

The king reached for the goblet, lifted it, and took a long drink of the water. He paused, still holding the cup in front of him, then lifted it again and drained its contents. He set the goblet back on the table with a loud *thunk*, puffed up his chest, and closed his eyes.

Zach measured the king's silence: fifteen heartbeats, fifteen breaths, fifteen steps up to his bedroom in a house that felt like another lifetime. The familiarity of the number should have comforted him. Instead, a cold sensation settled into his stomach.

Suddenly, another number intruded into his brain. *Ninety-nine.*

"Yes!" said the king. His eyes were bright, and a smile filled his face. "This god is indeed powerful!"

The king's enthusiasm frightened Zach. He had only been around the king a few times, but each time, the king had been reserved, calculated, and careful with his words. Not in this moment. In this moment he looked like an over-the-top character from an animated Disney film.

"We will begin preparations," said the king. He motioned to the high priest. The high priest turned to guide Zach and Akolo out of the throne room. But Zach wasn't ready to go. He had far too many questions. He gathered up all the courage he could muster and called back to the king.

"What do you mean, preparations?" he asked.

The king's cartoon-wide smile didn't fade. He tilted his head, as if to ask, *Don't you already know this?* then said, "We will be returning the artifacts to their rightful home. And our high priest will go with them. This will secure our standing with your god and become an anchor for the further expansion of our kingdom." Then, as if that was enough to explain everything, the king turned to walk away.

Zach couldn't help himself. As he was practically dragged toward the door by one of the high priest's companions, he called back, "When? When will you take it away?"

The king paused, turned toward Zach. His intensity seemed to grow. "When the time is right." The smile faded ever so slightly. "But don't worry," he said. "You both will be going too. Won't it be wonderful to be home again?" he said. His eyes were still wide-eyed with wonder.

"Home again?" asked Zach. His stomach clenched.

"Home again," said the king.

Zach looked at Akolo. His eyes were wide, too, but not with wonder. With hope.

"I'm going home," said Akolo. He smiled, but the smile didn't quite reach his eyes.

"Perhaps you'll find your answers there," added the king with a brush of his hand before turning away abruptly.

Zach felt the air go out of his lungs. Did the king know about their questions? How could he know?

"I'm going home," Akolo said again, this time in a whisper.

Zach said nothing. He couldn't leave this place. His only chance to find his way home was here. Instinctively he knew it was here, in this place. He couldn't leave the palace, or he'd be stuck in the past forever.

Maybe he already was.

FOURTEEN

THE ROOM WAS dark except for the soft blue glow from the clock on the bedside table.

3:17.

Was he asleep or awake? He closed his eyes, then opened them again.

4:11.

What? That can't be right.

Ian looked over at Lyana. She was little more than a silhouette. He kept watching until he saw her chest gently rising and falling. He breathed a quiet sigh of relief, then rolled over to face the bedside table again.

4:72.

No. Nope.

He blinked and looked again.

4:27.

That's better.

Images from a vivid dream congealed, then dissipated in Ian's head, straddling the line between asleep and awake. He got out of bed as quietly as possible, went to the closet and started putting on a bathrobe, only to realize it was much too small.

Lyana's robe.

He returned the robe to its peg and felt for the one next to it. This time the robe fit just fine. He glanced at the clock one more time before slipping out of the room and into the hallway.

4:51.

He desperately wanted coffee but didn't want to make a lot of noise in the kitchen, so he went to the refrigerator and grabbed a carton of orange juice instead, then carried it into his study, gently closing the door behind him. He didn't turn the light on, but simply moved the mouse on his desk. The screen came to life, brightening the cold room with the harsh white of a Word document that had been mocking him for days. His novel. His stalled novel.

He clicked behind the document on the browser. There were dozens of open tabs.

Ian lifted the orange juice carton to his lips and took a long swig, then randomly clicked on one of the tabs.

The webpage that appeared depicted an ancient carving of an ouroboros. Something in his brain clicked, like the pins of a lock falling into place.

"That's it!" he said. The sound of his own voice jarred him. Ian stood up and started pacing the small room. The recurring dream that teased him from the periphery of his brain came into focus. In that dream, Ian was following clue after clue in an attempt to solve the mystery of Zach's disappearance. And each one of those clues featured the image of the snake eating its own tail. It's an image he'd seen plenty in his study of ancient cultures.

He ticked off the places he'd recently seen the image in the waking world.

Zach's bracelet.

Marshall's cabin.

The lamppost? Was there something with the lamppost?

He made a mental note to check that out as soon as it got light outside.

Zach's drawing.

Ian walked back to his desk, sat down and shuffled through the stack in the overflowing paper tray until he found Zach's drawing.

Zach had showed it to him a couple of weeks after he'd returned from the hospital and Ian had asked if he could hang on to it. That Ian could recall this with clarity was new—every other time he'd tried to connect the dots with the symbol, the details would slither away, and he was left with little more than a vague idea that he was onto something.

But not this time. This time he saw the ouroboros in his thoughts as clearly as he saw the one on the screen.

But what's the connection? What does it mean?

Ian glanced at the time on his computer monitor.

5:11.

The ouroboros is a symbol of life and death. Infinite rebirth.

Infinity.

He grabbed the carton of orange juice and started to take a drink, but he was careless, and the orange juice poured out too quickly, spilling out the side of his mouth. He tried to catch it with the back of his hand, but the juice dripped onto Zach's drawing. Ian started to wipe it away but stopped mid-swipe as the orange juice swirled around on the page like a living thing, multiplying until it perfectly covered the image of the snake. The liquid changed color, first turning brown, then red, then solidified, growing into a three-dimensional depiction of the ouroboros.

This can't be happening, thought Ian.

But it was. Right there in front of him.

Ian reached forward to touch the snake, but in that instant, it untangled itself and the snake's head shot out toward Ian's hand. Ian recoiled, but not before feeling the sting of two fangs puncturing the skin between his thumb and forefinger. He scooted back in panic, nearly tipping the chair over. When he looked back at the desk, the picture was just that. A two-dimensional pencil drawing. A drop of orange juice had merely pooled atop the head of the snake, deforming it.

Ian tried steadying himself with slow, intentional breaths, but as he looked down to focus on his breathing, he noticed two bloody marks on his hand. His heart continued to race.

Did that really happen? The snake must have something to do with Zach's disappearance. He was sure of it now. *It's not just about the ouroboros,* he thought. *It's about this house.*

He recalled the time months earlier when he'd found a secret door in the hallway that led him to revisit a painful, life-changing moment from his childhood. He had come to accept that was a hallucination, but now? Now he was almost certain it had been real.

The answer to Zach's disappearance is here somewhere. In this house or on this property. But now that the memory of his childhood pain was vivid again, fear gripped him with ice-cold fingers. Ian glanced up at the bookshelf where the last bottle of whiskey sat, still mostly full.

He should be chasing an extra dose of liquid courage in this moment—it was what he had done numerous times over the past two weeks. But something in him had fundamentally changed. He could feel it.

He had absolutely no desire to drink.

Ian glanced again at the bite marks on his hand and shook his head in wonder.

"Huh," he said.

• • •

Lyana found her bathrobe on the floor of the closet, slipped it on, and headed downstairs to the kitchen. Ian's study door was closed. How long had he been up, obsessing over his theories about Zach?

She was surprised she had slept so deeply, considering the discovery of the mutilated chickens the day before. But she was thankful for the gift of sleep, nonetheless. And a dreamless one at that.

Lyana looked over at the espresso machine they had bought the day before Zach disappeared. It had sat there unused this whole time. And she wasn't going to use it today, either. She scooped coffee into the "old" coffeemaker and poured water into the holding tank, then pressed the button to brew the regular stuff. It had been good enough for them for years. It would be fine now, too. She half considered taking the espresso maker out to the garage so she wouldn't have to stare at it every morning and be reminded of the awful sinking feeling that had consumed her the very next day after they set it on the counter.

Trust, the voice had told her yesterday.

This was the same voice she'd heard months ago, when her world was turned upside down. Originally, she believed that it had been the voice of her mother, first offering encouragement when Lyana was feeling a little out of sorts in the new house, then providing an answer to the question that had plagued Lyana her entire adult life: *Why didn't you protect us when Eliza and I were children?* The answer she heard had brought Lyana peace. Her mother *couldn't* protect them; she was paralyzed from her own abusive relationship with their stepdad. *I have always loved you*, the voice had said. But now, after hearing the voice again, she wasn't so sure it was her mother speaking to her.

The sound of Ian's door opening caught Lyana by surprise. She turned to see him shuffling along the hallway, his hands spread out against the wall, feeling his way from one end to the other.

This again? thought Lyana.

"Ian," she called out. He didn't respond. She called again, "Ian!"

Ian stopped and looked over at her.

"I'm just… I need to…"

Were his words a little slurred?

"Why?" she said.

"Why what?" he asked. He had returned to brushing his open palms across the hallway wall.

"Why are you doing that?"

"The door," he said. "I need to find the door." He stopped suddenly, then walked directly to Lyana. He almost stumbled into her but caught himself on the kitchen counter. "It's all connected, Lyana. The door, the snake"—he spread his arms wide—"this house."

"What do you mean?"

"Zach isn't lost…out there…" His hands went wild, pointing this way and that. Lyana had never seen him so animated. He was almost manic. "He's lost…" His brow furrowed, then his eyes went wide. "He's lost here! In this house!" He shook his head like he was erasing a random thought.

"Ian, we've checked every room a hundred times," said Lyana. "Zach's not here."

"I know…but… I mean." Ian's face looked pained, like he was suffering from a migraine. He lifted his hand to grab his head, and that's when Lyana noticed the two marks.

"What happened to your hand?"

"It's the snake, Lyana! The ouroboros," he slurred. He started pacing around the kitchen, scratching at the back of his neck, pulling at his hair.

"Ian, you're scaring me," she said. She took a step toward him, but he stopped pacing suddenly and pointed directly at Lyana. His eyes were bloodshot and wide.

"Lyana, I know this doesn't make sense. Of course I know that. And no, if you're wondering, I haven't been drinking again. Zach didn't get lost in the woods, he wasn't mauled by a bear, and he wasn't kidnapped in his sleep or any other of the insane theories people have been tossing around at the diner. Yes, I know all about what people have been saying…"

"Ian…"

"Let me finish," said Ian.

Lyana nodded. "Okay. But please, Ian, slow down. It's me, your wife. I'll listen. Of course I'll listen."

Ian took a deep breath. Lyana guided him to sit down at the kitchen table. She sat across from him. He proceeded to tell her about his dreams and about his sudden clarity regarding the ouroboros.

"You and I have had strange experiences in this house," he said. "And Zach, too, with the bees."

"But not Ariel," added Lyana. This didn't provide her as much comfort as she'd hoped.

"No, not Ariel." Ian paused.

"You had impossible encounters with your mother and our unborn little girl," he said. "And I witnessed a scene from my childhood in person. I mean, it sure felt like it was real. It's like...I don't know, like we're in some kind of science fiction story that is making us relive tragic moments from our past."

Lyana gasped. "Time!"

"What?"

"It has something to do with time, right?"

"Yes! Time is all messed up in this house. What if...?"

Ian seemed to get lost in his thoughts. The next few moments of silence were pregnant with possibility and uncertainty.

"Ian, there's something else we need to talk about," Lyana began.

Ian turned his attention to his wife. She slid her coffee cup over to him.

"Drink some coffee first," she said. He didn't argue. After a few sips, he nodded to Lyana to continue. "I've been hearing the voice again." His eyebrows lifted. "But this time it sounds different." She paused for effect. "Like it's a part of me."

Ian tilted his head into a question.

"Ian, I've also seen more visions. I think it's her again. I think it's Avril."

Ian began shaking his head, slowly at first, then vigorously. "No, no, no. That can't be..."

Lyana let out a single laugh. "Ian, how is *that* any crazier than the rest of this stuff? Than you looking for a secret door in the hallway? Or me nearly losing my life because of some impossible connection with the wires in this house? Or bees suddenly showing up in Zach's..."

Ian waved her off. "Okay, okay. You're right. I'm sorry." He gestured for her to continue while he took another sip of coffee.

"Remember the vision in the mirror?"

He nodded.

"What if she's here? Not here, like in the flesh or anything. But... her spirit. That would fit the crazy science fiction theme, right?"

"What did the voice say?"

"The first time..."

"What? You mean you've heard it more than once? And you didn't tell me?"

Lyana took a deep breath. "We've been a little preoccupied. And, Ian, look in the mirror. You've not been in a good place lately. So, yeah, I didn't say anything."

Ian nodded solemnly. "I'm sorry...again."

"You can stop apologizing now," said Lyana. He opened his mouth to speak, but she interrupted him before he could apologize for apologizing too much. "The first time I heard a voice was a couple weeks ago. Not long after Zach went missing. The voice said, 'It's not what you think.'"

"What's not what you think?"

"I don't know. At the time, I thought it was talking about Zach being missing. But now? I'm not so sure."

"And the other time you heard the voice?"

Lyana sighed. She'd been doing a lot of that lately. "The *second* time was Friday. I thought I heard the voice say, 'She is hurting.' It was after Ariel had gone up to her room. But..."

"But what?" Ian slurped the last drips of coffee from Lyana's cup.

"That might have just been my instinct talking, you know? Because *of course* Ariel is hurting." She didn't say the rest of what she was thinking, that Ian's unpredictable behavior wasn't helping. He and Ariel had always been close, but Ian had been so distant of late, their relationship had taken a significant hit.

Ian walked over to the coffeemaker and refilled the cup. Lyana noticed that he paused to look at the unused espresso maker before rejoining Lyana at the table.

"I heard the voice yesterday, too," said Lyana. "After Sheriff Blackstone left. It just said one word: trust."

"Trust," Ian repeated.

"Yes."

"Why would…why would someone say that?"

"I think it's the house, Ian. I think it's trying to send me a message."

"But what does that have to do with the girl in the mirror?"

Lyana's frustration with Ian had been bubbling under the surface for a few days now. But she'd had enough. "You can't say her name, can you. Why can't you say her name?" Lyana was fighting tears. "Her name was Avril, Ian. We were so excited to meet her. Don't you remember? We were going to be a family of five, and she would be our second of three children. But after she was gone, we never talked about her again. I tried, Ian. You know I tried. But you wouldn't engage. I finally stopped trying, but that doesn't mean I stopped thinking about her." Lyana realized she'd folded her arms across her chest. She let them fall to her side.

Ian looked like a broken man. Part of Lyana felt bad for confronting him about this when their whole world was already in upheaval, but she needed this. It had been a long time coming.

"I'm…" began Ian.

"Please don't apologize again."

Ian closed his mouth and nodded.

"I need you to get through this, Ian," said Lyana. "I need you to come back to us. Ariel needs you. I need you. And Zach…" She stopped.

"I'm going to find him," said Ian. It was barely a whisper.

Lyana stood, walked around the table and placed her hand on Ian's shoulder. "I love you, Ian. I'm going to go for a little walk. If you want to join me…"

"In a few minutes," he said.

Lyana kissed the top of his head, then left through the front door. It was the right thing to confront Ian about Avril. But that only served to remind her of the heartbreaking conversation they'd had with her doctor soon after the miscarriage. He recommended that she not have any more children, as this miscarriage had caused some irreparable damage to her body.

• • •

The morning sun was just peeking over the trees and painting the house with an ethereal glow made more ominous by the still-lifting morning fog. Lyana shook her head at how "on the nose" the scene was. She had started to walk clockwise around the house, but quickly did an about-face and headed in the other direction. She didn't want to see the chicken coop again. Not yet anyway.

Halfway around the house, she stopped. A wide tangle of ivy had crawled almost to the roofline. The scene puzzled her. The chaotic brown vines that framed the front door and the picture window had captivated her when they first moved in. She thought they added to the charm of the Tudor-style house. But there were no vines anywhere else around the house. She was sure of it because Ian had said something when they were first inspecting the property. "Vines look great, but they can really cause problems with the stonework," he'd said, thankful that most of the house was clear of them. These couldn't have appeared overnight.

She stepped forward and ran her fingers across the brown tendrils and the small green leaves. Did they reach out to her as well? No, of course not. She was just imagining it.

It's stress, she thought. *I'm just under a lot of stress.*

Breathe.

There it was again. The voice. Lyana took the advice and breathed in deeply. An unfamiliar scent caught her attention. She glanced at the corner of the house and saw a flowering plant that hadn't been there the last time she was outside. Multiple umbrellas of tiny yellow flowers sprouted from a long green stalk. She'd never seen a plant like this before. She bent down and pulled off a sprig, lifted it to her nose. It had a vaguely medicinal smell. She rubbed the tiny flowers between her thumb and forefinger and felt a slight tingle.

"Huh," she said.

"Huh what?"

Lyana jumped as Ian appeared beside her.

"Do you notice anything unusual?" She spread her arms to indicate the house.

"Whoa," he said. "When did this happen?" He walked up to the ivy-covered wall and brushed his fingers across the vines just like Lyana had done.

"And look at this, Ian." She pointed to the flowering yellow plant. "This wasn't here yesterday."

Ian took a moment to inspect the plant.

"We need to talk to Marshall," he said. "I have a feeling he hasn't told us everything he knows about this house."

He took one step toward the backyard and stopped, then reached for Lyana's hand.

"Lyana," he began. "Please let me apologize one more time. I know I've been a mess. But I'm so close to solving this. I can feel it. I need you to trust me."

A shiver went down Lyana's spine. Was that what the voice meant? Was she supposed to trust Ian?

She took his hand.

"I trust you."

Ian began walking again, but Lyana tugged on his hand.

"Um, Ian?"

He turned to face her.

"Maybe we should get dressed first?"

They were still wearing their bathrobes.

"What?"

"Arthur Dent? Vogons? *The Hitchhiker's Guide to the Galaxy*?"

Ian looked puzzled for a moment, then nodded.

"You finally read it," he said, smiling.

"I did."

"Did you love it?"

"I did."

• • •

Back at the house, they changed into their clothes quietly to avoid waking Ariel. Then Ian led them to the cabin, but not without a few wrong turns. Why was it so difficult to find? It wasn't like the cabin moved from place to place. Did the trees? Treebeard and his ilk, the Ents, from *The Lord of the Rings* came to mind, but she shook away the thought. "That would be way too crazy," she said under her breath while they waited for a response to Ian's knock on the cabin door.

"What?" asked Ian.

"Nothing," she answered.

"Not home. Where does he go, anyway?" asked Ian. "You've talked with him more than anyone. What does he do with his day?"

Ian walked around to the back of the cabin. Lyana followed him.

"Well, that's new," said Ian. He was pointing to a path between the trees. The ground along the path was marked with two ruts—just the right distance apart for a vehicle. "Does Marshall have a car?"

Lyana shrugged. "Sure looks like it."

"I don't remember seeing a car, and I sure don't remember this dirt road." He started walking down the path that disappeared into the trees.

"Ian," said Lyana, eyeing the trees warily. "Maybe we should just head back to the house. We can come back later."

Ian stood in the middle of the rutted road for a moment longer, then turned and rejoined Lyana. "Yes. We'll do that."

As soon as they returned home, Ian disappeared into his study. He came out for mealtimes but spent the rest of the day hidden away. He seemed to have forgotten about Marshall. Ariel had remained in her room for most of the day, but after supper she joined Lyana in front of the TV for a re-watching of *The Lord of the Rings: The Two Towers*. The one with the Ents.

It had been Ariel's idea.

• • •

Monday came none too soon. Ariel had always liked school, but now she eagerly awaited the new week. She needed the break from her family, from her creepy house. And besides, that was the only time she got to see Garrett.

Ariel finished texting and slipped the phone into her backpack.

"They freak out if I don't show up exactly on time," she said. Garrett was sitting on the swing next to her. After school, they'd walked across the street to a small neighborhood park. There wasn't much to the playground—just a couple of slides, a spinning contraption, and four swings. A young woman was pushing a stroller along the sidewalk that bordered the playground and its adjacent soccer field.

Garrett played soccer. He'd spouted that little detail when they'd arrived at the park. He was odd that way, just saying random things out of the blue without elaboration. She liked that about him. He was unpredictable and succinct.

"Hey, I'm really sorry about your brother," said Garrett.

Ariel had grown tired of all the sympathy, but she didn't mind hearing this from Garrett.

"Thanks," she said.

Garrett started swinging, lifting his feet, then dropping them, going higher and higher.

"Whatcha waitin' for, Air? Let's see if you can make it all the way around."

"Did you just call me Air?"

"I did," he said, his voice passing as he swung backward.

Ariel reared up and started swinging too. She kicked hard to try and catch up with him. She couldn't remember the last time she'd been on a swing, but the exhilaration she felt was practically life changing. Butterflies flitted around her stomach, and not just from the motion of the swing.

"Air," she said as she swung forward. "I like it."

"Air is essential," Garrett added on an upswing.

Ariel couldn't have wiped the smile off her face if she'd tried.

She kicked her legs harder and yelled out, "Air is essential!"

Garrett synchronized his swinging with hers, and at the top of each forward swing, they yelled together, "Air is essential!"

The woman with the stroller had stopped on the sidewalk across the way and was watching them. Ariel wasn't sure, but she thought the woman gave them a thumbs-up.

If only this moment could last forever, Ariel thought.

FIFTEEN

"THE KING MUST be pleased with you."

Bijan sure doesn't sound too pleased, thought Zach.

Zach had been standing at the window of their room on the top level of a square tower that sat at the very back of the palace grounds. He hadn't even known the palace had such a structure until Bijan and the king himself took them there. The king called the tower a "work worthy of the gods" and praised his royal architect and the tireless workers who had built it, some of whom, he said with a strange pride, had died in the process. *It's impressive*, thought Zach. A long flight of stairs led to the first floor, then, around a corner, another flight of stairs led to the second floor. They had continued up a third flight, and then a fourth, to find themselves on the top floor of the tower in a small room that had windows on two of the walls.

Windows.

They finally had windows. This was no less a prison cell than their previous accommodations. It was just a nicer prison cell. But the best part of their new room was the view. The windows opened Zach's eyes to the wonders of the ancient world. Windows also meant they could enjoy a pleasant breeze now and then. Fresh air gave Zach hope that things would work out. It was a silly, small hope, but any hope was better than none, he reasoned.

What Zach had seen through the north window when they first arrived had taken his breath away. Situated in a valley, the sprawling city went on as far as he could see. Stone-and-clay buildings filled every inch of the scene before him. This reminded him of a puzzle he once worked on with Ariel—one based on a drawing by an artist whose name he couldn't recall. But it was all stone steps and ramps and columns and buildings, and everything was connected in ways that were impossible, where down was up and up was down. He wondered how people found their way amongst the tightly packed buildings.

Zach was looking out the south window now, watching the distant desert turn gold with the rise of the sun. He was mesmerized by the way the gold poured like liquid over the sand and scrub brush that went on forever just beyond the palace grounds.

A wide stone wall at least twenty feet high wound around the back of the palace. From his vantage point, Zach saw soldiers marching along the top of the wall. It seemed odd to Zach that the palace wasn't centrally located in the city for better protection against invading armies, but the more he studied the landscape, the more he realized how difficult an assault would be from the south. The palace sat on a high hill, easily defendable. To the south was nothing but sand and rocks and scrub brush. And even if an army did attempt an invasion, they'd be seen coming from miles away.

"What do you mean?" asked Akolo, snapping Zach back to the moment. Akolo was sitting on his bed, marveling at their "upscale" accommodations. The bed was an actual straw-filled mattress resting upon a wooden frame. Compared to their floor mats, it was a big improvement.

Bijan harrumphed at Akolo's question but didn't elaborate.

Zach had a pretty good idea what the guard meant. Moving them to the tower room was the king's way of acknowledging that Akolo and Zach had given the king an upper hand with this new god, but equally it was a way to keep a closer watch on the two people who were the king's only connection to the god's power.

Bijan had seemed more than a little perturbed that an additional guard now stood outside their room. It was as if the king didn't trust Bijan to keep the boys safe.

The other guard walked into the room. *No one knocks before entering in this world*, thought Zach. If Ariel had tried that, he would have yelled at her. Or maybe thrown a pillow at her.

"The king has decided that these boys are to visit the gardens," he said.

Bijan harrumphed again.

"I will be escorting them," the new guard added, staring daggers at Bijan.

"The gardens?" asked Akolo.

"Only the most magnificent gardens in all the land," said the new guard. His excitement was very un-soldierlike.

"Why would he want us to visit the gardens?" asked Akolo.

The new guard shrugged. "I only do as I'm told. We shall leave at once," he said. He turned to Bijan. "You will stay here and guard the room."

Zach watched Bijan's face for any sign of argument, but he simply nodded his acknowledgment of the apparent demotion and said nothing.

Down is up and up is down, thought Zach.

Zach started quietly counting the steps as they descended but was interrupted when Akolo spoke up.

"I can't wait to see the gardens," said Akolo. "Back home..." He paused. "The gardens back home were amazing. I loved visiting the gardens with my mother or my sisters."

"We had a small garden at my house," said Zach. *Have*, he quietly corrected himself. *Or will have. This time travel thing is so confusing*, he thought. *How many steps did I miss? Three? Four?* He went with four and continued counting.

"You had your very own garden? With fruit trees and flowers and everything?"

"Vegetables, mostly," Zach answered. But now that he thought about it, he wasn't entirely sure what his mother had planted. *Is it forty-six steps now?*

"Your family must be rich," said Akolo.

With difficulty, Zach abandoned the count. He would try again when they returned. "I don't know if we're rich," said Zach. Were they? They had pretty much everything they needed or wanted. "Maybe middle class or something."

"What's middle class?"

Zach sighed. "Like between rich and poor, I guess."

"Oh."

Akolo seemed truly puzzled that such a thing could exist. Maybe in his world there were only the rich and the poor.

Another guard joined them at the bottom of the tower steps and led them out of the palace, through a bustling market, where they endured the curious stares of shoppers and merchants alike, then up to a wide but simple-looking bridge that spanned a rapidly flowing river. He hadn't noticed the river from his north-facing window. As they reached the apex of the gently curved bridge, Zach couldn't believe what he was seeing. There before them to the west was a huge terrace-shaped structure at least a hundred feet high. It was at least two hundred feet across at the lowest level and he counted seven progressively smaller terraces rising from that foundation. Green leaves spilled out from each level of the terrace. It was as verdant as anything he'd ever seen, and such a contrast to the otherwise gray and tan of the city. The closer they got, the more Zach noticed other colors: bright yellows, reds, oranges, and even some blues and purples.

"Have you ever seen something like that before?" asked Zach. He turned to catch Akolo's expression, only to realize Akolo was frozen in place a few steps behind him, staring wide-eyed at the garden.

Zach walked back to his friend, and they stood side by side taking in the incredible view.

Their guards were content to let them stand there for a moment before urging them on, across the remainder of the bridge and then down a wide street that led to an immense, carved archway. The gardens appeared to grow bigger before them as they walked under the arch. The guards guided them to a stairway nearly hidden by surrounding foliage that led to the lowest level of the terrace and urged them upward. Zach didn't want to be rushed—there was so much to see—but he complied, following Akolo up the twenty-two steps.

Once on the lowest terrace level, Zach and Akolo followed a winding path amongst trees and bushes and flowers. Vines ripe with fruit hung along the interior stone wall. Zach paused to look at the very top of the garden terrace and nearly fell over, it was so dizzying. And the smells were overwhelming. Mostly there were pleasant smells—floral and fruity scents—but some awful odors occasionally found his nose, too. *Probably whatever they're using for fertilizer.* Zach shuddered to imagine what that could be.

"This way," said one of the guards. He led them to yet another set of stone steps that took them to the second level of the terrace. Here, they found rows and rows of flowering bushes and trees. The colors were so vivid, it felt unreal. A stray thought came to Zach. *Is this what heaven is like?* That thought gave way to a deep sadness. *What if that's what this all is? What if I died back in my time and this is the afterlife? Or some place you go between life and death.*

These and other questions swirled as Zach tried to stuff the thoughts away. Thoughts like these were too big of a distraction for the moment, and far too dire to consider. Akolo brought Zach back into the now with one of his million questions.

"What are those?" asked Akolo. He was pointing to a row of small trees along the outside of the terrace. Green-and-purple fruit could be spotted among the broad green leaves.

"Fig trees," said one of the guards.

"Oh, I love figs!" said Akolo. He looked as if he might bolt from the path to pull one off a tree, but a stern look from a guard kept him in line. Zach didn't care much for figs. At least he didn't think he liked them. *Have I ever had figs?* he wondered.

As they approached another set of stairs that led to the next terrace level, Zach noticed that the two guards were quietly arguing among themselves. They had stepped away, so Zach couldn't quite hear what they were saying, but a moment later one of the guards walked up to the boys and told them to follow him. The other guard stayed behind.

As they climbed the stairs, the guard nodded back at his compatriot and said, "This level scares him." Then he laughed as if that was the most ridiculous thing in the world.

They passed a row of lit torches at the top of the stairs. It didn't make sense to Zach that they'd keep torches lit in the bright daylight. Maybe they just hadn't yet extinguished them from the night before.

Zach heard the buzzing long before he saw the bees. The path they were on led to the interior of the terrace. And that was when he saw them. Makeshift hives. Rows and rows of ceramic pots and urns lined shelves that had been carved into the terrace wall. It made perfect sense to keep bees here. They would pollinate the flowers and plants and help this immense garden thrive. Zach was mildly surprised by how calm he remained as he walked just a few yards away from the buzzing bees going about their business. He had never really been afraid of bees before the incident in his room months before. And even then, he didn't really blame the bees for stinging him nearly to death. They were just doing what threatened bees do. It helped that Zach had studied bees on the internet for weeks after, trying to better understand them so as not to fear them.

Still, he felt just a little unsettled by the haphazard way the pots were arranged along the carved-out shelves. *How do they collect the honey from these, anyway?*

Akolo had maneuvered to Zach's right side, putting him between Zach and the bees as they walked.

"I like bees," said Akolo.

"I have...mixed feelings," said Zach. He decided not to share his saga. Not yet anyway. He still had to think of a way to tell it, so he didn't reveal the truth about where he came from. He'd tripped up more than a few times already using modern words or references that confounded Akolo, but always explained away his mistakes as nothing more than a cultural difference. His oft-spoken response, "I'm not from around here," had become something of an inside joke between them.

Their guard walked on ahead, a little briskly, Zach thought. Maybe he was more scared than he let on.

"They won't bother you if they don't think you're a threat," said Akolo.

Zach wasn't too sure about that statement. His experience with bees was very different. "How do they know if I'm a threat?"

Akolo laughed. "Good question."

They continued around the terrace, making a full circuit until they returned to the steps leading down to the second level. The guard sat on a stone bench there and encouraged the boys to do the same. He was sweating profusely.

Instead, Zach cautiously walked back toward the hives. Not far from the hives was a spread of flowering bushes he didn't recognize. Truthfully, he didn't recognize many of the plants they'd encountered. But this one reminded him of something out of a Dr. Seuss story. Long stalks of green held up umbrella-like spreads of tiny yellow flowers. He walked up to one and sniffed it, careful to avoid a bee that had landed nearby. It smelled like soap.

"Do you know what these are?" he asked Akolo.

"I don't know what they are called, but I have seen them before," he said. Akolo had walked up next to Zach, but the increased activity must have caught the attention of one of the drones. Zach started swatting his hands around, nearly hitting Akolo in the process.

"Ow!" shouted Zach. "One got me!"

Akolo turned to his friend. "What?"

"A bee! A bee stung me!"

Zach lifted his arm to show a rapidly growing red welt on his wrist. What was it with him and bees anyway?

"Hold still," said Akolo. He took Zach's hand in his and, as quickly and carefully as possible, tugged at the tiny stinger that was imbedded in Zach's skin. Zach tried to pull his arm away, but Akolo held tight, removing the stinger with ease. Then he grabbed some of the yellow flowers from the nearby plant and rubbed them between his fingers before spreading the dusty, waxy mixture on the site of Zach's sting.

"Ow...oh," said Zach. "That's...that feels okay."

He lifted his yellow-dusted arm to his nose and sniffed. *Yeah, like soap*, he thought.

"How did you know to do that?" asked Zach. The red welt had already started to fade.

"From watching my mom teach my sister," Akolo said. "She knows...knew a lot about plants."

"I wasn't threatening the bees," said Zach.

Akolo shrugged. "I guess bees can be a little unpredictable at times."

"Like people," said Zach. "Thanks, friend."

He gave Akolo an awkward side hug, then started walking briskly toward the stairs. Their guard was three steps ahead of them, urging them to hurry up.

"Wait," Akolo called after him. "I want to show you something else."

Akolo jogged up to the guard and whispered something. The guard shook his head and said, "No," but Akolo pressed him further. Finally, the guard relented. He pointed to the large jars sitting on the ground not far from the hives. Zach watched all this as he waited by the stairs.

"Have you ever tasted honey?" Akolo asked.

Zach shook his head. Of course they had honey in the house, but he had zero interest in trying it. Food texture mattered to Zach and honey had a strange texture. Something about it was just too unnatural for his senses. He realized how ironic that thought was.

Akolo started toward the jars and waved Zach to follow. Zach didn't move.

"That's okay," said Akolo. "Just wait there."

Akolo grabbed a stick and dipped it into a jar, then swirled it around. When he pulled the stick out, sure enough, the tip glistened. Akolo swiped at the honey with his fingers, then tasted it. He smiled and nodded, then walked over to Zach and held out the stick.

"Try it," said Akolo.

Zach stared at the stick, then carefully swiped at it with his index finger, catching just a tiny drop of honey. He stuck his finger in his mouth. His eyes went wide.

"It's sweet, but not like syrup," said Zach. "I don't hate it like I thought I would." A few bees started buzzing around the stick, and Zach took a step back. "But I think we should go now."

Akolo nodded, then handed the stick to the guard. They started to walk away. Zach glanced back over his shoulder just as the guard was licking his fingers, a broad smile on his face. Noticing Zach's gaze, the guard put on a serious expression, then tossed the stick aside.

On the way back to the tower, Zach briefly considered making a run for it. There were so many nooks and crannies along the narrow alleyways, he surely could have disappeared from sight. The guards weren't watching them too closely, after all. But where would he go? What would he do? And what would that mean for Akolo? He tossed the idea into his mental dumpster, noting as he did how many other thoughts he'd discarded in the past few weeks.

And besides, he reasoned, his legs were sore from all the walking and stair-climbing. Running was a bad idea in more ways than one.

Once back at the tower, he sighed at the sight of the first set of steps.

At least he could count them this time. Thankfully, Akolo remained silent as they ascended.

Sixty-six steps.

As Zach flopped onto his straw mattress, he mentally flipped the digits in his head and saw the number 99.

It was ninety-nine steps to the locked door from the bottom of the stairway where he'd first found himself weeks ago.

That means something. He was certain of it. Or maybe that was just hope talking.

• • •

When they'd returned to their room, Bijan was there waiting for them. He pointed matter-of-factly at a tray sitting on the small table in the middle of the room.

"Courtesy of the king," he said, none too happy about it.

The tray was overflowing with fruits and bread and some kind of cooked meat. It was a feast. Akolo went right to it and began gorging himself. Zach was still lying on his bed, his eyes closed.

"You better get some of this food before I eat it all," chided Akolo.

Zach opened his eyes. "Eat all you want."

"Does the bee sting still hurt?" asked Akolo.

Zach shook his head. "No. I'm…just not very hungry."

This troubled Akolo. How could Zach not be hungry? After all the walking they'd done.

Akolo began stuffing his face, but once Bijan left the room to stand guard outside, he took a split pomegranate over to Zach and sat on his bed, offering the seeds to his friend.

"You love these, remember?" Akolo said.

Zach sat up and offered a tired smile. "Thanks, Akolo."

They ate their pomegranate seeds in silence, then Akolo reached into his tunic pocket and pulled out his stone. A fire opal, Zach had called it. The stone had kept him connected to his home, to his past. It had been like a companion to him for all the weeks and months since he'd been torn from his family.

"Zach," Akolo began. He held out the stone to his friend. "I want you to have this."

Zach looked puzzled at first, then shook his head. "No. I can't take that. That's your special gemstone."

Akolo thrust his hand closer to Zach. "Please, Zach." Akolo felt tears welling in his eyes. "You're my best friend, Zach. You're… like family."

Zach reached out his hand and Akolo dropped the stone in it. Zach looked like he was going to say something, but instead he turned toward the wall, reached under his mattress and pulled something out from under it.

His bracelet. The one with the snake eating its tail carved into a stone.

Zach handed it to Akolo.

"Like family," he said.

"For me?" asked Akolo.

Zach merely nodded.

Just then a strong breeze blew in through the north window, swirling the day's dust into a tiny spinning storm in the middle of the room.

"A dust tornado," said Zach, pointing at it.

"Tornado?"

"That's what we call the spinning wind back home."

Tornado. Akolo added the word to his growing lexicon. There were too many to remember, but he didn't want to forget this one. He liked the sound of it.

Tornado.

Akolo watched the tiny tornado spin around the stone floor like a top. Then it disappeared as quickly as it had arrived.

SIXTEEN

ARIEL TURNED ON the TV and started randomly flipping through the myriad options afforded her. *Too many shows to choose from and nothing good to watch*, she thought. She got tired of scrolling and clicked on *The Wizard of Oz*. She didn't have any great love for the movie—she'd actually been scared by the flying monkeys when she first saw it as a child—but at least it was familiar. So little in her world felt familiar.

Her mother walked into the living room, stepping between Ariel and the TV.

"I'm going to say this again, because maybe you need to hear it again: I believe you, Ariel," she began. "But the hard truth is, I'm not convinced anyone else will. You know how parents can be—they'll stick up for their kids even when the kids do something wrong. I don't know Brooke's parents, so I don't really know what they'll do. But without any eyewitnesses, it's one of those 'she said, she said' situations. Based on what you've told me about Brooke, though, it kinda sounds like karma did its thing." She offered a bemused smile. "Not that I believe in karma or anything." She gently rubbed Ariel's shoulder and then headed back to the kitchen where she was making cookies.

Cookies. Ariel had just been suspended from school for pushing Brooke Chamberlin—something she absolutely didn't do—and her mother was baking cookies.

Make it all make sense! she thought. Because nothing made sense.

She was only half watching the movie while she sat on the floor, her back leaning up against the couch. She rewound the day to the moment when it all transpired. Ariel had been lost in thought then, too, revisiting the too-short hangout time with Garrett at the park, and didn't hear her teacher ask a direct question. Brooke didn't waste the opportunity to pick on her and had gently punched Ariel's shoulder as she walked by her desk.

It wasn't the punch that triggered Ariel, though. It was the "Your brother's dead, get over it!" that she mumbled under her breath while she walked by. She wanted to react to that, to grab Brooke by her starched white collar and shake some sense into her. But she didn't. She stuffed the anger and frustration deep inside.

After class was over, though, she made a beeline to the bathroom and stood at the sink, staring at her reflection and willing herself to calm down. To get control of her emotions.

Brooke must have followed Ariel into the bathroom. She stood in the doorway, her arms crossed in front of her, and sneered at Ariel. "What's your problem, anyway?"

Ariel was ready to explode, but instead of taking a swing at Brooke, she simply gripped the sink tighter and screamed.

"Arrgh!"

All her frustration and anger spilled out at once. In the very same instant, the lights flickered off and back on, the mirror shattered, and Brooke took an awkward step backward out of fear. One of her fancy shoes slipped on the wet floor and she fell, her head snapping against the metal hand dryer that hadn't worked since forever.

Ariel stood there in silence, stunned for a moment, then rushed over to Brooke to see if she was okay. Brooke aggressively brushed Ariel's offered hand aside and yelled, "Look what you did, you freak!" before stumbling out of the bathroom and, presumably, right to the office to make her accusations while the blood was still fresh.

Ariel hesitantly looked at her reflection in the cracked bathroom mirror, frozen and confused about the event that just took place. She hadn't even touched the mirror, let alone Brooke.

What was happening?

Ariel told the dean of students exactly what had happened, even owning up to the possibility that her scream had caused Brooke to lose her balance somehow. But the shattered mirror did more to support Brooke's claim of Ariel's aggression, and Ariel had no good explanation for how that could have happened.

Lyana was calm and collected in the meeting with the dean, offering little in the way of response to his decision to suspend both students for a couple of days until they could piece together the truth, or at least until things calmed down a bit. Ariel was thankful they had met separately from Brooke and her mother to discuss what had happened. She noted that the dean seemed sympathetic to Ariel's side of the story; he practically apologized about the suspension decision, considering their family's "special circumstance," as he put it.

Yeah. That her brother was missing. And probably dead. *That* special circumstance.

Ariel leaned against the couch, and it slid back an inch or two. When she turned to pull the couch back to its original position, she noticed the stereoscope slide she'd hidden there days before. She pulled it out from under the couch just as her dad walked into the living room. She hadn't even known that he was home.

"What's that?" he asked, looking slightly less grungy than the day before.

Ariel almost said "nothing" but decided instead to tell the truth.

"You know that stereoscope thing I found in the attic? The one you put in your office? This was one of the slides. It's…it's a picture of this house."

"Really? This house?"

"Yeah, while it was still being built. At least I think so."

"Huh."

"And there's something else," she added. This was a critical moment; she was about to jump with both feet into the craziness. "There's a man in the picture, too, and he looks just like Marshall."

"What? That doesn't make sense."

"I know."

"Why do you have it now?" Her dad was looking around the room, as if he might find a clue about why she was holding a stereoscope slide when the stereoscope and box of slides were sitting on a shelf in his study.

"I think the slide just sorta slipped under the couch or something," she said. It was partly true, anyway.

"Huh," said her dad. He'd been saying that a lot lately. "I need to see this," he added, then walked away to the study. He returned a moment later with the stereoscope. He slipped the slide into its holder and held the device up to his eyes.

"What in the…?" he began.

"It looks like him, doesn't it?" said Ariel. "But it can't be him."

"It sure does look like him. A little blurry, so I can't be sure. But this is from when?" He pulled the slide out and tried to read the fading description at the bottom.

"Most of the slides were from the late 1800s or something. This one seemed newer, but…I don't know when the house was built."

"Maybe it's his uncle?"

"Yeah, that must be it." *That has to be it*, thought Ariel. Because if it was Marshall in that picture, then… She couldn't even imagine what that might mean.

"I'm going to take this to Marshall. Sort this out," said Ian. He started to turn away, then froze, staring at the TV. Dorothy's house had just landed on the Wicked Witch of the East.

"Oh no," he said. "No, no, no." His face had gone white.

"It's just the Wicked Witch…" began Ariel.

Ian ignored her and raced to the kitchen. "Lyana!" he shouted, even though she was standing right there. "Where are the flashlights?"

Ariel started to feel panicked too but had no idea why.

"What is it, Ian? You look like you've seen a ghost."

"There's one place we haven't checked for Zach," he said. His words came out rapid-fire, like he had to get them out of his mouth before they burned him. "Under the house!"

Ariel felt like she was going to be sick.

"Under the house? What do you mean?" Lyana said.

"In the crawl space," said Ian.

"This house has a crawl space?" Ariel asked. Why didn't she know this?

"No, it's not possible. He couldn't be there," said Lyana. "We would know…"

Now Ariel was certain she was going to be sick. She ran to the bathroom and promptly threw up in the toilet. The thought of her brother being buried under the house for weeks was too much.

• • •

Ian rummaged through the junk drawer in the kitchen, not caring that he was knocking random items onto the floor. He finally found a small flashlight and clicked it on. Light shone out into his face. He clicked it off and turned to Lyana.

"Way back when we first moved in, Zach mentioned his disappointment that we don't have a basement. So, I told him about the crawl space. Showed him the access door outside."

"But the door had a padlock on it. Remember? You were going to ask Marshall about that. You don't think..."

"Zach could have talked to him about it. Zach could have gotten the key somehow."

"No," said Lyana. "He wouldn't do that without talking to us first. He's not down there, Ian! He can't be down there! After all this time..."

Ian took a deep breath and walked up to Lyana, placed his hands on her shoulders and looked into her panicked eyes. "Lyana, you're right. He's probably not down there. But if he found that key..."

Lyana shrugged out of Ian's hands and started for the front door. Ian followed, then ran ahead into the backyard where the thick span of lilac bushes sat against the façade of the house. They hadn't yet bloomed, but the swath of green did a fair job of hiding the metal door that rested up against the base of the house. It was barely big enough for an adult to squeeze through, meant to serve only as a last resort should someone have to go under the house to repair the aging pipes. Ian hadn't thought too much about the fact that it was locked—it kind of made sense to him. You wouldn't want some kid climbing in there in search of adventure, only to have the door close behind them. Did the previous owners have children?

Ian brushed the lilacs aside and stepped into the space between them and the house.

With his heart racing, he reached down and picked up an open rusted padlock that was sitting in the dirt, the key still in it. He was frozen for a moment, staring at the lock. Why would Marshall give Zach that key? His frustration with Marshall was quickly morphing into anger. The caretaker had helped them once before—he'd saved Lyana's life. So why would he be so careless about the crawlspace?

"Ian." Lyana was standing behind him, trying to get a look at what he was holding.

"It's the lock," he said. He lifted it up for Lyana to see.

"Oh no! No, Ian, no!"

Ian turned toward her. "Lyana, he could have done this a while ago. He probably took one look in there and decided it was a very bad idea to crawl in. I mean, imagine the spiders, right?"

Lyana was shaking her head. "No, I don't want to imagine the spiders. I don't want to imagine anything at all."

Ian clicked the flashlight on.

"I need to go in there," he said.

"Ian, no. You don't need to go in there. Please don't..."

"Lyana."

Ian stepped out from behind the lilac bushes, gently guiding Lyana away from the side of the house.

"Lyana, you need to check on Ariel. I'm going to crawl under the house. I'm going to crawl under the house and find that Zach isn't there and breathe a shaky sigh of relief that my panic was unnecessary. And then I'm going to crawl back out and find Marshall and get him to answer some questions. Okay?" Lyana didn't respond, so he repeated himself. "Okay?"

"Okay," said Lyana. She hesitated, then turned and jogged back around the house.

Ian bent down and opened the metal door. It squeaked on its hinges but swung open without difficulty until it rested against the wall. Ian lay down on the ground and scooted toward the opening, his flashlight in front of him. An unfamiliar smell greeted him.

It's just musty and old, he said to himself, shaking off the worst possible thought.

He expected to see a cramped space with dirt below and joists above. He saw something quite different. The ground below was indeed dirt, and joists marked the underside of the floor above, but the space wasn't nearly as cramped as he'd expected. He scooted in through the door and crawled down an incline until he was fully under the house. The space was nearly tall enough for him to stand, but not quite. As he shuffled forward, he stepped in a shallow pool of water. He shined the flashlight at the ground, then turned it this way and that, looking for the source of the leak. He traced old iron pipes with the flashlight's beam but saw no evidence of a leak. He continued exploring the dark, dank space until he believed he was under the kitchen.

To his great relief, there was no sign of Zach anywhere. Apart from the small pool of standing water, the dirt floor was dry and undisturbed. Ian confirmed that he was leaving footprints as he traveled, hunched down, from one end of the crawlspace to the other, and determined that he was the first person who had been down here in… well, in a long time anyway. He briefly considered what that meant for the house inspection they'd paid for before agreeing to buy the house but filed that question away for another day.

He listened for a moment to the footsteps above him, surprised at how muffled they sounded. This was an old house, built with old wood and old construction techniques, but there was nothing cheap about the materials used, and it showed, both above ground and below.

Ian looked back toward the opening he'd crawled through. He clicked off his flashlight and admired the strange beauty of the light coming through the door. It was an angular swath of daylight, a trapezoid pouring into the crawlspace. Dust motes danced in the light and Ian was mesmerized by the shimmer. He sniffed the air. Musty. That was all it was. He was sure of it now.

As he turned to make one last scan of the crawlspace, another shimmer caught his eye. Was there another door? Or a casement window he hadn't noticed before?

Ian flicked on the flashlight and began making his way toward the source of the shimmer. The flashlight flickered, then went out, and Ian slammed his head into a floor joist. He blinked at the pain. When he opened his eyes, he was no longer under the house.

Ian braced himself for a repeat of the flashback he'd experienced months earlier. He didn't want to watch that scene play out again. It was too much. But no, this wasn't his home. It wasn't a house at all. The ground below him was made of stone. A low fog obscured his view, but he could see the flicker of a small flame not far away. There was a new smell to this place. A familiar smell.

What is it?

Ian struggled to recall the sense memory. And then he suddenly had it.

Oil. That's the smell of a burning oil lamp!

"Zach?" he called out. There was no response. *Of course there was no response.*

Ian's head began to throb. He closed his eyes at the pain, and when he opened them, he was lying on the dirt of the crawlspace. His flashlight was still in his hand, the beam shining up at the floorboards above him. A massive spider web twinkled back at him. Ian rolled over onto all fours and crawled to the door. He climbed out and closed the door behind him, stretching to full height, only to scratch his cheek on the lilac bushes. When he pushed through them into the sunlight, Lyana was standing there. Her hand went to her mouth in surprise.

"Ian, you're bleeding," she said.

Ian ran his hand across his forehead and it came away red.

"I'm…I'm fine. I just hit my head on a floor joist," he said.

"And your cheek…" Lyana added.

Ian nodded. "The lilac bushes." He touched his cheek, felt the roughness of a wide scrape. At least that wasn't bleeding.

"Ian, I heard you call out for Zach. What did you see?"

Ian took a deep breath. "Nothing except for spiderwebs and a small pool of stale water. We'll need to call a plumber about that, just to be sure."

"Why did you call out Zach's name?"

"I don't know. I thought I saw something, but…it was just a trick of the light." He gently pulled Lyana into an embrace. "If Zach unlocked that door, he didn't go in there. I don't think anyone has been under this house in a long time."

Ian felt Lyana's relief in the way her shoulders relaxed. She pulled him tighter, then stepped back.

"I did some research on that yellow plant," she said.

"What did you find?"

"If it's what I think it is, that plant shouldn't exist."

"What do you mean?"

"It looks like something called..." Lyana pulled out her phone and clicked it awake. "Silphion, or maybe Silphium. There are entries for both spellings. But listen to this: Silphion was used to treat goiter, sciatica, epilepsy, tetanus, malignant tumors and—get this, was thought to have gone extinct two thousand years ago!"

"It can't be that. Maybe it's just something that looks similar."

"Maybe. But what if it is this Silphion? How would that be possible?"

"I don't know. We'll just have to add this to our unending list of mysteries yet to be solved."

"Maybe Marshall would know something about it."

Ian nodded. "Everything seems to be pointing at Marshall. I need to see him."

Lyana reached up and brushed Ian's hair away from his forehead.

"We should clean that up first," she said.

"But..."

Lyana gestured at his forehead. "If Marshall sees you looking like that, he's going to think you've gone insane."

Maybe I have.

Ian had another clue. A big one.

As crazy as it sounded, he was almost certain he knew where Zach was now.

Not just where, but *when.*

• • •

Marshall left his ancient truck in the Blue Job Mountain parking area and trekked the half mile to the fire tower. By the time he finally reached the top of the tower, he was gasping for air. He'd stood in this very spot many times before. On a clear day, the tower was a gift, providing inspiring views of the white mountains in one direction and the ocean in another. Today was not a clear day. The gray sky gathering in the east was a fitting metaphor for the past few months. He had been so sure things were finally falling into place with the arrival of the Keane family. He had waited so long for this.

But the events that soon followed continued to confound Marshall, even after careful, thoughtful reflection. First Zach was attacked by bees, then Lyana was attacked by the house. The Keanes had fallen in love with that house, and even after all the craziness, Lyana assured Marshall it was still her dream home—the very place she and her family were supposed to be.

Then Zach went missing and everything was thrown into chaos again.

Marshall had avoided the Keanes for days. He had mixed feelings about that decision—he had grown close to the family, after all—but everything was so out of sync, he didn't know what to say to them. Words mattered. If he'd learned anything of value over a lifetime, it was that.

What if his words made things worse?

Marshall got down on his knees. He couldn't remember the last time he'd done that. So many of his memories were cloudy of late. This troubled him most of all.

Marshall turned his eyes upward.

"This is not how it was supposed to go. What am I to do now?" he asked.

The clouds offered no reply.

• • •

Ian had just left to go to Marshall's cabin and Lyana was trying to come up with a dinner plan. She didn't really want to think about food, but the family still needed to eat, even if they didn't feel like it. Over the years, she had developed a skill of reinventing leftovers, mostly because Ian wasn't a fan of leftovers, which he would leave to die in the fridge, but also because she liked spending less time preparing a meal than one "from scratch" normally required. She was so creative with her leftover reinventions that most of the time Ian didn't even realize he was eating leftovers.

Lyana opened the fridge and stared inside. *Hmmm...looks like stir-fried rice with leftover pork*, she thought. As she crossed into the pantry to gather a few additional ingredients, she glanced in the mirror, expecting to see her tired face. What she saw instead froze her in place. A blurry image of a child stared back at her. Blood was dripping down the sides of the mirror and collecting on the floor.

"Zach?" she said, her voice cracking. "No, this is not happening. This is not real." Lyana shook the thought from her head and closed her eyes tightly, willing the image to go away. When she opened her eyes, the child was gone. In its place was a collection of random black shapes outlined in blood. She took a slow, deep breath to calm her racing heart.

"What is this?" she asked.

The image flickered at her words, reappeared, then vanished in a blink. Lyana closed her eyes again. The abstract images were still there, seared on the inside of her eyelids.

This means something!

Lyana took off down the hall toward the laundry room. There, next to the printer, was a stack of paper, and just below that, in the top drawer, were her paints. She grabbed a handful of paper and a large tube of black paint and practically ran to the foyer where there was plenty of space on the tiled floor to spread out.

She tossed the paper on the floor and stared at the random array, unsure what to do. She closed her eyes to see the image again—it was still there. Then, almost as if driven by outside forces, she fell to her knees and began squirting globs of paint on paper.

Fifteen, she said to herself. The number brought an awkward laugh of recognition. *There were fifteen abstract shapes.*

She counted out fifteen sheets of paper, tossing the remainder across the room, then frantically began to paint the shapes from memory, one each on a separate sheet. The first few shapes were easy, but then she began to struggle. She closed her eyes again.

No, no…!

The image had begun to fade. Lyana wasn't deterred. She doubled down and began painting faster, hoping that somehow, she could still paint the right shapes. Paint flew left and right, as much of it landing on the tile floor as on the paper. Somewhere in the midst of her frenzy, Lyana realized she was crying. She swiped away tears with paint-stained fingers.

"Mom? Mom!" It was Ariel.

Lyana didn't look up.

"No…wait!" said Lyana abruptly, waving her off. She had two more images to paint. Just two more. She squeezed her eyes closed again and caught just the faintest shadow of those remaining shapes, then opened them and quickly spread the black paint onto the last two sheets of paper. Totally drained, she sat and leaned back on her hands, feeling the paint beneath them slide against the smooth tile and rough grout.

"Mom! What are you doing?" The look on Ariel's face was utter shock.

"It's…" began Lyana. But what was it really? She took in the mess in front of her. Sheets of paper were scattered across the tile floor, fifteen of them bearing hastily painted abstract shapes. What did it mean? Did it mean anything at all? "It's something I saw," she said, finally. Ariel seemed stuck in place as she stared at the mess on the floor. Then, as if a switch was flicked on, she shouted.

"Daaad!" Ariel called out. "Dad!"

"He's not here," shouted Lyana. Then, in a calmer voice, she added, "He went to see Marshall. Ariel…I know how crazy this looks…"

Ariel spread her arms out, indicating the mess of paint and paper on the floor. "Do you?"

Lyana let out a laugh, then quickly realized how maniacal it must have sounded. "Ariel, this means something. I saw the shapes in the mirror…"

Ariel sighed. "The pantry mirror." It was a statement. Ariel knew the storied history of that mirror all too well.

"Yes. I saw these shapes. At least I'm pretty sure I got them right." Lyana decided not to say anything about the blood. "Count them, Ariel."

Ariel pointed to each one as she counted. When she got to fifteen, she gasped. "Fifteen. Like the steps. It's something about Zach, isn't it."

Lyana looked into Ariel's eyes. "I don't know. I just don't know. Maybe I'm going crazy…" She almost added, *again*.

Ariel stepped around the mess and sat down next to her mother, careful not to land on one of the many splotches of paint there.

"I've seen something like this before," said Ariel. "I mean, not this exactly, but something similar." After a pregnant pause, she shouted, "I know what this is!"

Lyana turned to look at her daughter. Her eyes were wide, and a smile had replaced the look of shock.

"It's a puzzle, Mom. I mean, I think it's a puzzle. Zach used to have an activity book with these sorts of puzzles in it. I think they're called tangrams, or something like that."

Lyana felt a glimmer of hope. She looked back at the shapes. "Yes, that has to be it," she said.

"Now all we have to do is figure out how they all fit together," said Ariel. She reached over and pinched her mother's sleeve between her fingers, lifted it to show Lyana the dripping paint. "Um...but you might want to clean up first?"

Lyana didn't want to clean up. She wanted to solve this puzzle as soon as possible. But a few more minutes to find some kind of calm might not be a bad idea. They needed clear minds to solve this puzzle. She nodded and squeezed her daughter's hand, leaving a smudge of black paint on it. "I'll only be a minute."

Lyana stood, somewhat unsteadily at first, then walked back to the kitchen. She took a brief detour to the pantry to glance in the mirror, fearing what she might see but unable to resist its lure. All she saw was her paint and tear-soaked face. That was frightening enough.

A vivid memory of Zach caught her by surprise, making her momentarily dizzy. She had come early to pick him up at kindergarten, only to find him covered head to toe in fingerpaints, a huge smile on his sweet face. She took a deep breath, steadied herself, then went to the kitchen sink to clean up. As she brought a wet cloth to her face to wipe off the paint, she heard Ariel call out.

"Mom! I think I figured it out!"

[illegible] she looked back at the [illegible]
[illegible] the [illegible]

[illegible] we [illegible] is figure [illegible] how they [illegible] together [illegible] between [illegible] the [illegible] point [illegible]

[illegible] wanted to solve this puzzle [illegible] something [illegible] to solve his [illegible] leaving [illegible]

[illegible]

[illegible] was [illegible] She had come [illegible]

[illegible]

SEVENTEEN

ZACH WAS RESTING on his bed, looking over at Akolo, who was standing at the southern window, craning his neck.

"It's a full moon tonight, right?" Akolo said. Zach rolled over to view the secret tally of days he'd scratched into the stone just behind the bed's frame. His insistence on getting the numbers right had seemed to intrigue Akolo.

"Full moon," said Zach as he rolled onto his back. "But not a blood moon. At least I don't think so. That would be way too soon."

"So, what's the total number?" Akolo asked.

"Fifty-two," said Zach.

Akolo surely already knew that. Zach had caught him counting the lines of his makeshift calendar earlier that day after he'd returned from relieving himself. But he didn't say anything about it. He wasn't saying much at all lately. The threat of their impending move had been weighing heavily on him, occupying every waking thought.

"Almost two months," Zach added quietly. He sat up and looked over at Akolo. "How long do you think it will be before the king sends us away?" He didn't expect Akolo to know the answer to that, but Akolo seemed interested in conversation, so he asked anyway.

Akolo shrugged. "He said 'when the time is right.' I don't know what he meant by that."

Zach nodded sadly. "You know, your home probably isn't going to look the same," he said.

"I know."

Zach recalled some of the many images Akolo had shared with him about his home: Akolo's sisters giggling outside the front door, the sharp edges of his father's silhouette, his mother smiling at him while he watched her baking bread. Even though he talked too much, at least most of what he said was interesting.

"What if the king is wrong?" Akolo said quietly, as if talking to himself. "Or what if he lied? What if my family members are still alive?"

Zach bit his lip to keep from saying what he thought.

A moment later, Akolo shook his head, answering his own question. "I know they're not. But it's still home," he said. "I miss it. Especially the way it smells."

This brought a small laugh from Zach.

"What's funny about that?" asked Akolo.

"I wasn't laughing because it was funny. I was laughing because it's true. I miss certain smells, too."

Akolo's dour expression morphed into a hopeful smile. "What smell do you miss the most?" he asked. "I miss the smell of the river. I mean, not always—sometimes it smells like rotten fish, but most of the time it smells like… I don't know how to describe it."

"Like home?" posed Zach.

"Yeah, that."

Zach's thoughts flooded with his favorite memories of home. When he was younger and his dad would return from a trip, they always enjoyed pizza night. This wasn't like more recent pizza nights when they'd order out. Back then, his mom would make homemade pizza dough, then invite everyone to personalize their portion of the pizza. He always grabbed the pepperoni first, then proceeded to cover every bit of sauce with as many slices as he could manage, usually to his sister's chagrin. After dinner they would pop popcorn and sit around the table and watch Ian and Lyana's favorite music videos. Zach knew that was a bit odd—most people he knew would watch movies or TV together on family nights. But Zach loved the way they filled their family nights with music. His mom had a story for every song. Zach's favorite video was the one for Phil Collins's "Take Me Home." As soon as the iconic drum loop started, everyone knew which song was coming up next.

Take that look of worry
I'm an ordinary man
They don't tell me nothin'
So I find out all I can
There's a fire that's been burnin'
Right outside my door
I can't see but I feel it
And it helps to keep me warm
So I, I don't mind
No I, I don't mind
So take, take me home, 'cause I don't remember
Take, take me home

"I miss the smell of pizza and popcorn on a Friday night," said Zach, returning from the vivid memory, the tune still bouncing around in his head.

"I don't know what that is," began Akolo.

They spoke at the same time:

"I'm not from around here," said Zach.

"You're not from around here," said Akolo.

• • •

Their laughter died down and they sat in silence for a long time. Then Bijan walked into the room without announcing himself. They hadn't seen much of him lately, since he'd been essentially replaced by the two guards who had escorted them to the grand gardens.

"Come," he commanded. He had his right hand on his short sword. A longer sword was stuffed in a sheath on his left side. Akolo had only ever seen him with his short sword. He didn't like the look in Bijan's eyes.

"Where are we going?" asked Zach.

"The king commands it," said Bijan. He pulled out the short sword and gestured with it toward the door.

Zach's worried expression confirmed what Akolo was feeling. Something wasn't right about this. The king didn't summon them at night. And the high priest had only done that once before.

But they could not say no to a guard with two swords.

Akolo and Zach left their room and started down the many stairs. Sixty-six of them, Zach had said. He himself hadn't counted. He had come to trust whatever Zach said was true, even the things he didn't understand. Maybe especially those things.

After leaving the tower, Bijan told them to be quiet—that this was a secret mission. He guided them through the hallways, across the courtyard and right up to the tent that stood in front of the temple doorway. They didn't really need the tent anymore—Akolo and Zach could just walk right into the temple without fear of harm. But the high priest had kept it as a deterrent to any others who might think themselves worthy of an audience with the god of Akolo's people. At least that was how Zach had explained it. Then he had to explain what *deterrent* meant.

"Where's the high priest?" asked Zach. "He's always here when we visit the temple."

"I told you; this is a secret mission on behalf of the king."

Akolo looked over at Zach. He was shaking his head ever so slightly. Whatever Bijan was up to, it wasn't right.

Bijan looked around nervously. Akolo knew what that meant. He had done the same thing many months ago when he'd sneaked out of the house to view the blood moon for the first time.

Bijan looked up at the moon, then back at the boys.

"Here," he said. He handed Akolo his bejeweled sword, but quickly removed his long sword from its sheath, holding it at the ready. "Take this into the temple and...do whatever it is you do."

Akolo held the short sword loosely in his hands, being careful not to cut himself with the sharp edges. It wasn't a blood moon. They couldn't bless the sword or anything else until a blood moon. That's what Zach had said.

"But it isn't the right..." began Akolo.

Zach interrupted him. "It isn't right for us to do this without the high priest here." Then he subtly shook his head again. Akolo got the message.

"Yeah, we need the high priest here," Akolo repeated.

Bijan lifted his long sword. "The king commands it!" he said, a bit too loudly, Akolo thought. Sure enough, he lowered his voice when he added, "Do not defy the king's orders!"

Bijan had never threatened them before, but the look in his eyes made it clear they had no choice but to comply.

"Okay," said Zach. He walked up and gently lifted the sword from Akolo's trembling hands. "We will see if our god will bless this sword. But can I ask why the king demands it?"

Bijan lowered his long sword. "He wants his guards to be strong," he said. "And soon I will be captain of the guard, so I must be the strongest of all."

Akolo thought his words sounded a little like a practiced speech.

Zach nodded toward the tent. "Maybe you should just take it in yourself," he said.

"What? You think me a fool?" Bijan lifted his long sword again. An evil smile came to his face. "You know, we don't really need two of you to do this job. I heard the high priest saying so just yesterday."

Akolo gulped. Surely this was a lie.

"So, if you value your friend's life…" Bijan stopped talking and pointed with his sword to the tent. That gesture was loud and clear.

"Let's go, Akolo," said Zach. "*The king demands it.*"

Zach opened the tent flap for Akolo to go in first, then followed him up the steps of the temple and into the darkened room. They approached the chest together as they had done numerous times before. Zach removed the fire opal Akolo had given him and set it on the chest, then Akolo did the same with the bracelet Zach had given him. The two items glowed just enough to reveal the boys' faces and the glint of the gems in the sword's hilt. Zach laid the sword on top of the chest.

"It's not a blood moon," whispered Akolo.

"I know," whispered Zach.

"The king didn't ask him to do this, did he?"

"I sure don't think so."

"Then what are we to do?"

"How good are you with a sword?" asked Zach.

Akolo's eyes went wide. "What? You don't mean…"

Zach smiled. "Kidding," he said. "We wouldn't stand a chance."

"Maybe someone will come looking for us?" Akolo knew the thought was little more than a wish. It was the middle of the night, and no one would be out wandering near the temple at this hour.

"As long as we stay in here, we're safe, right? Because Bijan won't come in. He can't."

"That's true. So, we wait?"

"We wait," said Zach. He sat down, leaning his back against the chest.

Akolo mimicked Zach's actions and sat next to him. "How long do you think we'll need to wait?"

Zach shrugged. "Maybe a long time. Maybe not."

It was only a matter of minutes before they heard Bijan's voice. He sounded much farther away than he was, but that was how it had always been when they were in the temple. Zach said it was almost like being in another world.

"How long will this take?" Bijan called out. When neither Zach nor Akolo responded, he repeated his question, this time much louder.

Zach put his finger to his lips and whispered, "If we don't answer, maybe he'll get tired of waiting and leave."

Akolo hoped so, but he didn't mind spending more time in the temple. It was a simple stone room that should feel cold at night, but no matter when he'd visited, he always felt warm and safe there.

Their stones threw a soft golden glow up to the ceiling that was dotted by colorful reflections from the sword's gemstones. He looked up, mesmerized by the gently swirling cloud of light.

"Why do we pray to the heavens if God is right here?" he asked Zach, pointing over his shoulder at the chest.

"I don't know. I was always taught that God is everywhere."

"What? How can that be?"

"Another mystery, I guess," said Zach.

Akolo thought for a moment. "Maybe we look up because God is bigger than us." He paused again. "Have you asked your question yet?"

Zach shifted on the floor next to Akolo. "No," he said.

"I think I already got my answer," said Akolo.

"What do you mean?"

"Well, I'll be going home soon. That's kind of like an answer, isn't it?"

Zach took a deep breath. Akolo noticed he'd been doing that a lot lately. "Yeah."

Bijan had called out a few more times, but neither boy responded. When it was quiet for a long while, Akolo wondered if he'd left. Or perhaps he'd just fallen asleep. Time worked differently in the temple. He wasn't sure how or why, but often when they exited, a lot more time had passed than Akolo had expected.

After some of that timeless time had passed, Akolo heard a voice calling from outside the temple. It didn't sound like Bijan.

"You can come out," said the voice.

"That's the high priest," said Zach.

Akolo wasn't sure if that was good news or bad. "Should we go?"

Zach stood and gathered the fire opal from atop the chest. Akolo stood as well and reached for his bracelet. As he did, he bumped the hilt of the sword. It slipped off the chest and fell onto the floor. The muffled sound of metal on stone was quickly followed by the gentle tinkle of something bouncing away toward the door. Akolo followed the sound and saw a fire opal sitting on the ground just like the one he'd given Zach. It was glowing, but only barely. He looked over at Zach, who had picked up the sword.

"It must have broken off," said Zach. He pointed to a small empty place on the hilt.

"What do we do? Bijan is going to be angry."

Zach walked over and collected the opal, then presented it to Akolo. "I don't think Bijan will notice."

"I can't take this," began Akolo.

"Sure you can. Now we'll both have one."

"But..."

Zach put the stone in Akolo's hand. "Maybe it's a gift from God," he said.

"Really?"

"Why not?"

"Yeah, why not?" said Akolo. He studied the stone, then pocketed it along with the bracelet.

Zach went first, descending the steps and then bending down to squeeze under the tent flap. When Akolo followed him, he was surprised to discover it was already morning. The high priest and his attendants were standing there, along with several of the king's guards.

Bijan was in chains, his head bowed in shame. Zach presented Bijan's sword to the high priest.

"We did what you asked, Bijan. But I don't think it worked."

The high priest nodded at one of his attendants and the man walked over to collect the sword. He took it to the high priest, who lifted it to the early morning light and studied it. *Did he notice the missing stone?* Akolo wondered.

"Take him away," the high priest said to the king's guards. Bijan didn't say a word as he was led away.

"What will happen to him?" asked Akolo.

The high priest was studying the sword's hilt again. Then he looked directly into Akolo's eyes. "He will be appropriately punished," he said. "And as for you two…"

Akolo's breath caught.

"I commend you," he continued. "It was wise to stay hidden in the temple." He raised his eyebrows into a question. "Did you hear from your god this time?"

Akolo started to shake his head, but Zach's voice stopped him. "He told us we shouldn't leave this place," he began. "He said we need to stay here a while longer. At least until the next blood moon."

Akolo hadn't heard anything of the sort while in the temple. Maybe God had spoken only to Zach?

"Ah, I see," said the high priest. "We will consider this." He gestured to the guards, and they guided Akolo and Zach back to their tower room.

• • •

"Why did God talk to you and not me?" asked Akolo after the guards had left.

"He didn't," answered Zach. He started pacing in the small room, walking from one window to the other, then back again. The sun was rising, but Zach didn't stop to watch the golden glow this time. He was preoccupied by something else. Something much bigger than a sunrise. "But I did hear something while I was in there."

"What did you hear?"

Zach stopped pacing and turned toward Akolo.

"I heard my father's voice."

"What?"

"I heard him call my name, Akolo. Just once, but I'm sure it was him."

"But…he's far away." Akolo's confused look turned to one of wonder. "Maybe he's not far away! Maybe he's here now and he's come to take you home! Maybe God answered your question after all!"

Akolo's capacity to hope was admirable. Zach wished he could have so much optimism. But no, his father wasn't here. At least he didn't think so. But his father was definitely looking for Zach. And maybe, just maybe, he was close to finding him. This was why he needed to stay put as long as possible—to give his dad enough time to solve the mystery.

"I don't think it's that simple," said Zach. "But I know it means something. And I know I have to remain here until it all makes sense."

"Ahh," said Akolo, clearly understanding now. "That's why you told the high priest we needed to stay longer."

Zach nodded.

"So, you lied?" Akolo's expression changed from wonder to concern.

"Well…technically yes."

"But…"

"Sometimes the whole truth is not helpful, Akolo. Sometimes you need to keep secrets, too." Zach remembered his mom telling him those same words when he was too blunt and honest with his friends. But this was different. His stomach began to churn.

Akolo tilted his head like a perplexed puppy.

"Do you keep secrets from me?" he asked.

"No," said Zach. "I don't keep them from you." Another lie flew out of his mouth and the nausea in his stomach increased. There was no way Zach could tell Akolo the truth of who he was and where he was from.

Zach's thoughts were all over the place. He didn't like lying to Akolo, but no one could know the truth. Instead, he had to focus on getting home. Had he really heard his father's voice? What did that mean? What was on the other side of the locked door at the ninety-ninth step in the lower level of the palace? Was that his way home? And what would happen to Akolo if he did indeed find his way home?

"Hey, it's okay," said Akolo. He was sitting across from Zach, staring at his face.

Zach felt a tear splash onto his folded arms. He didn't realize he'd been crying.

"You'll find your way home. Probably soon," Akolo said, a big smile on his dirty face. His enthusiasm faded into a look of sadness. "Soon," he repeated.

Zach reached over and ruffled Akolo's hair, just the way his own father would ruffle his. He felt old in that moment.

Soon, he thought.

EIGHTEEN

IAN WAS STANDING outside Marshall's cabin, having already determined that no one was home, when the rumble of an old truck drew his attention to the rutted dirt road out back. A few moments later, a pickup truck that must have been at least sixty years old sputtered to a stop just in front of him.

"Ian," said Marshall as he climbed out of the truck. The truck door could've used a healthy dose of WD-40, as it closed with a screech.

"Marshall," began Ian. He had so many questions, he didn't quite know where to start.

"Let's go inside," said Marshall. He pointed to the sky. "Storm's coming."

Ian looked up at the sky. It was a beautiful blue sky dotted with fluffy white clouds. Didn't look like much of a storm to him. He followed Marshall into the cabin.

"Tea?" asked Marshall. He'd walked directly to his kitchenette and was already filling a teapot with water.

"Marshall, I don't think we have time for a tea party..."

"It's always a good time for tea," said Marshall. He lifted an empty cup toward Ian.

"Fine." Ian walked over to one of Marshall's bookshelves. This one was filled to overflowing with old books. Ian pulled one from the shelf, bringing with it a year's worth of dust. "Are you a collector or something?" Ian asked, carefully turning the pages of the book. It was titled *Book of Hours*, author unknown. Ian looked at the verso page.

The publication date was 1350.

"This book is over six hundred years old!" he said. "Where did you get this?" Not waiting for the answer, Ian picked up another book. This one was so old it was wrapped in sheepskin with no title. Ian carefully opened it to find handwritten prayers and blessings in the Akkadian language, an ancient Semitic language spoken in Babylonia that Ian studied in his younger years.

"Uh…h-how…?" Ian stumbled over his words trying to ask Marshall how he possessed such a treasured piece of history.

"That's one of my favorites," said Marshall. He was standing beside Ian now. "It's incomplete, though. Time knows no mercy."

Ian carefully returned the book to the shelf. "These must be worth a fortune," he said.

Marshall shrugged. "Maybe. I haven't taken the time to find out. I just like having them."

Ian struggled to wrap his head around this latest discovery. Why would Marshall have such a collection? Shouldn't these be in a museum? He shook off the latest puzzle and turned his attention to the main reason for being here.

"Marshall, I'm so close to solving the puzzle of Zach's disappearance. But…"

"But you have some questions for me," said Marshall.

"Yes."

Thunder rolled in the distance. Ian pulled the stereoscope slide from his back pocket and held it out to Marshall.

"Ariel found this in the attic," said Ian.

Marshall took the slide and held it up in front of him, squinting. "Ah, yes. This is when the house, your house, was being built."

Ian pointed to the tiny image of the man standing next to the house. He realized then he should have brought the stereoscope, too. "Is that… It can't be you, can it?"

Marshall appeared to study the image for a long time.

"Striking resemblance, don't you think?" he said.

"That's not an answer," began Ian. But Marshall interrupted him.

"Ian, there are many great mysteries yet to be solved," he began. "But our primary goal right now is to find Zach."

"So...you don't think he's..."

"Dead? No."

"I've been researching, and I keep running into clues that seem to mean something but don't quite fit together. I think it has something to do with time travel. I know how crazy that sounds, but...it's the only explanation I can find for why we can't find Zach."

Marshall took the slide and set it on the table in front of him, then went to the stove to collect the teapot. He poured boiling water into two cups, then dropped tea bags into each.

"I ran out of my best tea, so this local brew will have to do," he said as he brought Ian a cup on a saucer, then sat at the table, setting his own tea down in front of him.

"There's another clue—one that's been plaguing me for a long time. The snake eating its own tail..."

"The ouroboros," said Marshall.

"Yes. I keep seeing it everywhere."

Marshall pulled back the sleeve on his left arm, revealing a small tattoo. "This," he said. It was the ouroboros.

Ian was surprised he hadn't noticed that before. "It has something to do with you?"

"It's a part of my heritage," said Marshall. "That's why you've seen the image around the property, too. It's been important to...to my family for years."

Ian's hope deflated. "I was so sure it had something to do with Zach's disappearance."

"I stopped being sure of anything a long time ago," said Marshall. "But there may be a connection."

"What do you mean?"

"The symbol is old. I have traced it back to the sixth century BC."

Ian looked over at the bookshelves. "You're not just a book collector. You're a history buff," he said. Of course, that made perfect sense.

"Mostly ancient history, like you," said Marshall. "But all history is interesting to me."

They were more similar than Ian had thought. Ian sipped his tea. He wasn't much of a tea drinker, but this was good. It was subtly sweet, with a hint of something almost floral that he couldn't quite identify. A loud clap of thunder brought him back to the purpose for his visit.

"You said there may be a connection. What do you mean by that? You must have some theories about Zach," said Ian. He hesitated, not sure if he should reveal the inexplicable visions he'd had in the past few days. Or had it been weeks? *Time*. There it was again, being unpredictable.

"Everything is connected, in a way," said Marshall. "But, like you, I'm still putting the puzzle together."

Ian's head began to throb. He reached up to touch the spot where he'd hit his head. It had started bleeding again.

"Whoa, what happened there?" asked Marshall, looking at Ian's head.

"I hit my head on a floor joist in the crawl space," said Ian.

"You went under the house?" Marshall's eyes went wide.

"I thought Zach…" Ian swallowed hard, unsure how to say it. "I worried that Zach might have gone exploring and that maybe…"

"I understand," said Marshall, thankfully cutting Ian's explanation short. He didn't want to imagine Zach's body rotting under the house again.

"Did you give Zach the key to the crawlspace padlock?" asked Ian.

"Did I? No."

"But it was locked before…"

Marshall waved Ian off. "No, no. I unlocked it. I had the same thought you did about Zach," he said.

Ian was confused. "Wait, you looked for Zach under the house and didn't tell us? Why would you do that?"

"Ian, he wasn't there. The door was still padlocked when I looked at it. I was the one who removed the lock."

This didn't make sense to Ian. "Why would you think he was there if the lock was still..." Ian paused. "This is about the house, isn't it? You thought the house had something to do with Zach's disappearance. Is that it?"

Marshall lifted his tea and took a long sip before replying. "Yes and no. It was a hunch, Ian. A wild, nonsensical hunch."

"But why under the house? Why would you look there?"

Marshall stood and walked over to a second bookshelf, one that was only partially filled with books. Looking past Marshall's shoulder, Ian saw *Mesopotamian Prayers and Incantations* by Tzvi Abusch and Sarah Johnston. *What a strange collection of books for a man who lives in the woods*, thought Ian. The rest of the shelves held all sorts of hand-carved items and collectibles. Ian was curious about it all. He wished he had the time to ask a hundred questions.

Marshall returned with a snow globe and set it down in front of Ian. "Shake that," he said.

Ian lifted the snow globe and shook it, then looked inside. The snow inside bounced around randomly at first, then began to spin in a clockwise motion, speeding up until it looked like a tornado. When the white flecks finally settled, Ian realized it was depicting a scene from a movie. *The Wizard of Oz*.

"What does this have to do with anything? I don't get it."

"You keep being drawn to the ouroboros," said Marshall. "I keep being drawn to this."

"To a snow globe?"

"To what's inside: a tornado. To unpredictability. To chaos."

"I still don't get how that's connected to the crawl space."

"In August of 1966, a rare tornado swept through the Littleton area," he began. "I was…I was visiting my uncle here, at the house. I visited often. I liked coming here. But when that tornado came, I was so scared." Lightning lit up the small cabin and, in that flash, Marshall's face had morphed into that of a frightened child. But it was just a trick of the light. His wrinkled features returned as he continued the story. "We had nowhere else to go, so we hid under the house until the tornado passed," he continued.

"There aren't many tornadoes out this way, are there?"

"No. In fact, none since that one almost sixty years ago. Frankly, and thankfully, it did very little damage. It was only an F1 in magnitude. But…that actually was the second tornado I…my uncle had faced. He wasn't going to be unprepared for a third, however unlikely. He decided then and there to build a shelter. A storm cellar, really, though he always called it his tornado shelter."

"The door in the floor!" said Ian.

"Yes. It's a tornado shelter. A totally unnecessary tornado shelter, I might add. And built in the most unlikely place, too far from the house, if you ask me. We haven't had a single tornado event since."

None of this was helping. Ian shook his head.

"There's more," said Marshall. "My uncle built that shelter twice."

Ian was more confused than ever. "What do you mean?"

"I mean he built it once, but something about it wasn't right." Marshall paused, then stood up and went to the stove to pour a second cup of tea. When he returned to the table, he didn't sit. He held his steaming teacup and shook his head slowly. "The first time he built it, it didn't have enough steps."

"I don't understand."

"The first build only had fifteen steps. I…" Marshall took a sip of tea. "Lyana isn't the only one to have visions around here. My uncle had a vision that the shelter needed more steps. I thought that was crazy, but he insisted. So, he tore down the first shelter, dug deeper, and built it a second time, this time with more steps."

Fifteen steps. *Fifteen steps!* Ian was so close to the answer, he could almost taste it.

"Marshall, the night before Zach went missing, he was counting the steps up to his room, like he always does," said Ian. "But he didn't stop at fifteen. I heard him count all the way to eighteen. I thought it was odd, but just wrote it off as Zach being Zach. He can be a little unpredictable sometimes. But then the next day, he was gone. What if these two things are connected somehow?" Ian shook his head. "But that makes no sense..."

Marshall stopped sipping his tea and stared straight ahead. The look in his eyes was one of sudden realization.

"What? What is it?"

"Could it be?" Marshall said. He was still staring off into the distance.

"Please, Marshall. Tell me this makes sense to you. I'm losing my mind over this. I've even been hallucinating..."

Marshall turned to look directly at Ian. "Hallucinating? What did you see, Ian?"

Ian described the ouroboros coming to life from Zach's drawing and biting him on the hand, then the brief smell of an oil lamp, and the feel of stone beneath his feet when he was exploring the crawl space. Almost as an afterthought, he lifted his hand to show Marshall the two bite marks.

Marshall set his cup down at the same time as a thunderclap. The conflation of these two things made Ian jump. The rain was a torrent now, pounding down on the small cabin's roof, making it harder to hear.

Marshall mumbled something about steps. Did he say ninety-nine? Or maybe nineteen?

"Ian, we need to get that shelter door open," Marshall said.

"But it's sealed shut. We both saw that. How could he have gotten in? You assured me there was no way..."

Marshall ignored him and grabbed a raincoat from a peg next to the front door, then tossed it to Ian. "I have a crowbar in the truck."

"It's cursed, isn't it," said Ian, suddenly resolute.

"What?"

"The tornado shelter. The house. This whole property. It's cursed somehow."

"I don't think..."

"Clearly you have studied ancient cultures. I've seen your book collection. So, you know many of these cultures believed in the power of curses and participated in ceremonies and practices to break those curses. If it is what I think it is, then I know what we need to do," said Ian.

He thought back to an article he'd come across, quite by accident, while searching for answers about Zach's disappearance. It was something he bookmarked weeks earlier, one of a dozen online articles he hoped could provide much needed inspiration for his novel.

"Do you have a bottle of wine?" Ian asked. He started looking around the cabin. "Bad wine, preferably, though I suppose it doesn't matter."

"What? Why do we need a bottle..." began Marshall.

"Some ancient cultures believed that only blood could break curses. That's why sacrifices were made to other gods. And many early and modern religions believe wine represents blood. But what am I saying? As a student of history, you already know this. You must know how the ancients sometimes poured out wine to break a curse." Ian found a bottle partially hidden by some books. "This will do." He grabbed it without reading the label, took two seconds to look for a corkscrew, then abandoned that search to follow Marshall outside.

"I am well aware of that practice," said Marshall as they stepped into the blinding rain, "but I think a crowbar is a far better option."

Ian knew how crazy it sounded, but what didn't sound crazy these days? Marshall opened the truck door and retrieved a rusty crowbar, then slammed the door shut. Lightning continued to flash, with thunderclaps not far behind. The sound of flowing water drew Ian's attention to the stream that ran through the forest and behind their house. It was no stream anymore. It was a river overflowing its banks, and the waterline was growing closer and closer to the house. Ian splashed behind Marshall through the backyard to the edge of the woods. He almost ran into Marshall when he stopped suddenly. There before them was the door in the dirt. The flood hadn't reached the door yet, but it was heading that way.

Marshall leveraged the crowbar and pulled hard, trying to pry the rusted door free. It didn't budge. He tried a second time with the same result.

Ian stared at the rusted door, his academic mind warring with his father's mind of desperation. Everything he learned in twenty years of studying ancient cultures screamed that this was nonsense—symbolic thinking, primitive superstition. But his son was missing, and logic had failed him completely.

"Blood opens what blood has sealed," he whispered, the ancient Mesopotamian words rising unsolicited from memory fragments of a text he'd translated in dusty archives years ago. At the time, he'd dismissed it as ritual poetry, but now… He held up the wine, then looked at Marshall's face. Marshall stared back with a blank look and said nothing.

"Look, I'm willing to try anything, Marshall." Ian stared at the wine bottle, reading the label for the first time. "Whoa, this isn't cheap wine. It's a Daríghe!"

Marshall shrugged. "I like good wine," he said.

Ian hesitated. It would be such a waste to dump all this wine, but he'd already made his decision. Without ceremony, he raised the crowbar like an ancient sword and brought it down onto the bottle's neck. The glass shattered in a burst of ruby spray, and the wine arced through the air like liquid fire. Expensive wine sprayed everywhere, including on Ian's rain-soaked shoes.

Here goes nothing, Ian thought, *or everything.*

He began to walk around the door, pouring out what was left of the wine onto the ground. He paused and hesitantly whispered, "Break the curse," and then something impossible occurred. The wine did not fall to the ground. Instead, it hung suspended in the air mere inches above the sodden soil, spreading outward like a crimson shield, defying the laws of nature.

This was not what Ian expected at all. Frustrated, he gathered all the belief he could muster and began chanting, "Break the curse! Break the curse!"

Ignoring Ian's chants, the wine continued to spread but refused to land on the ground. *I must be doing something wrong*, he thought. Clearly, he was onto something, but that something was also onto him. As the cursed soil continued resisting, a memory of his mother telling him a story about her struggles during her first year in America flooded his thoughts. In her darkest hours, she told him, *"The Heavens provided a 'but suddenly…' in the moments when all felt lost. In an unexpected way, as long as you hold on to hope, a supernatural intervention can occur."*

Filled with hope from his mother's words, Ian cried out, his voice cracking in desperation, "Break the curse! Break the curse that holds my son!"

Ian's breath caught in his throat. The ancient forces were stirring, responding to his plea. He raised his arms to the tempestuous heavens, rain streaming down his face like tears of supplication.

The suspended wine began to writhe and coalesce, forming a serpentine stream that rose through the air with ominous intent.

Lightning illuminated the impossible sight—a wine-wrought ouroboros, ancient and terrible, circling through the darkness.

The bottle began to glow—first a deep red hue, then slowly transforming into a blinding blue. Ian glanced at Marshall. His eyes were wide, his mouth open in surprise.

Without warning, the serpent coiled around Ian's chest and struck like lightning, sinking ethereal fangs into his hand—in the same spot as the snake from his vision. A surge of power—ancient, primal, and absolute—coursed through Ian's veins. His eyes blazed with otherworldly light as particles of luminous energy erupted from his very pores, transforming him into a beacon against the darkness. Impossibly, the power in the wine was now flowing through him.

But suddenly, as if possessed by some force, Ian began to shout, "Break the curse! Breāķ t'ħĕ ċůř… Ina šulmi edû ana nišiya ma-sar-ti u ma-na, ummânu bēlu, ma-sar-tu ana šalāmi u šulmi, lā ana lemutti, ana nadāni arkāni u tiklūti!"

Lightning struck a nearby tree, causing a bright flash of light. At the crack of thunder, the wine serpent burst from his chest in a spectacular fountain, spreading across the shelter door before slamming into the earth with explosive force.

When Ian came to, he tossed the bottle aside. His hands still glowing, he seized the crowbar with both hands and wedged it beneath the ancient door, then pulled hard. At first, nothing. Then, a small seam appeared.

"You're getting it!" said Marshall.

Ian took a deep breath and choked on a mouthful of rain. He coughed and steadied himself for another pull on the crowbar. This time there was a loud *snap*, and the door handle broke clear off. Ian reached down and tried to pull at the door, but it was still wedged shut. In one last desperate attempt, Ian resituated the crowbar near where the door handle had been and pulled with all his strength. The door popped free, and Ian fell backward to the ground. He groaned in pain.

"You did it!" said Marshall.

Ian was certain he had failed. But sure enough, the door was loose. Using the crowbar, they wedged the door up from the frame, then flipped it over on rusted hinges until it landed with a splash on the muddy ground. What Ian saw made his heart drop.

The shelter was filled with water.

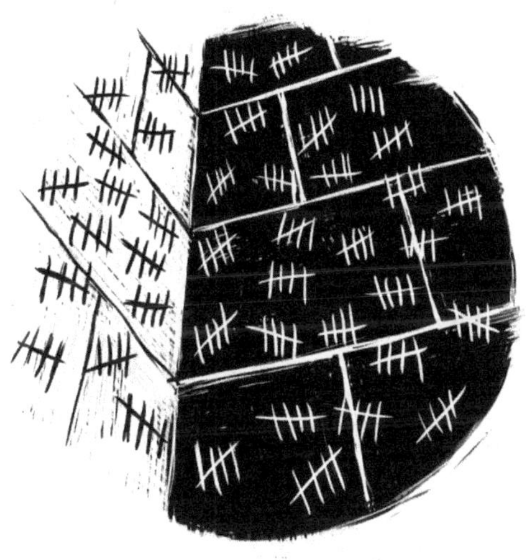

NINETEEN

AKOLO LOOKED OVER at Zach. He was scratching another mark into the stone behind his bed.

"Two hundred four," he said.

The announcement of Zach's days at the palace had become a morning ritual for Zach. In the early days, he called out the number in a big, dramatic voice, almost as if he were announcing it to a big crowd. But lately, his voice was little more than a rasp. Zach told Akolo he had all but given up on his dream of someday going home. Akolo tried to offer encouragement, but it was a mostly fruitless effort. The only time Zach seemed happy was when they visited the gardens. Thankfully, they spent lots of time there.

"It's a blood moon," said Zach. Akolo already knew this. Over the past few weeks, Zach and Akolo had talked at length with the high priest about how to identify a blood moon. There was some guesswork involved, but tonight it was assured.

"Maybe we can visit the gardens today," said Akolo.

"I just want to rest," said Zach.

"We could bathe in the river, or..."

"I said, I just want to rest."

Akolo recognized that tone of voice. It meant he should stop pestering Zach. *Pestering.* This was yet another word Akolo had learned from his friend. He didn't like this one as much as tornado, but it was fun to say. But he wasn't pestering Zach; he was just trying to cheer him up.

"Okay," said Akolo, but he was already cueing up two or three other suggestions for the day. Before he could pester Zach anymore, Abbas and Soroush entered the room. The two guards had become like big brothers to Zach and Akolo. At least when they weren't performing official duties. Based on their serious expressions, this was an official visit.

"Akolo," said Abbas. He was the bigger of the two guards, nearly a head taller than Soroush. But unlike his shorter partner, his voice was soft, gentle, even when giving orders. Soroush, on the other hand, had a piercing, brittle voice. Like the squeal the giant metal gate at the front of the palace made when it was opened. "The king requests your presence," he added.

Zach scooted to the edge of his bed and dropped his feet to the floor.

Soroush held up his hand. "Just Akolo," he screeched to Zach.

Akolo looked over at his friend. Zach didn't seem bothered by this slight. He shrugged, then lay back down on the bed, rolling over to face the calendar wall.

Akolo wasn't sure what to think. He and Zach had done practically everything together over the past two hundred days. He pondered this as the guards led him down the sixty-six steps and through the passageways and hallways and the courtyard until they reached the throne room. The king was waiting there for him, with the high priest standing to his left. The king wore a richly decorated crown and a broad necklace embellished with dozens of precious stones. He looked especially powerful sitting high on his throne wearing these adornments.

"Tonight is an important night," began the king. He motioned for Akolo to sit on a bench that faced the throne. "You will present my crown and my royal collar to your god." He indicated the crown and the necklace with a flourish of his small hands. "You will ask your god to bless the wearer and grant him wisdom in the ways of the world. Are you prepared for this task?"

Akolo's throat was dry. He cleared it and answered, "Yes. And Zach will be there too, right?"

The king didn't answer. He just indicated to the guards to take him away. As Akolo was being led away, he glanced back and saw that the king and the high priest were having a heated conversation. The high priest was shaking his head as if disagreeing with something the king said. Abbas reached over and gently steered Akolo's head to face forward as they exited into the grand auditorium.

"Best keep your eyes forward, Akolo," said Abbas. "The only good time to look behind is when you're being chased by an enemy. It's helpful to know just how close they are." Abbas ruffled Akolo's hair, then gently nudged him toward the passageways that led to the tower.

When he returned to his room, Zach was asleep. He wanted desperately to talk to Zach, to tell him what the king had said. But he didn't want Zach to be upset at him, so he remained silent. He spent the rest of the day attending to the small garden the high priest had allowed them to cultivate in a courtyard behind the tower. It was nothing like the grand garden terraces, of course, but it was his. Well, his and Zach's.

Akolo sat on his bed, wringing his hands. Dusk was approaching and the guards would soon appear to take him and Zach to the temple. Akolo liked the way he felt when he was inside the temple, but he was still nervous every time he slipped under the tent flap. The image of dead soldiers being pulled out by ropes had been seared into his brain. What if God decided he was no longer worthy to be in his presence? The thought brought a shiver, even though the day's heat lingered.

"Akolo." It was Soroush. "Come."

Akolo hesitated. "And Zach, too, right?"

Soroush shook his head. "Just you."

Zach had been silent most of the day, but Akolo was certain he would speak up now. They always did this together. Instead, Zach just nodded at Akolo and pointed to the door. Akolo's heart sank at the thought he would have to do this alone.

"Please," he said to Soroush. "Zach must come too."

Soroush shook his head. "This time, only you," he said. Soroush's hard edges seemed to soften in that moment. Akolo saw compassion in his dark eyes.

This unexpected change of plans unnerved Akolo. He had to comply, of course. But before he exited the room, he walked over to Zach and tried ruffling his hair as Zach had done to him once before. As Abbas had done to him as well. But the action startled Zach and he slapped Akolo's hand away.

"Just go!" he said, turning away from Akolo.

Akolo hid his tears as he left the room, following Soroush down the sixty-six stairs. Tears continued to fall all the way to the tent. The high priest was waiting for him with his two attendants. He was holding the king's crown and necklace out in front of him.

"Is something the matter?" the high priest asked Akolo.

Akolo wanted to tell him that he couldn't do this alone. That he needed Zach here with him. But no words came. The high priest walked up to Akolo and bent down on one knee. He reached a hand up to wipe Akolo's tears away.

"This is your destiny, Akolo," he said. "This is the role your god has prepared you for. You are uniquely blessed." He then gently placed the necklace around Akolo's neck. The weight of it bent him forward. The high priest handed him the crown, then walked up to the tent, pulled the flap open. Akolo had never seen him stand so close to the temple. He'd always had his attendants help with the tent flap.

"May God continue to bless you," he said, then gestured for Akolo to enter.

Once inside the tent, the flap closed behind him and Akolo paused to let his eyes adjust. As he climbed the steps into the temple, the gems decorating the crown and the necklace began to glow. He gently set the crown on the chest, then removed the necklace and draped it over the chest as well. Akolo reached into his pocket and pulled out his fire opal and held it in his hand. It had never glowed so bright.

Akolo sat down next to the chest and looked up at the ceiling. Colors began to swirl as if blown by a gentle breeze. Then that gentle breeze became insistent until the blues, reds, yellows, greens and golds were spinning violently, like the dust tornado in his room. This was new. Akolo sensed he should be frightened by the chaotic display, but fear seemed so far away he could barely recognize the feeling. The usually quiet temple grew loud with the sound of a terrible windstorm, and yet still Akolo was at peace. The world around him could have been ending, but he felt content. Hopeful. Happy, even.

And powerful.

He had never tasted such power.

Akolo lifted his fire opal and waved it in the air above him. The swirling colors paused their dance, then resumed spinning when he brought his hand down. He repeated the action, commanding the colors to pause with the swish of his hand, then releasing them again.

From somewhere deep in the whipping of the wind, Akolo heard a voice. He lowered his hand and strained to listen.

It is time to go home, the voice said.

Akolo waited for more words, but none came. The colors began to fade. Akolo slipped the stone into his pocket, where it clinked against the ouroboros bracelet. Before he gathered the necklace and the crown, he remembered what the king had said and asked God to bless the wearer with wisdom. Then he exited the temple and crawled through the tent flap into the dark of night. He was met there by a misting rain. Like every time before, he had no idea how long he'd been in the temple.

Only Soroush and a guard he didn't recognize were standing outside the tent. *What happened to Abbas?* he wondered. A moment later, the high priest appeared. One of his attendants was holding something over his head to keep the rain away. Akolo noticed movement behind the priest and a young girl about his age peeked around his robes. The high priest collected the crown and necklace from Akolo.

"Did you hear from God?"

Akolo repeated what he'd heard, then added, "There was a great power in the temple. I felt it in my bones." A remnant of that power had lingered, giving Akolo the confidence to speak plainly with the high priest.

The high priest studied the crown and the necklace for a moment, nodded his satisfaction, then walked away. His robes twirled with his departure, revealing the young girl who had been standing behind him. Her black hair was matted by the rain, and she was staring at Akolo with dark eyes.

The high priest paused and looked back. "Come, Esme," he said. The girl smiled at Akolo, then hurried to catch up to the high priest.

The rain began to fall heavier, but Akolo was frozen in place, lost in that too-brief glance from the girl.

Esme. Her name is Esme.

"Come, Akolo," said Soroush. "There is much to do, for today we begin our great journey."

Akolo wiped the rain from his face and looked up at the guard. "What do you mean?"

"When morning breaks, we leave. The king has decreed it."

"Leave for where?"

Soroush laughed. "For your home." A proud look appeared on his usually pained face. "We are going to rebuild the temple. Your temple!"

Akolo swallowed hard. "Nobody told me..."

"I'm telling you now," said Soroush. "Pack your things and get some sleep."

Akolo didn't have many "things" to pack. "What about Zach?"

The guard shrugged. "He will come, too."

Akolo wasn't comforted by that answer.

"Where is Abbas?" he asked.

"He is gone," said Soroush.

Akolo didn't understand. Why would he be gone? Did he get in trouble, like Bijan?

When he returned to the tower room, Zach was asleep. He waited until Soroush left, then sat on Zach's bed and tapped on his shoulder trying to wake him. Gentle touches didn't work, so he grabbed Zach's shoulder and shook him more violently.

"What? What are you doing?" Zach rolled over and looked like he might strike Akolo.

"I'm sorry, but I needed to wake you."

Thunder rolled outside, and with every gust of wind, rain blew into the room. Thankfully their beds were far from the windows, but Akolo felt the chill deep in his bones.

"Why, what's happening?"

Akolo proceeded to explain everything that had happened from the moment he left to see the king that morning until his return from the temple. He didn't say anything about the girl. About Esme. That was just for him to know.

"We're leaving!" he repeated after finishing his summary.

Zach sat up instantly. "When?"

"At daybreak."

"But I can't leave. I have to stay here in case..." He didn't finish his sentence, but Akolo knew what he meant.

"Zach, God spoke to me when I was in the temple."

Zach looked panicked. "What? What did he say?"

"I don't know what it means."

"Please, Akolo, tell me what you heard."

"The voice said, 'It is time to go home.'"

Zach stood up and started pacing in the small room, nearly slipping on a wet spot on the floor near the south-facing window. Periodically, lightning lit up the room, casting strange shadows on the stone walls. Akolo's confidence waned. The power he'd felt in the temple was all but gone now.

"What do you think it means?" asked Akolo.

"I don't know. Was the message just for you?"

"Maybe? But what if it was for both of us?"

Zach stopped pacing. He turned to look at Akolo.

"Ninety-nine steps!" he said. His eyes were wild. "I've been seeing that number in my head now for weeks. I thought it was just something that stuck, you know? Like an earworm?"

Akolo scrunched up his face. "Earworm?"

"Never mind. Look, I think the message was for me, too. And I think I know what I need to do."

Zach reached into his pocket and pulled out the fire opal Akolo had given him. A soft glow emanated from the stone.

"Akolo, I think it's finally time for me to go home," said Zach. He was wearing a wild smile, but soon the smile became a look of worry. "What if I'm wrong?"

"Then you can come with me," said Akolo. The words were almost swallowed up by the wind as it whipped through the room, stirring up dirt and straw. Some of that dirt got in Akolo's eyes, but that wasn't the only reason they were watering.

Zach walked up to Akolo and put his hands on Akolo's shoulders.

"This has to work, Akolo. I miss home so much."

"But how will it work?"

"Remember what I said about God being mysterious?"

Akolo nodded.

"I think it's like that. Something that's hard to explain."

"Will I ever see you again?" asked Akolo. He wished he could close his ears to the answer he knew was coming.

Zach's eyes went to his stone. "I don't know. My family is far away. It might be difficult to return. But no matter what happens, I'll never forget you. You are my friend, Akolo. The best friend I've ever had."

Akolo smiled through his tears. "Is it wrong for me to hope you can't find a way back? That you'll have to come with us to my home?" he said.

Zach laughed. "I like that you always tell the truth, Akolo. There aren't a lot of people like you. I'm going to miss you. If this crazy idea works, I mean." Zach's smile dropped.

Akolo sighed. "It's going to work, Zach. I know it is. I don't want it to, but also, I do. I really do. I want you to be happy."

"Thanks, Akolo."

Lightning lit up the room. Zach's face looked so much older in that flash.

"How will you get to the lower level?" asked Akolo.

Zach looked unsure for a moment, then his smile returned. "I have an idea."

• • •

Zach's plan had to work, or he was toast. He made Akolo promise that he'd tell the guards he didn't know anything about Zach's plan.

"Sometimes a lie is the right thing," Akolo had said.

"And this is one of those times," Zach replied. If they suspected Akolo had anything to do with Zach's disappearance, he might be punished. Zach couldn't live with himself if he caused his friend any harm.

They said their goodbyes before Akolo began his act. Zach hid in the shadows behind the always-open door to their room, waiting. He hoped the pile of tunics stuffed under his blanket on the bed might buy him more time before anyone realized he was missing. Akolo stood at the south-facing window and started yelling and pointing. His act was so convincing, even Zach wanted to rush over to see what he was pointing to. But when Soroush came running, Zach only had a moment to steal away. He moved as quickly and quietly as he could down the sixty-six stairs, counting each one as he went. Then he kept to the shadows as he raced down the pathways and through hallways until he reached the main courtyard. In a flash of lightning, he saw that two guards were patrolling the area. Neither of them looked very happy to be out in the rain. Zach marked the time between the lightning flashes and the thunderclaps. The storm was close. After a particularly bright flash, he dashed across the courtyard to his destination: the stairway that led down to the long hallway. The stairway he'd found himself on when he thought he was simply climbing up to his room so many months ago.

Down is up, he thought. Maybe he was wrong about the locked room, the ninety-nine steps. Maybe all he needed to do was go down these stairs. He held his breath, waited for the next flash of lightning, then descended, hoping, wishing that he'd find himself at home when he got to the bottom.

But when his feet hit the ground at the bottom of the stairway, he was still in the palace. Lamps lit the hallway ahead of him, if only barely.

Okay, it's not about the stairs. It's about the locked door, like I thought, he said to himself.

Just then, a wild gust of chilling wind whipped down the stairwell. All the oil lamps ahead of him blew out.

Zach was alone. And in complete darkness.

TWENTY

LYANA RACED BACK into the foyer area, her hands still dripping with water.

"Look, Mom." Ariel was standing at the top of the stairs. The papers had been neatly ordered into a five-by-three grid. It took a moment for Lyana to see it, but when she did, her heart nearly stopped.

"The storm shelter!" she said. "Or whatever that door in the dirt is."

"It has to be," said Ariel. "You even got the handle right. How in the world..."

"I have no idea." Lyana struggled to make sense of this madness. "But what does it mean?" She turned and grabbed Ariel by the shoulders. "It must be where Zach is. Oh, Ariel...we need to tell your dad. He needs to know right away. I'm going to put on a clean shirt and then go out and find him," she said. She raced up the stairs. At the landing, she stopped and spun, nearly running into her daughter. "No, wait! We need to go to the door. You know how to get there, right?"

Ariel squinted. "I...think so? But, Mom, the door is rusted..."

"You're right. Of course you're right. We need to find your dad first." She turned and frantically jogged down the hallway to her bedroom.

After changing her shirt, she paused at the top of the stairs to take a picture of the arranged paintings. *Ian needs to see this*, she thought. When she got to the bottom, she saw the mess she had left on the floor. She grabbed a rag from the sink and a trash bag from the kitchen and started to clean up, tossing the unused paper into the trash and wiping away the paint stains. She left the still-wet fifteen-piece mural on the floor where Ariel had neatly arranged it.

He must be found.

The faint voice caught Lyana off guard. She thought it was coming from Ian's office. She walked through the study door, nearly tripping on a bottle that had fallen out of a tipped-over trash can.

Lyana picked up the bottle and dropped it into the trash bag she was holding. "Is it the shelter? Is that where he is?" Lyana asked aloud.

"Mom." Ariel appeared in the doorway to the study.

Lyana dumped the rest of the office trash into the bag, fully aware she was stalling. She needed to go to the door in the dirt, but feared what she would discover.

"Mom," repeated Ariel. "I'm worried about Dad." This wasn't the first time Ariel had expressed her concern.

Lyana rattled the trash bag. "Do you mean because of this? He has promised he will stop drinking…"

"No, not about that," she said. "You said he went to see Marshall, but you know I don't trust Marshall. I think he's been lying to us."

"About what?"

Ariel waved her arms around. "About this. About everything!"

Lyana nodded. "Maybe you're right."

"Well, that's refreshing," said Ariel with more than a little snark in her voice.

"What?"

"You not telling me I'm wrong, for once."

Lyana was about to offer a clever reply, then decided against it. This wasn't the time for clever replies.

He must be found.

Lyana turned toward the sound of the voice. "I don't understand. What do you mean?"

"Mom? Who are you talking to?"

Lyana turned back to Ariel. "Look, Ariel. I need to tell you something. Don't freak out..."

"Um, it's a little late for that..."

"Ariel, I've been hearing a voice again..."

"Mom, no! You are not doing *that* again!"

"Wait, Ariel. It's not a bad thing this time. I think it's like...like the painting, you know. It's trying to help, give me clues."

"This is all just so impossible." Ariel stomped out of the room, then immediately turned around and walked right up to Lyana. "This house is making all of us crazy!"

Lyana reached out to touch Ariel's shoulder, but she shrugged her hand away.

"The voice said, 'He must be found,'" Lyana said. "But I don't understand. That's what we've been trying to do all this time. Find Zach."

"Why aren't you getting this, Mom? This place is..." Ariel's eyes went wide. "Maybe it's not Zach you're supposed to find. Maybe it's Dad. What if I'm right about Marshall? What if Dad's in danger?"

Ariel started toward the front door, then stopped. "We need to find him!"

Lyana dropped the trash bag and followed her. Ariel was putting on a raincoat. Lyana grabbed her own and an umbrella.

Ariel stopped. "Wait...there's something I need to do first. I'll catch up in a minute."

"But I'm not sure where to look," began Lyana. Ariel had already turned and raced up the stairs.

"Go find Dad. I'll be right behind you," Ariel called back as she disappeared into her room.

"Okay. I'll head toward Marshall's cabin."

Lyana opened her umbrella and stepped outside into the pouring rain. The driving wind immediately turned it inside out, rendering the umbrella useless. Lyana tried to close it, but a gust of wind whipped it from her hands, sending it high into the darkening sky.

• • •

Ariel waited until her mother was outside, then pressed the "talk" button on the intercom.

"Zach," she said. She waited for a reply. Nothing. "Zach, I don't know if you can hear me. But…we're going to find you."

Was that a voice she just heard? Or just more static.

She pressed the button again. "We'll find you. I promise."

Ariel let go of the button, listened to the silence for a moment, then took the stairs two at a time before racing out the front door into the rain.

• • •

Was there some truth to Ariel's assertion? Marshall had been absent of late, distant. Before Zach went missing, they had spent lots of time together. She usually did most of the talking in their conversations, but even though his words were few, they were almost always wise, and often just what Lyana needed to hear. She missed that.

What did she need to hear now? That Zach had been found. Alive. That was the *only* thing she wanted to hear.

• • •

Ariel jogged up beside Lyana.

"I'm never quite sure the best way to get there." Lyana had to shout to be heard over the pounding rain. She started walking toward the woods, but Ariel pulled back on her hand.

"They're not at the cabin," said Ariel. She shook her head and rain flew from her hair. "Why do I know that?" she said. "How in the world do I know that?" Then, without pause, she started walking in a different direction, tugging at her mother's hand. "This way!"

The ground was so saturated, every step brought a splash. Lyana didn't think she could be any wetter than she and Ariel were as they jogged toward the woods. When she looked off in the distance, she saw two rain-blurred figures standing just beyond the tree line.

"Dad!" Ariel let go of Lyana's hand and raced ahead. Lyana hurried to join her.

"Ariel, Lyana," said Ian. He was standing next to a water-filled hole in the ground. A metal door lay open next to it. "We have to pump the water out of the tornado shelter!"

Lyana's knees buckled. Ian grabbed her to keep her upright. "What? No! He can't be in there..."

Ariel started pacing back and forth, talking to herself. She looked almost manic.

"It's not what you think," said Ian. He reached out to Ariel and put his hand on her shoulder. "It's not what you think. I promise."

Lightning flashed, revealing a clear view of the flooded shelter. A memory flashed in Lyana's head at the very same time: an image of a baptismal pool. Was this her memory? It almost seemed like someone else's. *But how could that be?*

The loudest thunderclap yet snapped her out of this impossible thought and back to the moment.

"We need to get out of the rain," Ian said. He ushered them out of the woods and back to the house. When they stepped through the front door, all of them dripping wet, Ian addressed Marshall.

"Call your friend Herman," he said. Marshall started to object, but Ian pulled his phone out of his pocket and set it on the kitchen counter. "Tell him I'll be there as soon as possible."

"He could be out on a job somewhere..." began Marshall.

"Call him! Ariel, come with me. I'll explain everything." He pointed to Marshall. "Tell Lyana. We'll be back as soon as humanly possible."

Ian made a beeline for the garage door, pausing only long enough to call Ariel over to join him. The two of them exited. A moment later, Lyana watched through the window as the car disappeared into the pouring rain.

Lyana dropped into a chair. She reached up and squeezed water out of her rain-soaked hair. "Okay, Marshall. Tell me. What's going on?"

Marshall held up his finger as he held Ian's cell phone to his ear.

• • •

Marshall ended the call and sat down across from Lyana.

"Herman Kells," he said. "Runs a bunch of different businesses in town. He's the only one I know who has a pump truck."

"I don't understand, Marshall. What's going on? Why do you need to pump the water out of the shelter? And what was with the wine bottle on the ground. Yes, I saw that. Have you been drinking? Has Ian?"

Marshall pulled at his soaking sleeves. Water dripped relentlessly onto the table. "Sorry about this..."

"Marshall! Tell me."

Marshall brought Lyana up to date. He assured her neither he nor Ian had been drinking and explained all the clues they had uncovered and why they ended up at the door in the dirt. When Lyana showed him the picture of the paintings she'd made, his eyes grew wide, and he just stared at her. *How did she get the same message?*

After taking everything in, she sat in silence, surprisingly calm, considering everything that had happened. Oh, how he had missed talking with her these past few weeks. Her sincere interest in what he had to say made him feel important. He remembered that seductive feeling of importance all too well. And the cost, too.

"So…it's a portal?" Lyana's face had worn myriad expressions as he talked—everything from doubt to confusion to wonder. This one looked a little like hope.

"This house, this property," he began. How much could he say? "It wants you here. Dare I say it needs you. But not just some of you; *all* of you, including Zach. I don't understand it all myself, but I feel it in my bones; the tornado shelter is the answer. It's going to bring Zach to us."

"But why now? Why today?" she asked.

"With this rain, it's impossible to confirm, but if I'm right, it's a full moon."

Lyana laughed. "A full moon? You're not going to tell me this is about werewolves now, are you?"

Marshall couldn't suppress a small smile. "No werewolves are involved, I promise. But it's not just a full moon, Lyana—it's a blood moon. A much rarer event."

Lyana picked up her cell phone and wiped away a splash of water, then typed on it for a moment, clicking and swiping or whatever it was people did with cell phones. Marshall had chosen to stick with an old flip phone, and even that he rarely used.

"You're right, it is," Lyana said at last. "But why is that important?"

Marshall couldn't look Lyana in the eyes. She would see right through him, catch him in his lies of omission. *Sometimes the whole truth is not helpful. Sometimes you need to keep secrets.* So instead, he stood and walked into the kitchen. He grabbed a towel from the rack and glanced over at Lyana.

"May I?" he asked. She nodded. "Toss me one, too." Marshall tossed her a towel, then wiped the dripping water from his forehead. He looked out the kitchen window. Night would be here soon, but because of the storm, it was already dark outside. "There are some things that I can't talk about. Not yet anyway. But one thing I am almost certain of is that the blood moon is significant."

"Why do you say *almost* certain."

"There was a time when I would tell you things with certainty. That time has long passed." He turned back toward Lyana. "That's all I can say, Lyana. I'm afraid all I can do is ask you to trust me."

Lyana looked like she was going to say something, then closed her mouth and nodded.

"Trust you," she said with much hesitation.

"Yes. Trust me."

Oh, how he hoped he was right.

• • •

The rain continued, unabated. Night had already fallen when the truck finally backed up to the shelter, after getting stuck multiple times in the soggy grass. Lyana was surprised to see Lloyd driving the truck. "Herman was away on a business call," Ian explained. "One of his *other* businesses. Lloyd saw me pounding on Herman's shop door. It's just catty-corner from the diner. Anyway, Lloyd knows how to work this thing."

Small world, Lyana thought. And she was so thankful for that.

Lloyd invited Ariel and Lyana to sit in the truck out of the rain while he lowered the wide red hose into the flooded cellar. But they chose instead to hide from the rain under a sheet of plastic Ian had retrieved from the garage.

Lyana had her arm around Ariel. They were both shivering and the sound of rain hitting the plastic sheeting was relentless. Marshall and Ian paced back and forth near the shelter. Lloyd periodically checked the valves on the truck. Water poured out of the exit hose and into the lawn, quickly filling the ruts the truck had carved on its way to the shelter.

Lyana looked at the flooded cellar. The water level had barely dropped at all.

"Why isn't it working?" asked Ariel.

Lyana pulled her closer. Not one iota of this plan made any sense. But it *had* to work. If it didn't, it would be like losing Zach all over again.

Trust me, Marshall had said.

TWENTY-ONE

ZACH STRAINED TO see the top of the stairs. When the lightning flashed, he got a glimpse of the doorway twenty steps above him, but the light didn't reach the hall below. He inhaled a deep breath, tasting humidity and electricity in the air, then took his first step.

"One, two, three," he counted, quietly, in case any guards happened by the doorway at the top of the stairs. *Surely there's no one down here*, thought Zach. When he'd roomed down here with Akolo, he never saw another living soul, apart from their guard Bijan, who, he discovered, would sometimes nap in an adjoining room. The only other rooms he had been able to explore appeared to be used for storage. Still, there was something incredibly creepy about a long, dark hallway. Especially a quiet one. Except this wasn't exactly a quiet hallway. Zach had heard a voice. Someone calling his name. He was 93 percent certain of that.

"...twenty-seven, twenty-eight, twenty-nine..." Zach paused when he thought he heard something again. He turned his head slightly, trying to locate the source of the noise.

This wasn't a voice. It sounded like someone breathing.

Zach's heart started pounding fast. *Maybe it's just the sound of me*, he thought. He inhaled and held his breath. The muffled breathing sound continued. Zach took another step, moving even more quietly than before.

"...thirty, thirty-one, thirty-two..."

"Who's out there?"

The voice made Zach jump. He felt for the wall beside him and pressed himself against it.

"Is someone out there?" the muffled voice said.

Zach knew that voice. He abandoned his count and shuffled forward feeling his way along the wall until he came to a closed door. He pressed his ear up to it and waited.

"Please, if someone is out there, I need food. Rotten fruit, moldy bread...anything."

"Bijan?" Zach's voice cracked when he spoke, so he said again, a little louder, "Bijan? Is that you?"

"Young Zach?" came the reply.

"Why are you here?" Zach asked. But he already knew the answer. He had wondered if some of these lower rooms had been used to house prisoners. Like jail cells. Or a dungeon. Bijan was here because he hadn't followed the rules. He could have been holed up here for months. How was he still alive?

"Don't they feed you?" asked Zach.

"I fear they've forgotten me," said Bijan.

Zach glanced back toward the stairwell. A flash of lightning revealed just how far away it was. He didn't have time to find food for Bijan. And where would he look for it?

"Bijan, I'm sorry," he said. "I can't... I don't think I can help."

There was a soft sound, like someone sighing.

"It's okay, Zach. I won't ask you to break the rules on my behalf."

"Maybe I can search another room..." he began. He felt bad for Bijan, even if the guard had tried to use the boys for his own benefit.

"No."

Zach had lost count of his steps. He would need to return to the stairwell and start again.

"I'm sorry," he repeated.

"No, Zach, I'm sorry," said Bijan, causing Zach to pause. "I was wrong. Please, I beg of you: Can you forgive me for what I did?"

Zach didn't need to think too hard about that. He could list dozens of times he'd messed up and needed forgiveness. "I forgive you," he said. "And I'm sure Akolo does too."

"Thank you."

Zach waited to see if Bijan had more to say. But silence once again ruled the hallway. Carefully, Zach shuffled back to the bottom of the stairs. He turned around, resolute, and began counting his steps once again. This time, he counted in his head, marking every ten with his fingers to be certain of his count.

"...ninety-eight, ninety-nine." He stopped and reached his hand to the right side of the hallway. But there was no door. Had he miscounted? He shuffled forward one step, then two. Finally, with the third step, his hand found the edge of a closed door. He gently brushed his hand across it, feeling the grain of the old wood on his fingertips. His rain-soaked body shivered.

Zach looked down and saw his pocket glowing.

"Huh," he said. He pulled out the fire opal and held it up to his face. The stone glowed brighter. When Zach looked again at the door, an ouroboros symbol was glowing back at him from the very center of the door. He stepped back, and light began to stream out from the door's edges.

"Hey, what's going on down there?" a voice called out from down the hall. This was a voice he didn't recognize. When Zach turned his head to look, he saw a light coming toward him, and the sound of soldiers' boots on the stone floor was unmistakable.

Panic rose in Zach's stomach.

"It's the boy!" the soldier called out. A second, then a third torch joined the first. They were growing closer by the second.

Holding the fire opal tightly in his hand, Zach pushed on the door. It opened inward, then water from inside rushed past him, knocking him back into the hallway. He got up, glanced at the approaching torches, then fought his way through the current into the room. The second he was fully in the room, the door slammed closed. Water continued to flood around him, climbing up to his ankles, then his knees.

"Great," he said aloud. "Now I'm going to drown." He held the fire opal out in front of him, trying to identify the source of the water. What he saw made his heart swell with impossible hope.

Stairs! The water is pouring down a flight of stairs!

Is it just another entrance to the dungeon? he wondered. But why would they hide stairs in a locked room?

Someone was pounding on the door behind him. There was no time to consider the options.

"Up is the way out," he said. He inched toward the stairs, battling the rushing water, and began to climb.

"One, two, three…"

TWENTY-TWO

"WHY IS IT taking so long?" asked Ariel.

"It's this never-ending rain," said Ian. "It's filling up as fast as we can empty it." He turned to Lloyd. "Is there anything you can do?"

Lloyd shook his head. "It's pushed to the max," he said. Less than a minute later, the motor running the pump sputtered, then stopped. Lloyd jogged over and started it up again. It gurgled to life, ran for a few seconds, then died. He walked around to the other side of the truck, then swore under his breath.

He came over to Ian, shaking his head. "I'm sorry, Ian. We should have checked the fuel level. The pump uses a separate tank and I'm afraid it's empty."

Ian forced the rising panic down. *What to do? What to do?* "What if we siphoned some of the fuel from the gas tank…"

Lloyd nodded. "That might work. We'll need a shorter hose, or tubing of some kind…"

Ian started toward the garage.

"Dad, wait!" Ariel called out. "Look!"

He turned around to see Ariel pointing at the cellar. The water was receding. And quickly, like someone had pulled a drain plug below. He watched as the top step was revealed, then the next. But as the water level dropped further, a thick fog flowed into its place.

"What's happening?" asked Lyana.

Ian looked over at Lloyd. He shrugged. Ian turned his gaze to Marshall. Marshall had abandoned the umbrella Lyana offered him earlier and was standing at the far edge of the shelter opening, dripping wet like all of them. But he wasn't watching the water recede. His eyes were fixed to the skies.

"Marshall?" Ian began.

"Mom! Dad!" Ariel's shout turned everyone's attention back to the shelter.

"Shh, listen," said Lyana.

"...eleven, twelve, thirteen..."

Lyana's hands went to her face.

Ian raced to the edge of the opening. The fog swirled into shadow, then slowly, way too slowly, began to thin. Something was coming up the stairs, troubling the mist. No, not something...someone.

Ariel shouted, "Zach!"

The figure paused, then quickened his pace up the stairs. At the very top, he stopped, blinded by the truck's headlamps like he was standing onstage, lit by a spotlight.

It *was* Zach. But a different Zach. His hair was long and stringy, his clothing unfamiliar. Could it be he was taller? There was something about his eyes, too.

He looked for all the world like a bedraggled, sopping wet puppy.

When Zach saw his father, his eyes brightened. He ran into Ian's open arms and held him tight. Ian wrapped his arms around Zach, stunned into silence over the rare physical expression of affection. Lyana ran over and hugged the two of them, crying. Ariel stood back a few feet, her arms folded in front of her. Tears had joined the rain dripping down her face. Ian waved her over. She hesitated, then ran to join the family hug.

"Oh, Zach, I knew we'd find you," said Lyana.

"I knew it too," said Ariel.

"What do you mean?" he said. "I found *you*." Then he laughed and it was the best sound Ian had ever heard. Marshall hadn't moved from his perch on the opposite side of the hole in the ground, but the relief on his face was as palpable as the rain.

Ian glanced at Lloyd. His head was bowed. Ian knew his story well, how his wife and daughter had been killed in a tragic car accident years ago. When he looked up at Ian, he offered his typical Lloyd smile. It was the kind of smile that assured *everything's going to be okay*. Lloyd was a special kind of saint.

No one spoke for a long time. In any other circumstance, the lingering hug would have felt awkward long ago. Not this time. Ian ruffled his son's hair and said a silent prayer of thanks.

The rain continued, unabated, but Ian didn't care. His boy was home. His family was whole again.

Finally, Zach gently pulled away. "Boy, do I have a story to tell," he said. His voice sounded deeper. "But maybe we could go inside or something first?"

They ended the family hug, but Lyana wouldn't let go of Zach. She wrapped her arm around him, and they started walking back to the house.

"I'll move the truck," said Lloyd.

"Leave it," said Ian. "It's probably stuck anyway. We can move it in the morning. Come, let's get out of the rain." Ian looked at Marshall.

"Maybe we should close the shelter door?" Marshall said.

"Yes, that would be wise," said Ian. He jogged back, and together, the two of them lifted the heavy door and let it drop back into place. It landed with a squelching thud that made Ariel screech.

"Hey, you might warn a girl," she called back to them.

"Sorry," Ian replied.

He and Marshall stayed back a bit from the rest of the soggy travelers as they all exited the forest and tromped into the backyard. It was more like a pond than a yard. By the time they reached the empty chicken coop, the rain had subsided.

Ian looked up at the sky. The clouds began to part. It was like something out of a movie.

"Huh, would you look at that," he said. A pink moon blinked back at him.

He turned toward Marshall.

"What happened back there?" he asked, his voice low.

"What happened is you got your son back," Marshall said.

"But where did all that water go?"

"That, Ian, is a very good question."

They walked the rest of the way in silence. Ian sniffed the air. It smelled like rain, of course, but there was a hint of something else. Smoke, or maybe sulfur.

"What are we going to tell everyone? Our friends, the police, Zach's school. No one will ever believe this."

"You'll think of something," said Marshall. He gently grabbed Ian's arm before they entered the house. "Ian, thank you."

"For what?"

"For not giving up. For pushing me. For trusting me."

"We never would have figured this out without your help, Marshall."

"Well, actually, I think your wife had already figured it out."

"What?"

"Did you see her face when she arrived with Ariel? She knew."

Marshall squeezed Ian's arm, then stepped into the house. Ian followed him, still in shock that his son had returned. Where had he gone? And why did he look so much older? Ian had more questions than ever, but he would have to hold them for another time.

• • •

Everyone was standing in the kitchen, drying themselves off with an assortment of kitchen and bath towels. Zach was seated at the table, taking a long drink of water from the fading *Star Wars* cup he'd loved when he was six. He felt exhausted and a little bit lost, but his smile told a better story. He was relieved. He was happy.

He was home.

"Can I tell my story tomorrow?" Zach asked, his voice quieter than usual. He was fidgeting with the edge of his damp shirt. "I really just want to sleep in my own bed right now."

He looked around the room. Everyone was staring at him—Lloyd with his kind eyes, Marshall dripping in the doorway, and his family all waiting expectantly. Too many faces, too many questions for his exhausted mind to process. The kitchen felt smaller than it used to and the fluorescent light buzzed louder than he remembered.

"I know you probably want to know everything right away," Zach continued, still not meeting anyone's eyes. "But it's…it's a lot. Like, *really* a lot. And I need to sort it out in my head first, you know? Put it in the right order." He finally looked up at his dad. "When I try to tell big things too fast, it all comes out jumbled and then I get frustrated, and you guys get confused and…"

Zach trailed off, overwhelmed by even trying to explain. What he needed now, after his six-month ordeal, was the familiar cocoon of his weighted blanket and the comfort of his own room, surrounded by collections organized just the way he liked them. Not questions and explanations and everyone staring at him like he was some kind of miracle.

"I just need everything to be normal for a little bit first," he added quietly. "Before I try to make you understand how completely not normal it's been."

"Of course," said his mom. She ruffled his wet, tangled hair. "Maybe a quick shower first?"

Zach gave a big sigh. "Do I have to? Doesn't the rain count?"

Lyana laughed. "No, you don't have to. But you might feel better if you did."

"Okay." He looked around the kitchen. "If there are any dry towels left."

"There are some up in our bathroom," said Ariel.

"K. Thanks." Zach scooted back in his chair and stood. Ariel walked up behind him and wrapped him in a hug.

"I'm glad you're home, Zach," she said. Then she kissed the top of his head. Zach couldn't remember the last time she'd done that.

"Me too." Zach started to walk out of the kitchen, then stopped and turned. "Dad, I have a really important question."

"Yes?"

"Can we have pancakes for breakfast tomorrow?"

"Of course."

"Chocolate chip pancakes?"

"Well, let's not get greedy," his dad answered with a smile.

Zach was about to object, then he smirked and shook his head. "I think I'll want some toast, too." He turned to Marshall next. "And pomegranate seeds. I really like pomegranate seeds."

• • •

Zach left the kitchen and started up the stairs. Ian listened for his voice, for his counting, but all he heard was the sound of Zach's footsteps. Ian walked to the bottom of the stairs and watched Zach reach the landing. He turned around and caught his dad's gaze.

"Still here," he said.

"I'm so glad," Ian replied. He looked to his left and noticed a grid of papers on the tile floor, each one painted in Lyana's inimitable "rush-stroke" style, as she called it. If he squinted just a little, he could see the image of the shelter door in them. He looked back to Marshall as Lyana brushed past him.

"I'm not letting you out of my sight," Lyana said to Zach, taking two steps at a time.

"Mom, really? I'm showering!" said Zach.

"Fine. I'll wait outside the bathroom. But don't be surprised if I call out to you every ten seconds."

Ian watched until the two of them were out of sight, then returned to the kitchen.

"I didn't know he liked pomegranate seeds," said Ariel.

"I didn't know he even knew what they were," said Ian.

"Must be quite a story," said Lloyd.

Marshall was grinning.

"What are you smiling about, Marshall?" asked Ian.

"Me? Oh, I'm just happy Zach's home. He looks older, don't you think?"

Zach did appear more than a few weeks older. But maybe that was just because of his ordeal.

Just what was his ordeal?

Ian would have to wait another day for that.

• • •

Ariel pressed Send on her phone and waited for a reply. Minutes passed without a response. She was disappointed but not particularly surprised. Garrett's charming unpredictability meant she couldn't expect him to be staring at his phone every minute of the day like so many of her classmates. She had been mildly shocked to discover he owned a smartphone in the first place. He seemed like the kind of person to reject modern technology, just because.

She had typed and retyped the text at least ten times, ultimately deleting all the attempts at cleverness and deciding to go with a simple message: "Zach is home! We don't know what happened yet, but he's home and he's healthy and just as snarky as ever."

Ariel stopped willing the phone to ding with the notice of a reply and set it on her bedside table. She picked up her journal and began writing.

He's back! Zach is home and no one will ever believe how it happened. I saw it and I don't believe it. I'm not even sure what to write here.

Ariel's pen hovered over the paper, then she dropped it into the journal and closed it around the pen before placing it back on the bedside table. The insanity of the past few months wasn't something she could distill into a nice little journal entry. She might try another day, but not tonight. Tonight, she would simply pretend none of it happened and that she was living a perfectly normal life with a perfectly normal family in a perfectly normal house that wasn't trying to kill them.

She rolled over and closed her eyes, but her head was still piecing together all that had happened over the past few hours. After Zach had been found, everyone convened in the kitchen, but no one pressed Zach for answers. Didn't they need to know where he'd been? What he'd done? How he'd survived? And why of all places did he show up at the bottom of the locked tornado shelter? Ariel wanted to grill Zach right then and there, but kept her mouth shut. Everyone else seemed fine to wait until tomorrow.

Lloyd and Marshall left not long after Zach went up to shower. Ariel had heard Marshall say something about driving Lloyd back to the diner, but her dad had taken him back instead. She wasn't quite sure where Marshall ended up. Probably at his cabin.

Lyana said Zach fell asleep almost as soon as he'd climbed into bed. Ariel was certain her mom was still in his room, curled up under a blanket on his old *Death Star* rug, keeping close watch over him.

Ariel glanced at the intercom. "Welcome home, Zach," she whispered.

Ariel clicked off her reading lamp. She strained to hear sounds of life in the house, but it was deathly quiet.

The first wave was almost imperceptible. Like the way the floor vibrated when a heavy piece of furniture was being dragged across it. But the vibrations turned into a tremble, and the tremble into a shudder. Then the whole house shook.

And it didn't stop.

EPILOGUE

MARSHALL SAT AT his small table, shivering. Water dripped from his clothes, marking time with a steady *drip, drip, drip*. The rain outside had subsided, but the storm inside was only intensifying. He lifted the bracelet and turned it this way and that, as if he might find a clue hidden in the image. The leather straps had been replaced numerous times, but the stone looked no different than it had the first time he saw it. He folded his fingers over the cool stone and squeezed tight.

Marshall's thoughts were swirling, much like the image of the wine snake. What he had just witnessed was shocking, yet he had been waiting a long time to see it again—a very long time.

Thankfully, their last-minute plan had worked, but what if he hadn't listened to Ian? What if he'd stayed silent and let things play out without his intervention?

The thought of losing Zach forever brought an ache of another kind.

"What is the purpose of all this chaos?" he said to the empty room. "Where is this heading?" He shook his head. "You are a capricious God. An unpredictable force. How many times have I asked you to tell me what I must do?"

Marshall didn't expect an answer, and he didn't get one. He set the bracelet down, then shuffled over to his wood stove to stoke the fire he had prepared before Ian showed up to confront him. Marshall always knew when a storm was approaching. He felt it in his bones. But he paid the cost of that predictive ability with aching muscles and, often, respiratory struggles that lingered long after the storm had moved on.

This time the relentless, hacking cough had waited until his return to his cabin. Most men of a certain age would fear such ailments, seeing every cough and every ache as another tick on a countdown clock to certain death. Marshall would have welcomed that kind of thinking. He didn't fear death. He longed for it. Only then would he be reunited with his love.

With Esme.

ACKNOWLEDGEMENTS AND THANKS

Writing a meaningful, lasting story is a monumental task to take on, and we could not have done it without an incredible community of people.

We would first like to thank our friends Aaron and Jennifer Sanders for standing in the midst of the battle with us. We would not be standing, much less releasing a book, had they not willingly held us up in a very dark time.

A very special thanks to Lee and Charlotte Long for also joining in the battle and fighting alongside us.

A huge "thank you" to Stephen Parolini for helping us pull the hardest parts of our story together. Stephen, you know our life story, and we know your's. How perfect for us 3 to find each other and work through our stories together.

Everyone needs a Jill Pickering in their life. We cannot imagine our lives without her, her skills, her creativity and her talents. What a treasure you are to us.

And we are overflowing with gratitude for our precious Hope at Home community. Your support by always checking in on us, asking what we need, and just loving on us means more than you will ever know.

Writing Consultant | Stephen Parolini (steveparolini.com)
Cover Art and Illustrations | Charlie Swerdlow (HistoryDepicted.com)
Interior Layout | Alice Briggs (KingdomCovers.com)
Copy Editing | Lisa Gilliam
Lyric Permission Acquisition and Additional Photography | Emily Coey
(www.1885atelier.com)

ARCHITECT

Book 3

The Goodpasture Chronicles

Some blueprints take a lifetime to design.
Some take generations.

GoodpastureChronicles.com

About the Author

R.J. Halbert is a nine-time award-winning and best-selling husband and wife team who have collaborated as authors of The Goodpasture Chronicles, a supernatural fantasy trilogy that blends mystery, suspense, endurance, and triumph into an epic adventure.

Jason Halbert, one-half of R.J. Halbert, is an Emmy and Grammy Award winning producer and songwriter. His songs have reached millions of listeners worldwide through multiple #1 and Platinum selling albums. In addition to his 20+ year career as Music Director and Producer for Kelly Clarkson, he has left his creative mark on numerous works in film and television, and as well as a copious amount of recording artists over the years. When not creating music, he loves bee-keeping, Sci-Fi, and is known to be quite a storyteller.

After homeschooling their two children around the world on a tour bus, Rhonda Halbert, the second half of R.J. Halbert, has spent the past 10 years as a successful music and television manager, guiding her clients' relationships with labels, networks, and producers. She is also a published photographer, music supervisor, passionate cook, garden enthusiast, and spiritual practitioner.

Together, Jason and Rhonda have woven their 32+ years of life together into a riveting story, based somewhat on truth and experience, but even more so, brimming with imagination.

Learn more at rjhalbert.com